# What Guides Us

Dennis Joslyn

## DEDICATION

I dedicate this book to my family and friends, who have always supported me throughout this incredible journey, culminating in my second novel. Very special thanks to my editor, without whom I wouldn't have been able to complete such a grueling deadline, and to my two pugs. Thank you.

TABLE OF CONTENTS

# Prologue: STILL WAITING

1

The children sat in a circle around the old woman. Her light brown skin was weathered, her dark eyes calm and knowing. She sat in the chair the bookstore provided her—she came once a month to tell stories of her people's heritage, the Oneida Nation.

She traveled the region, and though her bones ached in the evenings and her muscles in the mornings, she still loved telling the stories of her people—especially the tale of Shukwayaʔtísu and Shakohlewátha?, the Good Twin and the Contrary Twin.

She waited patiently as the children settled, quieting almost instinctively, sensing she wouldn't begin until every eye was on her.

"Hello, little ones," she began. Her voice was soft but carried easily through the bookstore.

Some children murmured a hello back, but most simply stared, expecting a book to appear in her hands like at story-time. But that wasn't her way. This was a spoken history, and she would tell it from memory.

"Today, I'm going to tell you an ancient and very special story. A story about balance—about creation. About two brothers."

She leaned forward, her voice low, inviting. She'd been telling stories for thirty years, and she knew exactly how to hold a room.

"Long ago, before there was any land here, there was only water. The world was covered in it, and the only living things were the creatures below and the birds that flew above. But far above the sky, there was another world—a Sky World—and the people who lived there had great powers.

"At the center of their land stood a great tree. This tree gave light to their world, and from it grew many fruits. That's where the light came from—not a sun, but the fruit of that tree."

Her hands drifted out over the children like leaves falling.

"No one was allowed to harm the tree. That was the rule. But there was a young woman, heavy with child, who began to crave its roots and bark. She asked her husband to bring her some. He was terrified—no one disobeyed that law. But while no one was watching, he crept to the tree and began to dig."

The children's eyes widened. The woman smiled—she had them now.

"As he dug, the ground beneath the tree collapsed. A great hole opened up, right through the Sky World. The man ran back, frightened, and told his wife what had happened. She asked if he brought her what she wanted. When he said no, she became angry and went to the tree herself.

"She looked into the hole. Far below, she saw water and clouds swirling. She leaned closer—and fell. As she fell, she reached out to grab something, anything. All she caught were bits of dirt and root from the tree.

"The birds saw something falling through the sky and flew up to meet her. When they saw it was a woman, they rushed back to tell the water animals. They gathered to see who could carry her on their back. The great turtle agreed."

One child gasped. Another covered their mouth. The old woman's voice never wavered.

"The birds caught her gently and laid her on the turtle's back. She woke afraid and saw only water all around her. The animals told her where she was. She asked if there was any mud so she could use the dirt she'd held onto to build something—anything.

"The otter dove deep, but came back with nothing. So did the loon. Then the beaver tried, but he, too, returned empty-handed. The woman thanked everyone.

"Finally, the muskrat said he would go. He was gone for a long time. They feared he'd drowned. But at last, he floated to the surface, nearly lifeless—but clutching a small bit of earth in his paws."

A few kids gasped, eyes wide. One whispered, "He made it."

"She took the mud and mixed it with what she had from the Sky Tree, and she placed it on the turtle's back. It grew. It became the land. And from it, the plants grew. The woman gave birth to a daughter, and together they walked the earth, naming the plants, learning what they could be used for."

The woman took a slow breath. She glanced at her young audience—hooked, silent, waiting.

"Her daughter grew into a woman. One day she was walking very far from her mother and a man appeared to her. She became very terrified at seeing this man, and she fainted, and when she awoke, two arrows lay across her stomach— one sharp, one dull. Later, she gave birth to twins. One came the usual way. The other pushed out through her armpit. That's what killed her."

A few children recoiled. The woman nodded solemnly.

"The twins were opposites—one right-handed, one left-handed. One kind, one contrary. The right-handed twin made rivers, plants, medicines, and animals that helped the land. The left-handed twin followed behind—twisting plants into poisons, making predators to hunt the peaceful creatures.

"Later, the right-handed twin went back to look at all the things that he had created. He noticed the other differences in his creations and knew he hadn't created those things. He looked at everything he had made and saw the changes. This made him furious. As soon as he finished checking the things out, he set out to look for his brother. Soon he found him amusing himself by the ocean. The right-handed twin spoke sternly to his brother and told him he had no right to change the things that he had created. The left-handed twin replied to his brother and said that he wanted to create things too. He shouldn't be the only one creating things. So the right-handed twin said that it was time that they decided who would be the creator of all the things on Turtle Island.

"They fought even in the womb. They fought after birth. And one day, they challenged each other to decide who would rule Turtle Island. They played lacrosse, then a peach-stone game, but neither won. So they fought, thinking the only way to settle their differences was to kill the other."

She paused, letting the tension linger.

"The right-handed twin struck his brother with a deer antler. He thought he'd killed him. He placed him on a raft and set him out to sea. He became the Holder of the Sky and creator of all things. The left-handed twin—called Flint because of his rigidity—was not dead. He went on to create a world of his own, across the ocean."

She finished the tale slightly out of breath. The children sat wide-eyed, absorbing the story like roots drawing water.

Then, hands shot up all at once. Questions. Curiosity. Wonder.

The woman smiled. This—this moment—was why she still told the stories.

2

"Ryan! Put that down."

Jen's voice cracked through the stillness of the shop

like a snapped twig. Story time was over. The other parents had already picked up their kids, but Jen was late as always.

She was young—twenty—but life, and Ryan, had aged her early. There were tired smudges beneath her eyes that the concealer couldn't quite hide. These days, she looked closer to thirty.

Yet she was still young enough; the guys at the local bar never seemed to mind. When she found a sitter—which was rare; Ryan didn't get along with most of them.

So she came here. Used bookstores were quiet. Safe. A little world where no one screamed or spilled juice on the furniture.

Ryan stood frozen, his back to her. One small, pudgy hand clutched a black book. A strip of faded red lace bound its cracked leather cover, which looked like dried river mud.

It looked old. Important. And worst of all, expensive. Too expensive for this hole-in-the-wall used bookstore they killed time in every Monday.

Jen darted forward and yanked the book from his hands.
Ryan let out a sharp, guttural cry—not a tantrum. Not fear.

For one awful second, his eyes—wide and glassy—weren't his.
Something else blinked behind them.

She shook it off. Grabbed the book and put it back on the shelf.

"Let's go, you little hellion," she said, forcing a lightness into her voice. "I found a sitter, and it's Friday. Mommy needs a break."

They left.

The book sat on the shelf. Watching. Wanting.

Jen might've found Ryan a daddy that night. Many things might have been different…

If Ryan had gotten his new book.

But a city bus driver—distracted when a raven shattered against his windshield like spilled ink—slammed into their car two blocks from home.

Everyone called it a tragic accident. But it wasn't.

It was what happens when the book doesn't get its way.

*Same book.*
*Different reader.*
*Still waiting.*

# Chapter 1: ANTIQUARIUS BOOKS & THE ROAD TRIP

1

Maya sat in the back of the lecture hall, watching her dreams die to the soft drone of her Visual Programming professor's voice. Something about loops. Or maybe dictionaries. Who gave a shit?

She'd made the classic mistake: assuming that loving video games meant she'd love making them. Now, three years into a computer science degree, reality sat like a brick in her stomach.
A $125,000 brick.

She had the grades—made the Dean's List every semester. That wasn't the problem. The problem was, she hated this. All of it. Her heart? Fuck, her heart wasn't even in the building.

What she really loved—what she craved—was the smell of old paper, the thrill of the hunt. Dusty boxes at estate sales. Basements that hadn't seen light in decades. Half-burned piles outside condemned libraries. That tingle in her brain when she cracked the spine of something forgotten.

An English professor had started it—had turned her on to it. Well…he'd just turned her on, truthfully—but somewhere between the eye-fucking and the lectures on D.H. Lawrence, a fire caught.

Now it wouldn't go out. She wanted to—no, *needed* to—chase that feeling. To dig into language, history, stories no one was supposed to read.

But you don't just change your major three years in... Do you?

The room rustled to life—chairs scraping, bags zipping. Class was over. She looked down at her screen:

**print(f"Hello, {name}! Welcome to Fuck My Life!")**

A clever little title for a game she'd never finish, for a degree she didn't want, in a field she was learning to despise. She would never get out of debt.
Yes, *Fuck My Life* indeed.

It blinked back at her like it knew.
Knew she didn't care.
Knew she was already gone.

She shut her laptop with a quiet sigh and pulled out her phone.

Ping.
An alert:
*Antiquarius Books–Last Weekend Sale! Everything is 50% Off!*

Her mouth actually watered.

Mom-and-pop shops were goldmines. They never knew what they had—first editions, obscure banned texts, cracked leather grimoires written by someone who probably got burned at the stake.

She'd paid for half of last semester flipping weird stuff on eBay.

*This place...this could be the motherlode,* she thought.

She tapped the address.
Boonville, New York. Tiny. Off-the-map. Perfect. Four hours away though.

She chewed her thumbnail.
She'd need backup.


2


Ed was at the only decent place Boonville had—at least in his opinion—and sipped his coffee. Sure, you could get Dunkin' anywhere, but something about this one, across from the Tops, just tasted better.

The rest of the damn town could fall off the face of the Earth for all he cared.
But this? This little morning routine?
Yeah, he'd miss that.

Especially after he closed his father's old bookstore for good.

That place—like his dad with cancer—just wouldn't die.

He winced at the thought. Cruel.
But living in a small Upstate New York town makes you that way.
*Sorry, Dad,* he thought.

The sunny outlook on life fades when your only inheritance is a dusty, rotting bookstore full of forgotten relics—in a town that time never cared to remember.

He sighed. Took a sip. Scrolled through the ad he'd

blasted across social media one more time:
*50% OFF — EVERYTHING MUST GO.*
Big letters. Big dreams.

He didn't expect crowds. This wasn't Black Friday in
a Target parking lot.
But if twenty people showed up, he'd call it a miracle.

Maybe, with luck, he'd sell off some of the weirder
old stuff.
Maybe even the dusty candy—sure to lure in families.
Helping the local dentists could be his lasting legacy to a
town that always seemed to want him gone.

It hadn't.

He'd had a lot of ideas like that.
And Dad—Dad had always let him try.

Every doomed "get rich quick" scheme.
Every desperate "Let's be the next Amazon!" pitch.
Flyers. Blogs. A Twitter account no one followed.
Once, even a book-themed TikTok.

None of it ever worked.

And when his dad got sick, the energy shifted.
No more ideas.
No more storefront dreams.
Just long, silent drives to Upstate Medical in Syracuse.
Sometimes Rochester.

Hours on the road where neither of them knew what
to say—but both wanted to say so much.

Ed had wanted to tell him how much he loved him.
How grateful he was to the father who let him play CEO of
their tiny empire.

Even if that empire never made it past Boonville.
Even at its peak, it only cleared $250,000.

"The '80s," his dad used to say.
Ed never quite understood the reverence.
People read more, he guessed. Spent more. Cared more.

But that golden age was long gone.

And by the time Ed was ready to say the things that mattered,
His father was too sick to hear them.

The words dried up.
The car rides got quieter.
They sat silently, letting the years slip away like ash in the wind.

A tear pricked the corner of Ed's eye.
He blinked it back.

Enough of that.

He stood, took one last sip of cold coffee, and headed for the parking lot.

Outside, the traffic passed by in a steady, uncaring rhythm.
Just like always.

3

Matt sat in the car with all the essentials for a road trip—snacks, gas, a playlist, and the girl he'd been quietly pining for over two years.
Not that he'd ever tell her that.

In Maya's world, he was firmly placed in the *Break Glass in Case of Emergency* box.

And yeah, he knew it.

And yeah, he was pathetic enough to live with it.

Matt was short and stocky, which was the polite way of saying overweight. Not obese—*not yet*. But the train was on the tracks, coming faster than he liked.

His whole family was heavy. He didn't fully buy into the "blame DNA" thing, but he'd been to enough Thanksgivings to know he'd started behind the eight ball.

When Maya stepped out of the fitness center in her swimwear top and shorts, his heart stuttered.

He panicked, fumbling for the driver's door — *HONK. HONK.*

Commonwealth Avenue teemed with its usual chaos: engines growling, horns blaring beneath a thick afternoon haze.

Boston drivers didn't care that he'd scored a spot near the front—only that he'd dared open his door into traffic like some clueless Midwesterner.

"What the fuck are ya doin'?" someone screamed. "Jesus Christ, you fuckin' college kids!"

Matt flinched, but kept moving.

It all rolled off his back.

Because Maya Cartar was walking toward him, smiling—raven hair damp, olive skin glowing from chlorine and effort.

She was his friend. His favorite person.

Maybe even…something more.

At least in the version of the story he'd written in his own English Lit brain.

This was their budding-romance road trip to Upstate New York.

He opened the passenger door like a gentleman, took her gym bag, and tossed it into his not-great-but-respectable 2019 Chevy Cruze.
Then he dashed around the front of the car—tripped on the bumper.
Swore under his breath.
Opened his door into traffic again.

Boston let him know *exactly* how it felt.

"Fuckin' moron!" someone shouted.

But Matt was already in the car.
Door shut. Seatbelt on.
The world's chaos sealed outside.

Now it was just him.
And her.
A foot away.
And four hours of road to somewhere weird, quiet, and maybe—just maybe—meant for them.

An hour into the drive, Matt nearly jumped out of his seat when Maya howled in delight.
"I got one!"

The Cruze swerved slightly.

"Jesus, Matt—easy!" she laughed, clutching her phone.

"You're the one who screamed," he muttered, adjusting the wheel. "Got what?"

She turned her screen toward him, grinning. A photo showed a rundown but dignified Victorian house.

"A place to stay while we book-hunt this weekend— and cheap too. Listen to this."

She cleared her throat dramatically and began reading from the listing:

"The Queen's Quarters–Boonville, New York Tucked away in a quiet neighborhood, this grand 1860 Victorian once served as a bustling boarding house, welcoming travelers with its tall windows, wide porch, and timeless charm. Today, it still opens its doors—but now with a more private touch.

Suite #3 sits on the second floor, offering a peaceful retreat for guests who want both comfort and independence. Inside, a queen bed anchors the large room, with soft light pouring in through tall windows. There's a dining table for quiet meals, a desk for getting things done, and a cozy corner with a TV for winding down. A mini-fridge, microwave, and Keurig stocked with coffee and tea make it easy to settle in.

Guests come and go through their own dedicated entrance, separate from the first floor. With a full private bath and easy lockbox entry, everything feels effortless—like a boutique hotel stay, but with the warmth of a home. There's even a reserved spot in the driveway, so no need to worry about parking.

Once a boarding house, still a place to stay—just a little quieter now.

$450 for five nights," Maya said. "It's perfect. I'm booking it."

Her fingers danced across the screen.

"Wait—*five* nights? You said—"

"Matt," she whined playfully, cutting him off. "You're not gonna make me come all the way up here and *not* check out a few other places, are you? Come on…please?"

She leaned in slightly, her hand resting on his forearm.

He caved instantly.
After all, Matt thought…

Queen-size bed.
Anything could happen.

---

Meanwhile, in Boonville…

Miranda Callahan scowled at the new Airbnb reservation glowing on her ancient desktop screen.

She wore her usual uniform: tired jeans, a bleach-stained hoodie, and that faded pink Red Cross vest she refused to throw out.
Her hair snapped back into a brittle gray ponytail, wiry strands springing loose like they couldn't wait to escape her scalp.

She had a smoker's voice, a coffee drinker's teeth, and a face carved deep by upstate winters and disappointment.

The folks in Boonville would call her mean and dumb—if they bothered to describe her at all.

"College kids," she muttered.

She didn't know why they were coming, and she didn't care.
She just hoped it wouldn't be another *Peterson incident*. Those shitheads nearly burnt the place to the ground.

All college kids ever brought were too many hormones and too much booze.
And she didn't want *her girl* anywhere near it.

Still…they'd already paid.
And winter had been brutal.

The furnace needed repairs—hell, if she was honest, it needed replacing.
So their $500 would go some of the way toward that.

And who knows?
Maybe the dumb little shits had wealthy parents and would break something.
Something old.
Something *replaceable*.

She snorted.

"Boston," she said, reading the billing address aloud. "Fucking typical."

She shoved her chair back. The floor creaked under her weight.

"Probably Red Sox fans too," she muttered, as if it were the ultimate insult.

# Chapter 2: THE BLACK BOOK ON THE COUNTER

1

E d unlocked the entrance to the bookstore, as he had every day for the past five years. The weight of the place pressed down on him the moment the door chime let out its tired little *ding*.

He passed the alarm panel without even looking at it. That thing hadn't barked to life since Clinton was in office, collecting dust while the world moved on without it.

"Who's gonna rob a bookstore in Boonville?" his dad used to say—half-laughing, a cold Labatt's in hand down at the Elks Lodge.

Turns out, no one ever had.
And no one ever would.

At the end of this summer, Antiquarius Books would be just another empty shop.
Another obituary on Main Street.

A shame, really—considering it survived the fire.
To go out with a whimper.

But that was Ed's life to a tee, wasn't it?
One long, quiet whimper.

High school football star—until his knee gave out in twelfth grade.

College scouts were supposedly in the stands.
It didn't matter now.

What mattered now was this:
He was about to sell his family's legacy for pennies on the dollar.
Running while he still could from this tundra of Upstate New York.

Someplace where terrible things happened to *other* people for a change.
Where little kids didn't get hit by buses two blocks from your front door.

The local high schoolers had loved that one.
"The Cursed Bookshop."
They even made TikToks.

Ed shook his head, stepped inside—and stopped.

There, in the middle of the floor, was the book.
Just lying there.
No reason. No explanation.

That same fucking book.

Black leather. Red lace. Waiting.

The one he'd shelved twenty times this month.
The one the high schoolers always moved, always joked about.

"Fucking black book," he muttered, stomping across the warped floorboards.

His boots hit heavily, angrily.

He bent down.
His hand curled around the leather.

Picked it up.

Only this time, he didn't put it back on the shelf.

Instead, Ed walked it to the front counter.

He dropped it like any other object—like it wasn't
something he resented, something he'd hauled from place to
place more times than he could count.
Like it belonged there.

Then he flipped on the lights.

The store came to life—or its version of it.
Rows of old paperbacks and dusty hardcovers blinked into
being under flickering fluorescents.
A lazy loop of NPR crackled through ancient ceiling speakers,
full of voices too calm to change anything.

Ed moved behind the counter, switched on the
register, and opened the cash drawer.
Just a few twenties, some fives, and quarters.

He snorted.

"As if," he muttered, slamming the drawer shut.

Then he sank into the chair—the one with the bad leg
and the duct tape patch across the armrest.
Pulled his laptop from under the counter.
Woke it up.

The black book sat just to the left of the keyboard.
Quiet. Innocent.

Ed didn't move it.
He didn't open it.
He didn't touch it again.

But he didn't put it away either.
And that was new.


2


Amanda Rodrick sat at the red light in her brand-new 2023 red Tesla Model X.

Did she care, even though Ed had begged her not to buy it?
No.

She deserved it.
She'd stayed in this goddamn town three years longer than necessary, trying to save that decaying bookstore.
As if saving it would bring Charles back.
As if Charles was even *worth* bringing back.

The man was barely worth $100,000 when he died— and that was *before* the medical debt.

Ed had promised her a life of travel.
Comfort.
A second act somewhere warm.

And yeah, sure—he blew his knee out in high school. But she gave things up too.

She *could've* been with someone else.
Anyone, really.

Not that it meant much—when Boonville's most significant exports were cow juice and trees.
But still.

If she'd left earlier?

She could've been someone.
Or at least fucked someone who *could've* been someone.

The car behind her honked.

Amanda snapped out of her daydream, eyes flicking up to the gray morning sky hanging heavily over Upstate New York.

Soon.
Soon, they'd leave this frozen graveyard of a town.
Someplace warm.
Somewhere this car didn't need to be put away six months out of the year.

Maybe Ed would get an actual job.
Maybe he'd finally make good on the life he promised.

And if not?

She glanced in the rearview mirror.
Her reflection stared back: 31, sleek-blonde, green eyes hard with hunger.

She could still grab a man who could.

"At least one who fucks better," Amanda muttered aloud to no one but the morning DJ rambling through static on the radio.

She flipped off the impatient driver behind her without even glancing.
An old woman, by the looks of it.
Whatever.

She yanked the Tesla into the bookstore parking lot a little too fast.
The tires hissed against the wet pavement as she parked

crookedly, killed the engine, and grabbed her bag.

Time for her daily fight with Ed.
What about? She didn't know. Didn't care.

It didn't matter.
She was in a pissy mood.
So he had to be in one too.

Fair was fair.


3


Ed watched through the front window as Amanda cut off a Buick and whipped the Tesla into the parking lot—too fast, too confident.
He winced.
That car cost more than he'd make in two years.

But she had to have it.
No—she *needed* it, she'd said.

As if anyone *needed* a $1,400-a-month car note for something she wouldn't even drive if the weather so much as *threatened* snow.
All-wheel drive or not, she'd rather die than get salt on the tires.

He sighed.

She was probably fuming over the ad.
Ready to storm into the store and let him have it.

Didn't matter.
In a few more months, it'd all be over.
That's what he told himself.

Then he felt it.

A low hum.

Not loud. Not physical. Just...*present.*

He glanced at the counter.

The book?

No.

Had to be the laptop fan. Probably dying.

Great. Another expense to justify.

The Tesla's gullwing door hissed open.

Amanda stepped out like she was walking a red carpet in a town that didn't deserve her.

Ed didn't move.

Ding.

The bell rang above the door.

"Really, Ed? Twelve hundred dollars for ads?"

*Why not say hello?* he thought.

Not even *good morning.*

Not even *go fuck yourself.*

Just straight into—Jesus, Ed, you're a shit husband.

And a terrible lay.

And a waste of skin—all tucked snugly into those few words, delivered like a slap.

"Yes, sweetheart," Ed said without looking up.

"That's how business works."

He knew she hated that tone.

*Mansplaining,* she called it.

"I fucking know how business works," she snapped.

"Let me know when you find one, Ed."

She tossed a few bills onto the counter like breadcrumbs to a beggar.

"Until then, no more fucking ads."

Then she spun—perfect heels, perfect timing—and walked out with that practiced sway in her hips.
She knew he was watching.
And she made sure he knew exactly what he wouldn't be touching tonight.
Or the rest of the week.

Ed sighed.

He bent to scoop up the mail she'd knocked loose—and saw it.

The book.

Open.

Not wide.
Just enough.
As if someone had been...*reading it.*

He stared at the page.

The words swam into focus, like they'd been waiting just behind the ink for him to *look.*

His name sat at the top in crisp, elegant script:

*Edward Rodrick*

A sentence appeared beneath it, forming line by line—like breath fogging on glass:

*She'll never respect you again, Edward. But I can get it for you. Make them ALL respect you...*

*FEAR you... Like they used to...*

His fingers hovered.
Trembled.

The hum beneath his skin grew louder—low, electric, almost tender.
Like something inside him was...*opening.*

Ed's breath hitched.

No.

No, no, *no.*

He slammed the book shut.
It *snapped,* loud in the quiet shop.

The bell above the door gave a faint answering jingle—like it had *heard* the snap.
The lights flickered. Twice.

Ed backed away from the counter fast, chest heaving.

The bills Amanda had tossed slipped from his hand, fluttering across the worn floor like fallen leaves.

He stared at the book.
Closed now.
Still.

But somehow, it felt like it was watching him anyway—with red eyes and a smile full of sharp teeth.

The NPR feed went silent.

Ed stumbled back another step.
Breath shallow.
Hands trembling.

The bookstore was *too* quiet now.

Like even the building was holding its breath.

Then— Ding.

The door chime.

Soft.

Innocent.

Final.

# Chapter 3: WELCOME TO BOONVILLE

1

Evelyn Callahan stood in her mother's driveway, sweeping for reasons she never understood.

"Get it clean, Eve," was the daily order.

So she did.
Even if she didn't know why.

She looked up as a blue Chevy with Massachusetts plates rolled to a stop at the curb.

"Massholes," her mother always called them.

Evelyn never got the reference.
People from there seemed nice enough.
Sure, they drove like shit.
But didn't *everyone* think everyone else drove like shit?

Evelyn preferred to judge people by how they treated her.
And in her experience, the locals treated her like crap.

"Massholes?"
Usually polite.

She adjusted her grip on the broom, pretending to sweep as two people her age climbed out of the car.
The girl was striking—raven hair, olive skin, confidence in

her stride.

The guy—stocky, maybe a little soft, but cute in a sweet, round-faced kind of way—trailed behind her like a loyal spaniel.

Evelyn didn't need to guess how their dynamic worked.

The girl turned heads.

The guy carried bags.

She sighed.

Evelyn had been called ugly—more than once.

A few guys had asked her out, only to tell her she needed to "girl it up" more.

She'd stopped seeing them after that.

This was her style.

Take it or fuck off.

She was drifting in her own head when the guy showed up—too close, too fast—snapping her back to the moment.

"Excuse me!" he shouted, like she had earbuds in.

Evelyn jumped, startled.

He jumped too—then tripped and hit the pavement hard.

"Ow."

"Why are you screaming?" she asked flatly, brow raised.

The guy looked up, red-faced.

"I…uh…"

"Are you the staff here?" the pretty one asked,

ignoring her friend still sitting on the asphalt.

Evelyn smirked.

"Staff? Yes. As close as you're going to get."

She offered a hand to help him up.

"I'm Evelyn Callahan," she said, glancing at the boy now being pulled up by his rather attractive companion. "Is he okay?"

"I'm fine," he said quickly, brushing himself off. "Just slipped. My rather large ass broke the fall."

"Oh, Matt." The girl rolled her eyes with an air of long-suffering affection.

"I'm Maya Cartar," she said, offering a practiced smile. "And this one here is Matt LaFord. We've got a room here... Do we check in with...?"

She let the question dangle, glancing around the house as if it might produce a concierge desk.

"Nope," Evelyn said. "With my mother. She's the friendly one inside."

She snickered, imagining the warm, likely profanity-laced greeting that awaited them.

"Nice meeting you guys. If you need help finding stuff around town...I'm around."

Evelyn watched them go inside.
She decided she liked Matt—but the jury was still out on Maya.

The girl gave off *smartest-person-in-the-room* energy. Which was fine.

As long as she didn't act like it.

Evelyn shrugged and went back to sweeping, her mother's voice already echoing through the walls—loud enough to carry out the front door.

2

Maya stepped into the overheated front hall, ready to check in—and stopped cold.

Miranda Callahan stood with her arms crossed, cheeks flushed, eyes sharp.

"Just what the hell are you doing in my home?"

The words hit like a slap.

Maya froze.
Unsure if she'd just committed a crime.

"Uh… Airbnb?" she stammered, fumbling with her phone.
"I can show you the—"

Miranda waved a hand, already over it.

"Oh, well." She raised an unkempt eyebrow. "You ought to learn to knock or something."

She handed over a crumpled folder and a pair of keys.

"Here's your welcome kit. Local info. Wi-Fi password. Instructions on how to rate us. Five stars, we hope."

Her smile was as thin as a fishing line.

"My daughter'll take your bags up. You two make a cute couple, by the way."

The sarcasm wasn't subtle.

Maya accepted the keys.

"We're not a couple."

"Oh?" Miranda raised a brow. "There's only one bed."

Matt and Maya hadn't noticed Miranda's hands—tight little fists, balled with something more than sarcasm.

"Hope you don't plan on making the poor boy sleep in the tub."

Maya smirked.

"Nah. He's resourceful."

That was the wrong answer.

Miranda's smile vanished.
Her face darkened like a storm cloud.

"Is that right?" she said, eyes narrowing. "You...resourceful?"

She stepped closer, eyes locking on Matt.

"You planning on sneaking off into someone else's room later? Is that it?"

She took another step forward.

Matt blinked.

"W–what?"

Miranda's voice dropped, low and dangerous.

"I'll tell you something, boy," she said.
"Reconsider that. Lest you miss a few things you came with.
You understand? No one is stealing away my little girl."

Matt swallowed hard.

Maya stepped forward, placing herself between them.

"I'm sure there won't be any funny business," she
said evenly.

Miranda sniffed.

"See that there isn't."

She jabbed a finger at Matt's chest.

"My daughter's not some roadside attraction."

Before either of them could respond, Miranda turned
on her heel.

"Eve!" she shouted.
"Come get our guests' bags and take them to their room!"

3

Evelyn chuckled as she led them upstairs, two steps
ahead with the keys.

Matt, ever the good guy, had refused to let her carry
the bags.
Maya already had her nose buried in her phone—scrolling,
tapping—probably checking the bookstore's hours.

"So…is it Eve or Evelyn?" Matt asked as they
climbed.

He'd noticed the soft red of her hair, the freckles
across her nose, the sharp hazel of her eyes.
She wasn't flashy—nothing about her screamed for attention.
But if you looked closely, it was all there.
And Matt found…he liked that.

She glanced at him sideways. "Either's fine. Most
people call me Eve. Or 'bitch.' Depends on the mood."
She smirked.

Matt grinned. "I'll stick with Eve then. Seems safer,"
he said, slightly out of breath on the narrow stairway. "Gotta
protect the old balls."

"Your mom made…an impression," he added,
smirking.

Evelyn laughed. "Yeah, she does that. Especially with
guys our age who pass through."

They reached the landing.

"Now, if you were some shit-shoveling dairy farmer
from up the hill talkin' about sneakin' into my room
tonight…" Evelyn paused, then finished, "she'd sell you the
flashlight."

Matt barked a laugh. "Jesus."

"She's got a system," Eve said with a shrug, unlocking
the door. "Terrible, but consistent."

The door creaked open.

Matt stepped inside—and felt it.
Cool. Still.
Like the air hadn't moved in days.

Evelyn moved straight to the window and cranked it

open, letting in a gust of late spring air that sliced through the stillness like a knife.

"There," she said. "Better already."

She crossed to the closet and popped it open.

"There's a cot, by the way," she said, pointing to the folded frame in the corner.
"Pretty sure Mom put you two in here just to mess with you. Thought it'd be funny. Until it backfired."

She turned back toward them with a smirk.

"I'll grab you some extra blankets—unless you're planning a midnight stroll down the hall?"

Matt flushed crimson.
"I—I wasn't."

"Relax, stud," Evelyn laughed.
"Your friend's gonna keep you busy enough book hunting for any reindeer games."
She winked.

Matt opened his mouth. Closed it.
Smiled despite himself.

Maya, still buried in her phone, nodded without looking up.
"Yeah…right. Tip her, Matty. I'll get you later. The bookstore closes soon—we need to go."

Matt blinked. "What?"

Maya glanced up, all business. "We're on the clock. Let's move."

She breezed past them into the hallway, already

texting again.

Evelyn raised an eyebrow as she disappeared.
"She always like that?" she asked, half-teasing.

Matt shrugged. "Only when she's awake."

Evelyn grinned and grabbed the doorframe.
"I'll get those blankets. Watch out for the spring in the cot—
it bites."

4

In the car, Maya could feel Matt's frustration.
She ignored it.

"Up here," she said, tapping the GPS. "Take a left,
then at the light—you should see it."

Matt said nothing at first.
Then — "Fine."
His voice was tight. Flat.

Maya glanced over and nudged him with her elbow.
"Come on, Matt, don't be like that," she said, still glued to
her phone. "You can flirt with the local talent after I get my
books."
She smirked. "She likes you."

"Shut up," Matt muttered. "She doesn't."

He stared ahead, knuckles white on the wheel.

"Besides, you've got me driving you all over the
middle of nowhere in search of…what, exactly?"

As he eased to a stop at the light, a sleek red Tesla

blew through the intersection, tires hissing.
Matt blinked. "Damn. Nice car." He followed it with his eyes.
"Did you see that?"

Maya didn't look up.
"See what?"

"Never mind," he muttered. "We're here."

He turned the wheel and pulled into a cracked,
narrow parking lot beside a sagging, two-story building.
The paint had faded. The sign above the door looked like it
had given up years ago.

"Charming," Maya said flatly.

Matt killed the engine.

They stared at the storefront.
Neither of them moved.

The wind kicked up a swirl of dead leaves along the
curb—odd for spring.

"Just…don't be you in there," Matt said, trying to
joke. It came out wrong—too sharp.
He winced. "I mean—you know. Sometimes you can
be…intense."

Maya gave him that sideways smile. The one that
smoothed everything over.
The one that always meant she'd won.

Then she got out of the car.

Matt watched her go—her hair catching the breeze,
her walk confident, like nothing in the world could knock her
off balance.

She was already inside when he noticed.
She'd forgotten her bag.
Of course she had.

He sighed, grabbed it off the seat, and followed her
into the bookstore.

5

Ed watched her walk in like she owned the place.
Tall. Sharp. Sure of herself.
Like the store had been waiting for her.
Hell, maybe it had.

*Here you go, ma'am,* he thought bitterly. *It's all yours. Just
sign the deed. Sign your life away. This nightmare can be yours now too.*

Her eyes met his.
Blue. Intense.
Not the kind of eyes that belonged in a dead-end shop in a
dying town.
They flicked over the shelves, the floors, the dust—and
finally, to him.
Sizing him up.

Ed could tell she'd already found him wanting.
That was fine.
He wanted her.

He was older than her—by more than enough to
matter.
And the gold band on his finger still meant something to
him...
Even if it meant less than shit to Amanda.

"Can I help you?" he asked.

It came out rough. Too soft. Like a schoolboy's voice cracking through his first crush.
*Why the hell did I say it like that?*

Maya smiled—and for a second, Ed forgot what year it was.

She stepped toward the counter, smooth, her eyes grazing over the titles like they were old friends she hadn't seen in years.
Ed had to check that his mouth was still closed.
It was.
Just barely.

The bell above the door dinged again, snapping the moment in half.

A heavyset guy shuffled in, slightly out of breath, clutching a purse like it was radioactive.

Maya didn't look back.
Ed did.

Matt—or Matt-something. That type always had a name like that.

The moment was over.
The spell shattered.

Ed cleared his throat, straightening behind the counter.
Back to business.

Maya might've talked her way into some serious discounts—if she'd left the puppy in the car.

# Chapter 4: THE MILK WAR

1

Boonville, tucked between the woods and hills at the foot of the Adirondack Mountains, was no stranger to hard times.
By the 1930s, its cobbled Main Street bore the weight of them—weathered storefronts with fading signs.
The Depression had reached Upstate New York, but folks around here just called it *living*.
Only now, milk prices—the lifeblood of the town—were being threatened.

And on one sultry July night, Stanley Millard stood before his neighbors.

He stood in the bed of a rusted-out pickup, hand trembling around a black book.
Its leather cover was warm in his palm.
It hummed—not loud, not out loud—but deep behind his ribs.

He railed against the governor. Against the League. Against those goddamn suits in Albany.
"They're *supposed* to be on the farmer's side," he growled.
But were they?

*No*, the book whispered.
A bloom of pain flared behind his eyes.

"No!" Stanley shouted, louder now. "They aren't on our side!"

47

The crowd stirred—farmers, wives, teens in sweat-stained shirts and worn shoes.
People who'd had enough.
People ready to be heard.

"A milk day!" someone called out.

"Milk holiday!" another agreed.

*Milk war*, the book said.
It didn't speak in words — It stamped the idea behind Stanley's eyes.
One word.
Big.
Blocky.

**WAR.**

Stanley straightened. His grip tightened.

"No," he said slowly. "This ain't a holiday."
He scanned their faces—sunburned, tired, hungry.

"This is a fight. For our families. For our lives."

He raised the book high.

"Albany don't give a damn about a *Milk Day*. And the city folks'll just laugh at a holiday," he said, fire now burning in his voice.

He held the book aloft again—
So everyone could see it.
Or so *it* could see *them*.

"No," he said, a sick smile creeping across his face. "What we've got here…is a war."

A beat.

Then:
**"A Milk War."**

The crowd erupted.
Fists raised. Voices overlapping.

A chant rose like fire:

**"Milk War! Milk War! Milk War!"**

And in Stanley's hand, the book pulsed.
It liked the sound of that.

"That's right!" Stanley shouted.
"Milk War tomorrow! Depression or not, those bastards
don't get a *drop* of our milk until they pay what it's worth!"

The book surged in his grip.
It wasn't power.
It wasn't faith.

It was hate.

2

An hour had passed since the crowd had thinned at
Stanley's farm.

His wife offered lemonade and weak coffee to the
few who lingered. A handful of men stood around in clumps,
smoking, talking low.

Stanley sat alone on the porch. The black book rested
in his lap. A cigarette hung from his lips, forgotten.

Tom Eastwood made his way over—slowly,
cautiously. He glanced at the book, frowning.

Tom had known Stan since they were kids—played together, worked together. Hell, Stan had been his best man.
So Tom figured it fell to him to talk some damn sense into him.

"I didn't even know you could read, Stan," he said after a long pause.

Stanley smiled down at him—too calm. Too still.

"Oh, this?" He held up the black book. Its leather cover seemed to drink the moonlight, the red lace like dried blood.
"I don't read it. I just like to hold it."

He flicked ash off the porch railing.

"Truth be told, it's not even in English."
Stanley stroked the book softly, almost like a pet. "I think...Latin."

He stood, stepping down toward Tom.

"How are you, Tom?"

"I... I'm doing okay." Tom scratched the back of his neck.
"Truth is, Stan, I came over to talk about this war of yours."

Stanley's smile vanished.

"Not my war, Tom," he said sharply.

Tom flinched.

Stanley's voice softened—but his eyes didn't.

"No... *Our* war," Stanley said, fire rising behind his gaze. "They mean to push us out, Tom. Take our land. You'll see."

He looked out over his fields, as if peering into the future.

"I already have."

"Seen it?" Tom asked, uncertain.

"Oh, yes." Stanley nodded, placing a hand on Tom's shoulder.

"I've seen what happens when the suits get their way. When Albany forgets who feeds them. That we feed the whole damn state."

He leaned in. His breath reeked of ash and something hotter.

"They think Wall Street pays the bills. But without us?"

He waved a hand in the air.

"Pfft."

Tom shifted, unease crawling up his spine.

"People get worked up when you talk like that, Stan. When you use words like *war*. Someone could get hurt."

Stanley's grip tightened—too hard now.

"And what of it, Tom?" he whispered. "Maybe someone *should* get hurt."

Tom winced. He could feel the heat rolling off Stanley's skin.

"Forget I said anything. I should get going. Pigs need feeding and—"

Stanley didn't let go.

"Walk with me, Tom."

His voice was low. Steady.

"I want to show you something. Something that'll help you understand where I'm coming from."

Tom hesitated, tense—but relented, following Stanley around the side of the house.

Stan said little as they walked—just that eerie silence between men who had nothing safe left to say.

The night air was heavy, thick with humidity and the quiet hum of crickets. Fireflies blinked across the dark like sparks from a dying fire.
The scent of hay and manure hung low—familiar, but sour tonight.

They followed a worn dirt path toward the animal barn.

That's when Tom noticed it.

No grunts. No shuffling. None of the usual pig noise.

Just a low, constant buzzing.
Deep. Unnatural.
It vibrated in his chest. In his bones.

His heart picked up. His stomach turned.

He slowed.

Stanley's hand landed on his back—firm. Too firm.

"Not much farther now, Tom," he said.

There was a smile on Stanley's face.
But it didn't reach his eyes.

Tom gave a hesitant nod, glancing back toward the house—maybe for help, maybe for a reason.

But the porch was empty.
Everyone was gone.

Just him.
Just Stan.
And that sound.

They reached the barn.

Stanley flung open the door, and the smell hit Tom like a brick wall.

He staggered back, but Stanley's hand was there again, pressing him forward.

When had he gotten behind him?

The barn was hot. Dark. The air was thick with rot, old blood, and something fouler still.

Flies buzzed in clouds above them—but strangely, they didn't land on Stanley.
They hovered close...but never touched him.

Tom didn't know why.
Didn't *want* to.

"Sorry, old friend," Stanley said, voice sticky-sweet—wrong for the moment. "It's dark in here."

He lit a lantern.

And horror bloomed into light.

Two sows lay in the far corner, bellies split wide open.
Intestines spilled like ropes onto blood-slick floorboards.
The air stank of iron and rot. The pigs' eyes had gone milky
— no.

Not milky.

*Milk*, Tom thought, and his stomach pitched.

He turned, desperate to look away—only to catch sight of the far side of the barn.

The piglets.

They'd been…opened. Dissected. Rearranged.

No science. No purpose. Just cruelty.

Blood had been used to write something on the wall behind them.
Words. Symbols.
A prayer in red.

Tom bolted through the side door and doubled over, vomiting hard into the dirt.

His wife's mashed potatoes hit the ground in pale clumps.

Behind him, Stanley's voice floated out of the barn—cheerful. Calm.

"The book told me it would please it," he said, as the sound of vomit splattered the hard-packed earth.
"Just like tomorrow will please it, Tom."

Then colder:

"You've been telling folks to stay calm. Trust that bastard Governor Lehman.
You think he won't run us off this land? You think Wall Street gives a shit about your pigs?"

Stanley looked at Tom for a long moment—his lifelong friend.

And for that brief moment, he *saw* him.

Tom turned, staggering.

The pitchfork came down hard in a blur of black iron and brown wood.

It drove deep into Tom's back with a sickening crunch.
Metal pierced spine, lung, and hope in a single, practiced motion.

Tom convulsed forward. The air left him in a wet, rattling gasp.

No scream.
No fight.
Just blood.
Just silence.

Stanley leaned down, eyes glassy—far too bright.

"The book said this would please it too," he whispered.

Then he dragged Tom's body back inside the barn, one leg at a time, and closed the door behind him.

The buzzing flies settled once more.

3

The book hummed softly as Stanley walked back toward the house, his hands still red from the work.

It whispered in his mind.
Assurances. Promises.

This was important work. Sacred work.
*His* work.

He'd asked the book once—just once—who he was.
And what the book showed him...

A vision so unspeakably horrible—and so
wonderful—that Stanley never dared think of it again.

But he remembered how it made him feel.
Small.
Chosen.
Loved.

He wanted to please *him*.
He wanted to please the book. To make it happy.

His thumb stroked the spine as he walked—reverent,
almost shy. Tom's blood still coated his fingers, soaking into
the cracked black leather like the book was drinking it.

He reached the old hand pump in the front yard and
set the book down.

Instantly, a pang of longing hit him—deep, like
withdrawal.
But he gritted through it.

He pumped the handle twice.
Cold well water splashed over his hands.

Tom's blood swirled pink in the basin, then clear.
Gone.

Stanley dried his hands on his jeans and picked the
book back up.
And just like that, he felt whole again.

The hum returned.

So did the whispers.

But Stanley didn't go back into the house that night.

There were still steps to take.
More work to do.

4

Mary Rodrick had just put her baby down when she spotted a man walking down Main Street toward the Elks Lodge.

It was late, but the lodge was open—and so was that worthless Hulbert House—so at first, she thought nothing of it.

Except—it was Stanley Millard.

He'd just given a speech that afternoon out at his farm.

She stepped out onto the porch.

"Stanley?" Mary called, walking into the light. "Is everything okay?"
Her voice carried a hint of concern.
"Is Alice with you?" she asked, taking a cautious step toward the street.

Stanley looked over, but his eyes seemed...far away. He waved with one hand. In the other, he clutched a small black book. She couldn't make out the title.

"No," he said. "She stayed back at the farm. Cleaning up after her husband—as always, I'm afraid."

He smiled, but it didn't reach his eyes.
"Just need to see to a few things in town."

"Well," Mary said, trying to keep her tone light, "aren't you a man of the people these days? Will it be Mayor Millard someday soon?"

Stanley stopped walking.
Just for a second.

Something about the way he tilted his head—slightly toward the book in his hand—made Mary's chest tighten. Then he looked at her again.

That grin.
Too wide. Too knowing.

"No," he intoned. "I don't think politics is in my future…"

He paused.

"Maybe your great-grandson's though."

The words hit her wrong.
She didn't know why.

She stepped back, still smiling politely, but suddenly cold with unease.
"Well—I should check on Ronald. Have a good night, Stan. Give my best to Alice."

She didn't wait for a reply.

Mary slipped back into the house, shut the door, and—for the first time since her husband came back from France—locked it.

# Chapter 5: THE SALE AND THE COLLAPSE

1

"**I**'m looking for first editions," Maya repeated, her voice even and patient.

It wasn't the first time she'd had to say it twice.

Men rarely heard her the first time—at least, not the words. But she didn't mind. Not really.

She'd figured it out young—thirteen, maybe.

That everyone with a penis wanted to sleep with her.

And if the world insisted on treating her that way? Fine. She'd use it.

The bookstore, though… Something felt off.

Even for this town—which was saying something.

She'd read about the tragedy.

She'd seen the TikToks—grainy footage, exaggerated stories, all trying to go viral.

The so-called "cursed bookstore," the local lore.

High schoolers chasing clout with shaky phone footage and bad editing.

But now that she was *standing* in it?

It felt…different.

Heavier.

Then she saw it.
On the counter.

The book.

Ed seemed to snap out of whatever daze he was in—
right as Matt came crashing through the door behind her like
a confused Labrador.

Great. There went her discount.

"The old rare stuff is over there," Ed said, pointing to
a locked cabinet.

Maya's heart sank a little.
Damn. He knew what he had.
No clueless shopkeeper to take advantage of today.

Still…maybe.

She nodded toward the black book on the counter.
"What about that one?"

Ed followed her finger.
His hand moved before he really thought.

"That?" His voice tightened. "Not for sale."

She smiled. Not too big—just enough to blur the line
between flirtation and challenge.

"Your sign says *everything* must go."

It was the kind of smile that usually came with 20%
off and lingering eye contact.
The kind that made older men feel young—and stupid—
again.

And for a second, it almost worked.

Ed's grip loosened. His eyes flicked to her mouth.

Then he seemed to catch himself.

"Just look at our other stock," he said, firmer now.

Maya didn't argue.

She just turned and walked away—slowly, deliberately—letting him watch her go.

2

Matt stood back, watching the whole thing play out.
The walk-up.
The lean forward.
The smile that said, *Maybe I'll let you think I like you.*

It always played the same.
And he always hated it.

Not her—never her.
Just the way it made him feel.
That pang of jealousy. Shame. Resignation.

Maybe it held up a mirror.
Showed him Future Matt—a thirty-something shopkeeper handing a pretty girl an extra book, a free weekend, a better price.

He knew exactly what it was.
And still didn't care.
Not with Maya.

He took a few tentative steps closer, as he always did when she was working her charm.

And then—a whisper.

At first, he thought it was NPR static.
Something low and garbled, bleeding through the store speakers.

*She'll love you…if you get me for her…*

Matt blinked.

That wasn't NPR.
That wasn't a commercial.

He looked around.
Ed hadn't moved.
Maya was flipping through a shelf, oblivious.

*Get me…and you'll get her…*

There it was again.
Not loud.
But clear.

Matt spun, heart pounding, and his foot caught the edge of a low comic rack.
The whole thing tipped, a fan of brightly colored covers scattering across the floor with a clatter.

Maya didn't even look.
Just sighed and pinched the bridge of her nose.

"You're like a springer spaniel, Matt."
She smiled though.
"Go…find something better to do, please."

She patted his shoulder like he was a child who kept screwing up.

That stung more than the comment.

Matt knelt, scooping up the comics as fast as he

could.

Every eye was on him.

When he stood, Ed raised an eyebrow but chuckled.

"Everything okay over there?"

Matt flushed. "Yeah. Yeah, just…clumsy."

No point trying to be invisible now.

He walked up to the counter, where Ed was smoothing the black book's cover like it was a pet.

Matt nodded toward it. "What's the deal with that one?"

Ed didn't look up.

"Haven't you heard? It's cursed. Kills toddlers and single moms."

He paused.

"Then it kills bookstores."

The words came out flat. Bitter.

"Then why not sell it?"

Ed paused again.

"It's not up to me who buys it," he whispered.

And part of him believed that was true.

He didn't get it. But something in Ed's voice made him not want to.

3

Amanda sat in the nail salon, nearly done—just a chip from scraping the Tesla in a grocery lot—goddamn teenager's fault.

"You're a lifesaver, Angelina," Amanda said—and she meant it.
If she could pack up her nail girl and bring her with her, she would.
"Best in the area," she added, not looking up, letting her hand dangle while scrolling through her phone.

On a whim, she opened the security camera app. Might as well see if her worthless husband was actually working today.

To her surprise, the bookstore wasn't empty.

There were customers.

*Maybe those ridiculous ads worked,* she thought.
Not that she'd ever admit it to Ed.
She'd rather blow him tonight than give him the satisfaction.

She toggled to the interior cam.

And there she was.
Tall. Thin. Young.
Standing at the counter, smiling at Ed.

For way too long.

"What the fuck is this?" Amanda muttered.

Then louder: "No, not you, Lina. You're great."

But something twisted in her gut.

Jealousy.
Sharp. Immediate. Ugly.

And she didn't fucking like it.
Not one damn bit.

Still, she watched the girl work her magic on her husband—*when had she started thinking of him like that again?* Amanda shook the thought off.

Then she saw it.

On the counter.

The black book.

She zoomed in—impressive, considering Angelina was still working on her nail—but she managed.
And in a blink, it was like a film reel unfurling behind her eyes:

Their courtship in high school.
The good times.
None of the bad.
Their marriage...the good years...
All rushing back, uninvited.

The closer she zoomed, the worse it felt—the faster those memories flooded in.

*That girl.*
That girl had her hands too close to the book...
Too close to her husband.

Help.

The whisper slipped behind her eyes.
Not a sound.
A command.

SERVE ME.

It flashed like a neon sign across the back of her mind.

Amanda blinked. Dazed.

Her hand buzzed faintly, like holding a phone mid-vibration, but nothing moved.

Her phone was dead.
Just a black screen.
Battery gone.

A bead of sweat clung to her temple.

Angelina finished with a flourish.

"Perfect, as always," Amanda murmured, staring at her flawless nails.

It wouldn't do to have a chip.

Not today.

4

Ed sat back and enjoyed the show.

Literally.

Did that make him a perv? Yes.
But she was doing it on purpose, and it would've felt rude *not* to look.

Besides, Matt had bailed hours ago when Evelyn came sniffing around for dinner, and Ed figured—at this point—all was fair in love and books.

"Listen, Maya…you've been at this for two hours

now," Ed said, resting his elbows on the counter.
"Not that I mind the company, but at some point, you're
gonna get me rezoned as a library."

Maya smiled her too-charming, too-practiced smile
and placed another two first editions on the counter.

"Sell me the TikTok book," she said, winking. "And
I'm gone."

Ed looked at her—visions of the empty register, the
money he just blew on social media ads, and that goddamn
Tesla payment flashing through his mind.

"Five thousand dollars."

The number dropped from his mouth before he
could stop it—and pain spiked behind his eyes, like someone
had driven a nail into the base of his skull.

"Deal," Maya said instantly, already reaching into her
bag.

Too fast.
Too eager.

Shit.

Matt was going to kill her.
That was almost all the money they had — No, all the money
*he* had.

She knew it.
She had five hundred on a credit card.
Matt had saved—nearly every cent—for these trips, with the
promise of repayment someday.

Maya often flaked.
But she'd never spent this much before.

She wanted that book.
No—she *needed* it.

Ed's hands moved on their own.
He slid her card through the reader, numb.

"Six thousand, three twenty-five. Sign at the bottom."

He handed her the receipt.
A sharp pain shot through his arm, causing him to wince.
But Maya, absorbed in the book, didn't see.

She signed without hesitation.

He exhaled—and the pain left his body the moment her signature dried.

Guilt rushed in.
Not for the money.
Not for the lie.

But for the book.

The one his father refused to sell.
Ever.
Too late now.

He boxed up the black book — and three rare first editions that had been in his family since the 1930s — and handed them across the counter to a college student from Boston.

Maya beamed.

A sunbeam.
A thief.

"Will you be in town long?" Ed asked.
His hands itched. Skin crawling.

His stomach lurched like he'd been vomiting all night.

Maya glanced at the box, then back at him.

"Oh yes. I want to check out Rome and Utica. See if I can find more treasures."
She smiled again. "But I doubt I'll find anything quite like *this* one."

"That I can promise," Ed whispered.

He watched her go, head pounding now.
He should've asked for ten grand.
No—ten *million*.

The bell jingled.

Matt and Evelyn walked in, carrying a bag of Burger King.

"Looks like your dinner's here," Ed muttered.

He looked defeated.
Not like someone who just made more money in one transaction than in the last six months.

Maya smiled. Colder this time.

Transaction complete.

"Thanks for the books," she said with a wink, lifting the box.

Then she turned and walked out the door.

The chime echoed behind her.
The lights buzzed.

Ed stood there, rubbing at his temple, already missing something he never should've given away.

The book was gone.

But the store still remembered.

It had sat there for ninety-two years.

The fluorescents flickered.
The floor swayed — Not like an earthquake.
More like the building itself was…unsettled.

Wrong.

Ed stepped out from behind the counter.
His knees buckled.

Pressure bloomed behind his eyes—the kind that
comes before a nosebleed.
Or a scream.

But there was no sound.
Just absence.

Something had been ripped out of the room.
And the room didn't know how to hold itself together
without it.

He reached for his chair—his familiar anchor.

Didn't make it.

His legs gave out.
He crumpled to the floor, shoulder-first, into a shelf.
Wood cracked.
Books tumbled.

Hardcovers rained down like stones.

One hit his shoulder. Another, his head.
One caught him…lower.
Of course it did.

He winced.

But his last thought wasn't pain.

It was a question:

*Is this where they found my dad?*

Then the dark came for him.
And the store was quiet again.

# Chapter 6: CLAVIS NUMQUAM FUIT SANGUIS

1

Maya sat in the back seat.

*For once—the back seat.*

It annoyed her, but she let it go. She'd need to piss Matt off later, and letting Miss Local ride up front felt like a fair trade.

Let the boy win something for once.

She held the box in her lap as they drove south on Route 46 toward Rome, New York.
The sun was setting—cows and cornfields casting long shadows across the fields.
Evelyn had mentioned a shop that might have books.
Maya had a few bucks left on her credit card.

Good enough.

She opened the box.
Lifted the black book out—heavier than it looked—and set the rest of the books beside her on the seat.

The leather felt old but soft. No title. No author.
She raised it to her nose. Inhaled.

The scent made her shiver.

God, she loved that smell.

She rotated the book, inspecting the spine, the edges.

She decided she could open it carefully.

So she did.

The world tilted.

The first page was blank.
Like most books.

But the second one wasn't.

A faded inscription in delicate cursive sprawled across the top:

*The time may come when the light will fade, and time will stop. To whoever finds this first, know that I did not mean for any of this to come to pass.*

Maya squinted at the name underneath.

Unreadable.

She turned the page.

At the center—set apart like a commandment chiseled in stone—was a single Latin phrase:

*Clavis numquam fuit sanguis... sed voluntas.*

"Fuck," Maya muttered.

"Something wrong?" Matt asked, glancing at her in the mirror. Their debate over which version of Commander Shepard was superior now paused.

"Yeah. I don't know Latin. Professor Taylor always said it'd bite me in the ass... Well—ass, meet teeth."

"I know Latin," Evelyn said, spinning around in her seat. Her hazel eyes lit up, practically glowing with gotcha pride.

"To quote Stu Redman: 'Country don't mean dumb.'"

Maya raised the book so she could see.

Evelyn mouthed the words, then read aloud:

*"Clavis numquam fuit sanguis... sed voluntas..."*
"The key was never blood... but will."

She shivered.

"That's creepy as fuck."

Then she turned back around and nudged Matt, like she hadn't just read something out of a cursed grimoire.

Maya didn't answer.
She was still holding the phrase in her head—like it was alive.

*The key was never blood... but will.*

Her blood ran cold.

The car dimmed around her.
Or maybe it was the light outside.

But the book?

The book seemed brighter.
Alive on her lap.

She turned the page.
Didn't know why.
Didn't care.

The words didn't matter anymore.
The book mattered.

It felt right in her hand. Like it had been waiting.

"Hey, Eve?" Maya asked, her voice lower now.
Slower.

Not bubbly. Not sarcastic.
Something else.

*Something beneath.*

"When we stop…can you read more of this to me? I think it wants to tell me something."

Evelyn smiled, oblivious.
"Sure. Happy to help."

Outside the window, the sky darkened.
The cows and cornfields blurred past, indifferent.

What Evelyn didn't see—couldn't see—was the book already working.

Shaping.
Twisting.

Not just Maya.

All of them.

2

They made it to Rome in about thirty minutes.

Maya couldn't tell whether that was fast or slow.

She didn't care.

She was starting not to care about *anything* but the book.

Which was…odd.

Matt and Evelyn—now full-on lovebirds—had gone inside to ask if the shop had old books.

Maya hadn't moved.
Didn't look up.
Didn't want to.

She turned another page.

Her hand brushed over the paper—worn, soft, almost warm.

It thrilled her.
Like a new crush might.
Sitting in the car outside a party, heart racing, wondering if the guy would grow a pair and kiss you.

A flash—Matt kissing her.

Maya blinked. Shook it off.

What the fuck was that?

She'd never—not once—considered Matt anything more than a tagalong. A friend.
*Barely* that.

He was nice. Sweet.
But once college was over?
She doubted they'd ever talk again.

She turned another page.

And something shifted.

The Latin...made sense.
No effort. No translation.
Just meaning—flowing straight into her mind as if it had always been there, waiting.

Numbers.
Passages beneath them.

Symbols curled in the margins like thoughts you shouldn't think.

And then—a passage:

---

Then rose Asem, first among the Gathered, whose heart was heavy with yearning, and whose mind did tremble at the edge of the Abyss.
He spake not, for words do falter before the Voice.
But he approached the altar with feet bare, and soul bared...

And he took up the *Blade of Unseeing*, forged in silence, quenched in ash.
With hand unwavering, he drew it across the sockets of his sight...

Blood fell in rivers, black and slow, and each drop sang a name long forgotten.
His eyes, he placed upon the altar stone, lids open, staring into nothing, as an offering unto *He Who Sees Without*.

And lo, the altar groaned, and the stone did drink.

Then came the *Veiled One*, who reached forth and touched Asem's brow with a finger of shadow and spake:

*"Thou hast severed the lesser sight, and I bestow the greater."*

And behold: where once were eyes, now bloomed voids—black stars, still and seeing.
Asem beheld the truth behind truths, the shapes that move beneath thought, the light that devours...

He fell not, nor did he cry, for his soul was bound in iron.
But his voice was broken, and thenceforth he spake only in

riddles and grief…

The Gathered beheld him and despaired, for they knew the price—and yet their feet did not flee.

Thus was he sanctified in blindness, and through his wound was wisdom poured like oil.

And his name was struck from the records,
*for those who see with the inner eye have no need of remembrance.*

---

Maya's breath hitched.
Her fingers twitched.
She couldn't feel the seat beneath her.

Her eyes had gone glassy.
Not blinking.
Not seeing.

But reading.

Even the sky outside seemed darker now.

The book hummed.
Vibrated in her hands.

Without looking down.
Without *reading*—

Maya spoke.

And her voice…wasn't hers.

---

"*Per velamen carnis, undique viscus quaero…*
**Through the veil of flesh, I seek the gaze that sears.**

*Visus meus non deficiat; ut veritati testimonium perhibeam sub veritate…*

**Let my sight be unmade, that I may witness the truth beneath truth.**

*Vexillifer Lucis, Custos Oculi Qui Foris Videt; aperi me…*

**O Bearer of the Unlight, Keeper of the Eye That Sees Without, open me.**

*Non ad salutem… sed ad denudationem…*

**Not for salvation… but for unveiling.**

*Lumina detrahe minora; nisi inane relinquere…*

**Strip these lesser eyes; leave only void.**

*Lux falsa uratur. Figura post figuram reveletur…*

**Let the false light be burned away. Let the shape behind the shape be revealed.**

*Visionem meam praebeo; pro claritate…*

**I offer my vision in exchange for clarity.**

*Nomen meum offero; in commutatione ad cognoscendum…*

**I offer my name in exchange for knowing.**

*Me praebeo…*

**I offer myself.**

*Fiat. Fiat…*

**So be it.”**

---

Then silence.

She closed the book.

And smiled.

Not her usual smile.
Not *Maya's* smile.

Something was wrong about it now.
There was something older in her eyes.
Something deeper.
Someone else.

A single drop of blood slipped from her nose and struck the pavement.

No one noticed.

Least of all her.

She was staring into the bookstore.

Still.

Unblinking.

Like something inside was staring back.

Yet the window's reflection showed nothing but her own blank stare.

3

Evelyn glanced out the big glass window of the bookstore.

Maya sat on the hood of Matt's car, just staring at the book.

Not reading it.
Just…looking.

Like it was talking to her.

She kept petting the damn thing too—stroking the leather like it might *purr*.

Creepy as hell.

"Matt," Evelyn said, nudging him. "Is she, uh…okay?"

In her head, she'd said:
*Hey, I think your friend's losing the plot and maybe we need to take her somewhere.*
But she didn't know them well enough yet.

So she settled for the nudge.
For now.

Matt barely looked up.
"She's fine," he mumbled, digging through a shelf of trade paperbacks.

Still hunting for something to impress Maya.
Still trying to win her favor—for some fucking reason that Evelyn couldn't wrap her head around.

Here she was—right here—flirting with him the whole drive down,
laughing at his dumb jokes,
dropping hints like bricks.

And he was still carrying a torch.
Typical.

She sighed and went back to scanning spines—but not before elbowing him again.

Just hard enough.
A little jolt.
As if to say:
"Hey, dipshit. Someone actually wants your attention.

Someone who doesn't give a shit about your car or

your wallet."

Matt grunted and gave her that crooked Midwestern smile—the one that looked like he wasn't sure if he'd left his boots under your bed or someone else's.

God, she hated how much she liked that smile.

Fucking hormones.

She rolled her eyes, grabbed a first edition medical text, and held it up like bait.
"Hey, nerd. You want to impress a girl?
Try giving her something she *can't* read for once."

Matt took it, laughing.

And for just a second, Evelyn forgot all about the weird girl on the hood
with the book that hummed like it was dreaming.

4

He needed to find something.
Anything.

It didn't matter what—he just wanted to show Maya he wasn't some clumsy, forgettable fool.

Evelyn stood by the window, arms crossed, staring out at the car.

At Maya.

What the hell was she doing?

Didn't matter.

She was fine.
She was *always* fine.

He turned back to the books.
Focus.
Find something good.
Something rare.
Something impressive.

He flipped through brittle pages, hands shaking.

*She has me...*

The voice again.
Same whisper from Boonville.
Soft—curling behind his ears like smoke.

He clenched his jaw.
"Fuck off," he muttered.

It didn't scare him this time.
It pissed him off.

She could have anyone.
And it was never him.
Never Matt.

Heat flooded his chest—fast, angry, buzzing.

Then — a hard nudge to his side.

Cool fingers.
Warm eyes.
Evelyn.

She grinned up at him—crooked and cocky.
A lifeline.

"Hey, nerd. You wanna impress a girl?" she said.

"Try giving her something she can't read for once."

Matt laughed—really laughed—and took the book from her hand.

It felt good.
Better than it should have.

And yet...

He glanced out the window again.
Maya was still there.

Still staring at the book in her lap — like it was whispering secrets into her bones.

And now...

She was looking at them.
Through the glass.
Smiling.

Only—it didn't feel right.

That smile.
It didn't reach her eyes.

Something about her eyes—wrong. Watching, but not seeing. Or maybe seeing too much.
Didn't feel like her at all.

The medical text slipped from Matt's hand.
He didn't notice.

Instead,
his fingers found Evelyn's.

And this time...
he didn't let go.

# Chapter 7: DYNAMITE AND A TALKING BOOK

1

Stanley walked into the dark room of the Hulbert House — smoke thick, laughter low, whiskey flowing in cracked-glass tumblers no one bothered to hide anymore.

Prohibition was dying. And with it, any pretense of law.

Besides, they had bigger problems now.

He smiled as he sat at the bar.
A glass of amber appeared without a word.

He nodded to the bartender, took a slow sip, and set the black book gently on the polished wood.

The room went quiet.

Men turned in their seats.
A few women leaned in.
Waiting.

"Tonight," Stanley said, fingers brushing the book's spine like checking for a pulse, "we block the highway."

A murmur rippled.

"They'll come fast, trying to break us up.
The Millers won't help—they've got a shipment heading out at dawn.

Jenkins, you stop it.
Dump it in the fields if you have to.
No milk leaves this town."

He stood straighter.

"Albany will send its goons. You know that.
And we will meet them.
We will defend our homes. Our farms."

For a moment, no one moved.

Then:
A man spat into a jar.
Another muttered a curse.

"Damn right!" someone barked.
"You tell 'em, Stanley!"

Stanley drained his glass and set it down with a hard
clink.

"If something happens to me," he said — slower
now.
His voice dipped into something harder.
Older.

"This book goes to the old shop on Main.
Rodrick will keep it safe.
Until I'm back."

No one asked *from what.*

"Get some sleep.
Load your weapons.
Tomorrow—bring war."

He turned.
Boots thudded toward the door.

The bar slowly returned to motion—chairs shifting, glasses clinking, low voices rising.

And the black book sat on the counter.
Quiet.
Waiting.

Not for Stanley.

The book had already charted his course.

It waited now…
for its next vessel.

2

Joshua Miller had just filled the last of the milk cans and was loading them onto the wagon when the first edge of sunlight crested the eastern tree line.

Maples and oaks stood in still rows, the morning fog pulling back from the fields like a curtain.

It was shaping up to be a beautiful August morning.

The cows lowed lazily, content with the dew and the quiet—as if they, too, agreed it would be a fine day.

Joshua wiped his brow.
Already in the sixties, and humid—another warm one.

*Weather that makes men do stupid things.*

His eyes drifted to the loaded cart.
He sighed.

He knew it was a risk—going against the others.

But he needed the money. Desperately.
And a little money now was worth more than Stanley's
maybe-money later.

He climbed into the old horse-drawn wagon—the
one he swore, every damn spring, he'd replace with a proper
truck.

But not this year.
Not with the prices what they were.

He snapped the reins.
The horse let out a soft protest, then lurched forward, hooves
echoing in the dirt.

Joshua glanced back at the farm as it receded behind
him.
His wife would be up by now, probably coaxing their
daughter from bed for morning lessons.

Life on a farm never stopped.
Not for politics.
Not for protests.
And sure as hell not for some madman's war.

Two miles down the road,
Joshua spotted Andy Jenkins standing near the ditch, waving
him down.

Joshua muttered, *"What the hell is this now…"*
and slowed the wagon, pulling back on the reins.

The horse snorted and came to a stop.

"What's the matter, Andy?" he asked, the irritation
plain in his voice.

"Oh, I'm glad I caught you," Andy said, already

climbing up into the cart like it was his.
"Hoping to catch a ride into town, if that's alright."

"Into town? It's gotta be barely six," Joshua said, squinting at him—confused and still annoyed.
He just wanted the delivery done.
Wanted the milk off the cart before Stanley tried something stupid.
Before any of this turned into more than talk.

Andy didn't answer.
Just smiled and leaned back on the wagon seat.

Joshua frowned.

Then, reluctantly, he snapped the reins again.

The horse groaned and walked.
And Andy smiled a little wider.

Something about that smile sat wrong with Josh.
But the road rolled on.

3

Stanley needed supplies—but not the kind you picked up at Woolworth's.

No, these were *special* supplies.
The kind that killed state troopers.
Politicians.
Hell—anyone who got in his way.

He moved through the overgrown grass behind the Department of Public Works, boots damp with morning dew, air thick with heat—and coming violence.

Somewhere in the dark guts of that building was what he needed.

Andy Jenkins had let it slip one night, whiskey loosening his tongue—the DPW still had a case of dynamite left over from the Route 46 project.
Forgotten.
Unsecured.

Stanley smiled at the thought.
A few well-placed charges would send a message to Albany— a fitting end.

The book liked that.
Which meant *he* liked that.

He didn't have it with him anymore.
Didn't matter.

It spoke regardless—inside his skull, behind his eyes, like a memory turned inside out.

It told him what to do.
Where to go.
What to burn.

And Stanley obeyed.

He reached the building just as the sun cleared the treetops.
"Locked," he muttered, testing the door.

Footsteps.

A man rounded the corner—John Turner.
Stanley recognized him from another town.
Quiet.
Nice enough.

Didn't matter.

Stanley slipped into the shadows and waited.
When John stepped up and unlocked the door, Stanley was on him.

He slammed his full weight into the man, driving John's head into the steel door with a sickening crack.
They hit the pavement.

Stanley was already on top—hands clawing at John's face.

Searching.

Then—found them.
Two hollows.
Perfect.

Stanley drove his thumbs in.
John screamed. Wetly.

A pop. Slick.
His screams turned to gasps.

Then silence.

Stanley lifted John's head and slammed it into the concrete.
Once.
Twice.
Five times.

Until the body twitched.
Then seized.

Calm now—methodically—Stanley wiped his hands on John's shirt, pulled the keys from his pocket, and slipped inside.

The book wasn't with him.
It didn't need to be.

It was within him.
And it wanted dynamite.

---

Inside, Stanley moved with purpose.
He knew exactly what he was looking for—and found it.

A dusty wooden crate marked:
**DANGER — EXPLOSIVES**
sat in a supply room corner.

But there was more.

Propped against the wall beside it:
A Winchester Model 42 pump-action shotgun.

Ten shells in a rusted metal tin.

His grin widened.

A green canvas bag hung near the door.
Stanley loaded his new toys with care—first the dynamite,
then the shotgun and shells.

Everything had its place.

Before leaving, Stanley turned back toward the
entrance.

John Turner's body still twitched.

Stanley grabbed him by the shoulders
and dragged him inside, propping him just behind the utility
sink.

Then he closed the door.
And locked it.

It would be a full week before anyone found John's body.

And when they did, they discovered something worse.

His fingernails had been peeled off one by one—not by another man, but by his own raw desperation.

He'd clawed at the inside of the locked door.

Blind.
Alone.
And alive.
For days.

4

Captain Leon Webb sat alone at Trooper Barracks 30, just south of Boonville, when the phone rang.

Something about farmers.
Uprising.
Milk prices.

He sighed.
Rubbed his temples.

"Christ. Don't they know there's a Depression?"

He grabbed the receiver and barked into it, already dialing the other barracks.

"Darren? It's Leon. Something's brewing up north— Boonville."

A pause.

"What do you mean it's already in three counties?"

Webb sat up straighter, the receiver suddenly slick in his hand.

"Four hundred men?"

He hung up.
Dialed Albany.
His voice was calmer than he felt.

"This is Webb, Lee Barracks. We're going to need backup. A lot."

He stared at the wall, mind racing.
Something was happening in Boonville.
And it wasn't just about milk anymore.

---

Outside, the morning had gone unnaturally still.
No birdsong.
Not even the wind.

Just that dead quiet that makes the back of a man's neck go cold.

Webb cracked the radio.

"Dispatch, this is Webb. Full mobilization. North route. All of it. Now."

As he reached for his sidearm,
A whisper came then.

Or so he thought...
behind him.

*He walks along the road.*

*He walks along the road.*
*He walks along the road...*

Webb turned fast—but the room was empty.

Just the map on the wall.
His eyes were drawn to Boonville.
Like a heartbeat.

And somewhere out there, walking a dirt road with a shotgun slung low and someone else's blood already staining his jeans, Stanley Millard was humming.

*Love is the sweetest thing...*
**Click.**
*What else on earth could ever bring...*
**Click.**
*Such happiness to everything...*
**Click.**
*As love's old story...*
**Click.**
*Love is the strangest thing...*

# Chapter 8: AFTERMATH AND DARK BARGAINS

1

Ed woke up on the floor.
His back cramped.
His ass was numb.
And—yep—his balls ached like hell.

He groaned as he sat up. The world tilted, pulsing in sync with his heartbeat. The edges of his vision went dark, threatening another blackout. But after a few shallow breaths, he brought himself back.

It was nighttime now.

The street outside the window lay dark and quiet. Inside the shop, the lights were off—just the faint red glow of the IR camera in the corner and a pale wash of moonlight leaking through the blinds.

He didn't move.
Just sat there, letting the same words loop through his mind:

*It's gone.*
*The book is gone.*
*But something else had left with it.*

The weight.

The bookstore—always heavy with dust, silence, and

something *unseen*—felt...lighter.
Like it had finally exhaled.
For the first time, the place didn't press on his chest.

Ed grunted, reached for the counter, and hauled
himself upright.
His body complained—loudly—but he made it.

He shuffled to the light switches.
Flicked them on — and froze.

What if it were all gone?
What if someone came in while he was out cold, cleaned him
out, took everything?

But the lights buzzed on—row by row.
NPR crackled back to life through the overhead speakers.

The shelves were still full.

The store was still his.

Not just his father's dream.
Not just a burden.
His.

He smiled. Turned toward the counter.
Ran a hand across the old wood and whispered,

"I can't sell you, old girl."

---

"Really, Ed?"

He jumped.

Amanda was sitting in his chair.
Arms crossed.
Eyes blazing.

He hadn't even seen her there.

"Keeping the store, are we?" she asked, her voice tight.

"I…just…mean… Well," Ed stammered. His head was still spinning. His back throbbed. Hell, everything hurt. And here she was—already laying into him like he hadn't just passed out on the goddamn floor.

"We are not keeping this damn store, Ed."
Her voice cut clean and sharp.
"You promised me. You assured me we'd be out of this godforsaken state by October—at the latest."

"I—" he tried.

"I don't want to hear it.
*You*. It's always *you*. Never me.

While you sat here flirting with that little high school thing—college? Whatever—selling what? One book?

Not that it matters.
Unless pretty Miss Flirts-a-Lot is going to buy this place. Or suck your dick. Is she, Ed?

Is she going to fuck you, marry your worthless ass, and stay in this town where there are more goddamn cows than people?"

Her voice cracked. But she kept going.

"Because I am *done*.
You hear me?

You keep this store—*you lose me*.

And best believe, Ed—my lawyer will make sure I *still*

get this piece-of-shit bookstore.

And when I do?"

She stood.

"I'll sell it. Burn it to the ground.
Hell, I'll piss on the ashes just for fun."

She shoved past him.
The bell above the door chimed as she left.

Her Tesla started before she even reached it — the gullwing door hissing open like a threat.

Ed watched her go—again.

She nearly clipped some poor bastard driving past; the Tesla fishtailed for a second before it roared down Main Street.

He didn't move.
Just stood there.

Watching.

But the longer he stood, the more it gnawed at him.

The thought of her getting her hands on the store—his store—didn't just bother him.

It *infuriated* him.

This wasn't just square footage and old paper.
This was his family's story.

No.

It was his story now.

And Amanda?

She wouldn't touch a goddamn page of it.

Not now.
Never.

2

Maya drove.

Yes—now she was *fucking driving*.

Just one more indignity to suffer on this goddamn trip.

The *lovebirds*—as she now thought of them—cuddled in the back seat, whispering, giggling, warm and tangled like teenagers who'd just discovered touching.

The black book sat in the passenger seat beside her.

Where it belonged.

It whispered to her as they sped down the blacktop, slicing past Delta Lake, the moon casting silver across its glassy surface. The water shimmered as if it held secrets, as if it was waiting for something.

Then the radio crackled to life.

Unprompted.

A song from another time wheezed through the static:

*"Love is the sweetest thing*
*What else on earth could ever bring*
*Such happiness to everything*
*As love's old story…"*

"That's an old-ass song," Matt said from the back, half-laughing, unsure if he was amused or creeped out.

"The book likes it," Evelyn murmured, her head resting on his shoulder, eyes half-lidded.

Maya nodded.

Didn't speak.
Just turned it up.

Matt blinked. He looked down at Evelyn, confused. Unsure if he'd actually heard her say that—or if he was ready to admit it.

*"Love is the strongest thing*
*The oldest yet, the latest thing*
*I hope only that fate may bring..."*

Static.

Hard.
Sharp.
Wrong.
Like something *sucked* the sound out of the air, yanking it back into a silence that wasn't natural.

The song vanished.

Maya didn't flinch.

She leaned in just slightly, lips close to the book's cover, and whispered—just loud enough for it to hear:

"Play it again."

And it did.

Not through the speakers.

In her head.

The music returned—smooth, rich, otherworldly—curling through her mind like smoke. Maya swayed gently to the phantom tune, humming along with a voice only she could hear.

Matt watched her in the mirror.
Watched her sway.

And the fear in his chest…grew teeth.

3

"I wish I could do more to help," Matt said, looking at her from across the small, plastic table at the Dunkin'.

Evelyn bit her lower lip, her pulse quickening as the weight of his words settled over her.
More.
A single syllable, dense with unspoken possibilities—each one both thrilling and terrifying.

She took a shaky breath, emboldened by the warmth of his hand over hers and the sincerity in his eyes.

"M—more?" she asked, voice smaller than she meant. "For example?"
She looked into his eyes, hoping—begging—for something. A hint, anything.

Matt hesitated.
"I don't know…"

Evelyn held her breath. Her heart pounded.
Hope clawed at her chest even as fear told her to run.
Still, she leaned in slightly.

*Come on, Matt.*

"Take you. Run away together," he said, eyes blazing.

She gasped. Her eyes widened.
A flush crept up her neck as the words settled in—reckless, beautiful, impossible.

"Run away together?" she echoed, barely a whisper.

"It's just...a silly notion that popped into my head," Matt said quickly, walking it back.

A pang of disappointment flickered through her—tangled with relief.
She laughed softly, shaking her head.

"Silly notions are the most compelling, don't you think?" she said.
"There's a kind of freedom in indulging them—even if only for a moment."

Matt didn't smile.

He just looked at her.

"The best ones..." he said, "you just get in the car. Go west."

Evelyn inhaled sharply. The image flared in her mind—empty highways, freedom, escape.
Her heart raced.

"West, huh?" she said, letting the idea bloom.
A new life. Away from here.

"Or flip a coin," he offered.

She chuckled.
Absurd. Intoxicating.

"Flip a coin, hmm? Heads we flee, tails I stay chained to this misery…"

Matt reached into his pocket.
Produced a silver coin. Slid it across the table.

"I've carried that Liberty dollar every day for the last twelve years—except during surgeries, of course. If you want to leave it to fate…that's the vessel I'm letting fate drive."

Evelyn stared at it.

Her fingers brushed the cool metal. She picked it up reverently, turning it over.
It felt solid. Real.

"A Liberty dollar," she murmured.
"How fitting."

She looked up at him.

"Considering the gravity of the decision we'd be making."

"I know," Matt said.

She took a deep breath.
The coin grounded her.
The moment tilted.

Then—without a word—she flicked her wrist and sent it spinning.

It danced through the air, silver catching the light.
One bounce.
Two.
Three.

It landed.

Heads.

Lady Liberty glinted back at them—clear and undeniable.

Neither of them moved.

Evelyn slowly looked up.

Her hazel eyes shimmered—uncertainty, excitement, and something new.
Something electric took root.

Outside, a crow let out a low, rasping caw.
The wind, dead all day, scratched at the glass like fingernails.

Evelyn blinked, as if she'd just remembered she had a body.

Her eyes were too wide now.
Too bright.

Hunger.

"Well…" she whispered.

"Well…" Matt echoed, that crooked farm-boy smile tugging at his lips—the one that always made Evelyn feel like her knees didn't quite work right.

"All we need to do," he said, like a man soothing a child mid-fire alarm, "is help Maya. Serve the book."

His eyes didn't flicker.
His voice didn't rise.

"You want this too. I know you do."

His hand rose—slow and reverent—and cupped her face.

"You'll make it right...for us."

His thumb brushed just under her eye.
And for a moment, Evelyn forgot how to breathe.

The fluorescent lights buzzed.
Outside, the sky dimmed another shade—like it was listening.

And inside her chest, something shifted.
Hardened.
Settled.

She nodded. Just once.

A small, traitorous motion.

Outside, the Dunkin' windows went black—not from the hour, but from the sky itself folding in on the sun like it was ashamed.

The air thickened. Humid. Heavy. Like the world was holding its breath.

Then — Thunder.
Close.
Wrong.

Evelyn flinched.

Matt didn't.

He was still smiling. Like he'd just asked her to elope, or go halfsies on a road trip.

And something inside her—something still and dark and waking—smiled back.

"Yes," she said.

The word left her lips like a vow.

A tremor ran through her.

The book wasn't even there.
But it was watching.
Like a cat waiting for a bird to twitch.

Matt reached across the table and tucked a curl behind her ear.
His touch was gentle.
Warm.
Possessive.

"That's my girl," he whispered.

Outside, the wind picked up.

The world bent.

———

Far up Route 46, Maya drove on, the black book nestled beside her like a lover.

She hummed that old tune—the one the book liked.

And somewhere inside Evelyn's chest... her heart hummed it too.

She dreamed of Matt.
Of helping Maya.
Of doing unspeakable things.

Ahead, Route 46 stretched like a promise.

In the driver's seat, Maya hummed a song only she could hear.

Matt looked down at Evelyn and brushed her hair from her eyes.

This was all going very wrong.

And he knew it.

But he didn't know how to stop it.

And Maya?
She didn't see the darkness on the road ahead.

She barely saw anything anymore.

Except the book.

It pulsed beside her like a second heart.

She hummed.

*"Love is the sweetest thing…"*

And the book?

It sang back.

# Chapter 9: HE WALKS THE ROAD

1

They came from everywhere—Lee, Holland Patent, Westernville, even as far as Alder Creek.

Trucks rattled down dirt roads.

Men marched on foot, pitchforks over shoulders.

Some brought hunting rifles. Others just brought rage.

Stanley watched from the treeline, a slow smile creeping across his face.

Pride bloomed in his chest.

The men of this land were ready to stand up.

To fight for something that mattered.

But that wasn't what he was doing.

Not anymore.

Let someone else whip the crowd into a frenzy.

Let them block roads, tip over milk carts, chant in the streets.

Stanley had bigger plans.

Older ones.

He slipped into the trees, shotgun slung over one shoulder, the canvas bag of explosives heavy on the other. The woods swallowed him whole.

And somewhere, the book—though far from his hands—was smiling too.

Twenty minutes later, Stanley stepped out of the forest onto a dirt road just outside town.

The Miller cart was already there.
Tipped over.
Milk cans lined up like little tombstones along the ditch.

Andy had tied the horse to a tree.

Along with Miller.

Andy had done his part.

Stanley was soaked in sweat, his red-stained jeans and shirt clinging to his chest.
He set the bag down, then walked to the horse.

One pat on the hindquarters.
Then the shotgun barked.

Half of the horse's head disappeared.
It staggered once, blood arcing hot across the dirt road, painting it dark.

It didn't fall right away.
Part of its brain was still trying to figure out what had happened.

Then, slowly, it collapsed.

Andy stared. That dumb half-grin still on his face —
until Stanley turned the gun on him.

The blast hit Andy in the chest.
He dropped beside the horse, hands scrabbling at the hole where his lung used to be, gurgling like a clogged drain.

Stanley stepped over his twitching leg, calm as ever.

Joshua Miller thrashed against the ropes, wrists raw and bleeding from trying to break free.
His mouth moved, but no sound came.

"Won't work," Stanley said, crouching beside him. "Andy ties a hell of a knot."

He leaned in close, breath hot against Josh's face.

"Why?" Josh rasped. The word barely made it out.

Stanley smiled.
"I stopped asking why the book wants things."
He knelt lower. "Safer that way."

Then, gently, he wiped the sweat from Miller's forehead—like a father tending a fever.

"For example—why does it want you alive?"

He stood.

"Not my concern.

You're lucky. Sort of. You get to sit here and breathe this in until someone finds you. Lucky might be a stretch, but hey—you're not going to hell today."

He glanced back at the wreckage.
"Guess you'll need that new truck after all."

Stanley turned and kicked over each milk can, one by one, until the air reeked of sour cream and blood.

He hefted the bag, reloading his shotgun as he walked.

And hummed sweetly, like a lullaby:

"Love is the sweetest thing…"

2

Captain Webb sat behind the wheel of his patrol car, sweat clinging to his brow.

They'd made it to Boonville in record time—if anyone asked—but it still didn't feel fast enough.

Farmers were massing in the fields just outside town. Too many. Too fast.

He couldn't move yet—not without backup.

The radios crackled with half-clear reports:
Blockades. Armed men.
Rumors of dynamite.

Webb didn't trust rumors.
But he trusted panic.

And this?
This was starting to feel like the kind of thing you didn't walk away from clean.

He glanced up at the town clock: 9:20 a.m.
Already in the seventies. Humid.
His forearm came away wet when he wiped his face.

"Damn," he muttered, staring down the narrow main road.
Boonville sat ahead—quiet. Watching.
Like it was waiting for something to begin.

From somewhere in the back of his skull, an old memory surfaced:
Nickel novels from his childhood—pulp Westerns where the

sheriff rides into town just before everything goes to hell.

"He walks the road…"
The whisper slid through his mind again.

Webb clenched his jaw and shoved it away.

He drove slowly.

The town felt wrong.
Empty, but not silent. As if something just under the surface
was humming—waiting.
Eyes peered out from windows and vanished.
Curtains twitched.
Doors creaked shut as he passed.

This wasn't the Boonville he knew.
Not the sleepy hamlet that always waved when the trooper
car rolled through.
Even in the '30s, cars were still a kind of magic out here—
people noticed. People smiled.

Today, no one smiled.

Webb pulled up outside the Hulbert House, killed the
engine, and stepped into the thick morning heat.

He adjusted his belt.
Placed his hat carefully on his head.

Then looked up and down the street — Like a man
about to draw.

---

The Hulbert wasn't just an inn. Everyone knew that.
During Prohibition, it had become a not-so-secret speakeasy.
Still was, even with repeal in the air.

He didn't care about the liquor. Not today.

He needed answers.

Webb pushed open the door.

Inside, the bar smelled of sweat, wood rot, and yesterday's regrets.
A few local drunks hunched in their usual spots, nursing glassy amber pours and bloodshot hangovers.

Webb let the door swing shut behind him and raised both hands.

"Relax. I'm not here for that."

He stepped to the bar, pulled out a stool, and set his hat down.

"I'll buy you a bottle. Your choice. Just tell me what the hell is going on out there today."

That got their attention.

Jeff Kidd—already halfway back into last night's buzz—blinked, squinted, and swiveled in his seat.

"A...a bottle? No shit?"

"That's what I said."

A black coffee slid across the bar.
Webb nodded to the bartender. Took a sip.

Jeff stumbled over, swaying like a barn door in the wind.

"You're a trooper... Since when do you boys buyin' booze?"

"That's a fair question..."

"Jeff."

"Jeff. Right. Still a fair question. I guess the new policy went into effect this morning—assuming you can give me something worth hearing."

Jeff leaned in, breath thick with whiskey and guilt. He dropped his voice.

"You didn't hear it from me, yeah? He'll kill me if he knows I said anything."

Webb didn't respond. Just took another sip.

"It's Stanley."
Jeff whispered the name as if it were poison.
"Got everyone fired up about the milk prices. But it ain't just that anymore. He's got a book."

Webb raised an eyebrow.
"A book."

"A black one. Real old. Smells wrong."
Jeff crossed himself.
"And it talks to him."

Webb lowered his coffee slowly.

"What do you mean, talks to him?"

"I mean, he listens to it. Follows it. He's not leadin' the protest anymore, far as I can tell. Think he's got other plans."

"What plans?"

Jeff scratched the back of his neck. Looked toward the door as if he expected Stanley to walk in.

"I don't know. But if Stanley thinks the book told

him to do it… Well. You'd best check his farm."

Webb tapped the bottle still sitting behind the bar. The bartender nodded and slid it over.

Webb kept a hand on it.

"What's the address?"

Jeff rattled it off like a parishioner naming a saint.

Webb pushed the bottle across the bar.

Jeff's eyes lit up as if it were Christmas.

But Webb leaned in, voice like a whip crack:

"But, Jeff—if I find out you've misbehaved because of that bottle… I'll see that the only thing you drink for the next ten years is warm toilet water in a state pen. Understood?"

Jeff swallowed and nodded.

Webb tipped his hat, stood, and stepped out into the blinding heat of the Boonville morning — heading straight for the heart of whatever this was.

---

Outside, he paused by the cruiser, hand on the door.

He took one last look at the town square — quiet. Too quiet.

Curtains twitched in windows.
A dog barked once and fell silent.

Even the sky felt wrong.

Webb slid behind the wheel; the old Ford groaning beneath him.

The engine coughed, caught, and purred low.
He wasted no time.

Gravel crunched under the tires as he pointed the car north—toward the Millard farm.

Stanley Millard.

The name twisted in his gut now.
He couldn't say why—not exactly.

But something in that bar...
Something in Jeff's eyes...

It wasn't just drunken nerves.

It was fear.
Real, bone-deep.

Webb pressed the gas.
The town slipped behind him in the rearview.

If he were lucky, he'd find nothing but a busted fence and a few bad tempers.

If he wasn't...

He tightened his grip on the wheel.

This wasn't about milk anymore.

3

John Westcott walked alone, a wooden box tucked tight beneath one arm.

Oak—polished to a mirror shine.
Brass hinges—bright, flawless.

Craftsmanship that made a man proud.

And yet...
He carried it like a coffin.

The box gleamed too much in the sun.
Almost desperate in its beauty.
As if trying to *hide* what was inside.

Lined with deep red velvet.
Locked tight.
And nestled within: the book.

Black leather, cracked with age.
Pages inked in Latin.

And if you opened the box — if you even *dared*
unlatch the lock — it would whisper.

It always whispered.

John didn't know Latin.
He didn't need to.
The words still found their way in.

Soft.
Sickly sweet.
Like oil sliding into his ears and down into his gut.

He knew better than to open it now.
Not again.

His hands gripped the polished oak tighter.
One more stop before delivering the thing to the new
bookstore.

Just one.

The church.

Father Patrick would bless the box.

Not the book — it was too far gone for that.

But maybe the box could *hold* it.
Maybe that was enough.

John climbed the stone steps of the old church, the oak box clutched close.

The building rose tall and white against a blur of summer green.
Its steeple stabbed the sky like a warning.

There had been a breeze.

It died the moment John stepped off the road.

Even the birds fell silent.

All except one.

A crow let out a rasping caw from above—like it knew what John carried.

He wiped his brow.
Sweat slicked his grip.

The box slipped—just a second — but he caught it.

Fingers locked tight before the polished oak shattered on the stone steps.

The church door creaked open.

Father Patrick stood in the doorway.
Crisp collar. Brows drawn—half concern, half amusement.

"Welcome, John," the priest said. "I see you've brought your box."

A small smile.

"Though I don't make a habit of blessing furniture."

John managed a weak smile.

"Thank you, Father. I know it sounds odd. But please—it's important."

He stepped inside.

The church was cool.

Stone and silence.

But something felt *off*—the echo of the room didn't sit right. Like the building itself didn't want them there.

John set the box on the side table near the altar.

The table creaked.

The floor *tilted*.

"There's something inside," John said quietly. "Something wrong. I won't ask you to bless it. I wouldn't dare."

He looked up, eyes glassy.

"But the box...if it's strong—if it's holy—maybe that's enough."

Father Patrick approached slowly.

He placed his hand on the lid.

Then recoiled.

Not dramatically.

Just a flicker.

Like touching a stove you *thought* was cold.

He cleared his throat.

"Feels...warm."

"It wasn't before," John said.

The box sat in silence.
But both men *felt* it watching.

After a beat, the priest found a logical foothold.

The warmth. The air. The tilt.

"The sun must've heated the wood on your walk here, that's all," he said, chuckling softly.
"No need for dramatics, John. Oak holds heat—especially with a lacquer like that."

Relief washed over John's face.
His shoulders dropped.

"If you still want me to bless your fancy box, I'll be glad to."

He patted the lid again.
"Cool now," he added with a small shrug.

"Thank you, Father," John said, exhaling like a drowning man breaking the surface.
"It means more than I can say."

Father Patrick nodded and turned toward his chambers.

John watched him go.

Alone now.

He reached out and touched the side of the box.

Still warm.
Still *humming* under his fingers.

This time, it *hummed back*.

But not in sound.

In thought.

*Open me.*

"I...I...can't."

He staggered back, hands on his head.
Breath jagged. Vision pulsing.

Then came the pain.
White-hot.
Blinding.

## *OPEN ME. NOW.*

He dropped to his knees, mouth open in a scream
that made no sound.
His voice—gone.
Just *gone.*

He clawed through his coat, fingers trembling.
Brushed the key.
Missed it.

The book punished him again.

Another wave of pain—ripping through his nervous
system like wildfire.

*Unlock this box before that clown gets back.*

*Or I will make you pluck your own eyes out and eat them,*
*John.*
*Do you understand me?*

He nodded.

He understood.

He found the key again.
Forced it into the lock.

Click.

Something in the room *changed.*

A pressure—like air squeezed through the eye of a needle.

The candles by the altar *bent away* from the box.
The copper taste of blood filled John's mouth.

And something else did too.

Clink.
The latch hit the stone floor.

So did John's sanity.

He lifted the book from its velvet nest—hands trembling—and set it on the altar.
Where the Bible would go.

And *something inside him fractured.*

Permanently.

He would never speak again.
Never meet another person's eyes.
Not after what he saw in those pages.
Not after what he became.

Because if they knew what waited inside that book...
If they saw what he saw...

They wouldn't either.

4

John woke with a start—except he hadn't known he was asleep.

Everything was different now.

Older.

The church was gone.
So was the altar.
He stood upright in a place that reeked of rot and damp stone.
Walls pressed in close—sweating, slick. A cave.

*Walk*, the book said.

Not loud.
Not cruel.
It didn't need to be.

John obeyed.

Not out of fear—but because resistance no longer lived in him.

He shuffled forward.
Bare feet slap wet stone.
The ground sloped gently ahead, toward a strange light.

Firelight?

No.

Not a fire.

The glow pulsed steadily—too cold to be flame.
Gold through smoke.
Unnatural.

Wrong.

He heard chanting.

Not in English, French, or German—he spoke all three.

This was older.
Older than roots.
Older than man.

He walked slowly at first.

With each step, the voices thickened—bending syllables into impossible shapes, collapsing language.

His hand slid along the wall.

Slippery.

Not water.

A viscous film clung to his skin—gleaming, dark.

His stomach rolled.

Still, he walked.

The light drew him.
Not warm, not flickering—but steady. Like a star being born underground.

*Is there anyone?*

His voice echoed.

Once.
Twice...

The second echo twisted—warped—like it had too many teeth.

No response.

Only the chant, gnawing at the edges of thought.

The light brightened, flooding the passage.
Its source: *within*.

Something was waiting there.
Ancient.
And it already knew his name.

Then—white-hot brilliance.

No sound.

No time.

John opened his mouth to scream—arms flung wide—and the world *shifted*.

---

He stood in a field now.

A bruised purple sky boiled overhead.
Motionless storm clouds churned without wind.

His hands dripped thick, warm blood—black and glistening.

He stared at them, trembling.

Before him, in a perfect circle, a fire burned—no wood, no smoke. Just flames.
Breathing. *Observing*.

Figures surrounded it, backs turned.

Unmoving.

"Hello?" he called, voice fractured, static—like a broken radio.

No answer.

The circle didn't stir.

Beyond the fire, a man stood at an altar—stone, streaked red.

He wore white robes stained with blood.
He raised a curved blade—face calm, hands steady.

John's legs moved on their own.

The blade sliced clean across the man's eye.

*Pop.*

Then the other.

No scream.

Only blood—streaming down like tears.

With trembling fingers, the man lifted both ruined eyes.
Held them aloft.

And placed them on the altar.
Two coins.

Buying something back.

The flames leapt higher.
The figure swayed.

And John understood:

This wasn't a sacrifice.

It was an *invitation.*

The man whispered a prayer—low, guttural.
Smoke carried it skyward.

John didn't know the words.
But he *felt* them.

That's when he saw it:

The book.

Black leather.
Cracked.
Perched beside the altar.

Drinking the blood.

Not soaking.
Not absorbing.

Drinking.

The others began chanting—voices folding in on themselves—prayers warping into screams.

Then — the man rose.

Lifted off the ground.

Rigid.

John gasped.

Something stepped out of the fire.

Not fully *there*.
Shimmering.
*Wrong.*

A translucent hand reached out.
Touched the man's forehead.

The man fell—boneless.

John staggered back, eyes wide.

"Jesus protect us," he whispered.

He regretted it instantly.

The thing turned.

Not toward him.

*Into* him.

He felt its gaze scrape down to his marrow.

The book looked.

And in his skull, a voice replied:

"Now you see…and now you will see."

The demon appeared before him.

Shadows wrapped its frame.

No face.

Only *intent*.

"I give unto thee the sight of the future, John Westcott. This sight is a magnificent gift, this sight. *Do not fail me.*"

It paused.

Then smiled.

"Or Him."

A finger rose—long, skeletal.

It pointed *up*.

John's eyes followed.

The demon placed its palm on his forehead.

And the world broke.

---

Pain.

Electric fire shot through his limbs.
Muscles seized.

His mouth vanished.

He could not scream.

Then—visions.

A deluge.

The book consuming souls,
murder committed in its name.

The blind man from the firelight.
Children.
Soldiers.
Lovers.
Martyrs.

A car.
The book purred in the passenger seat.

More people.
More death.
Devastation.

Time unraveled.
A thread of blood woven through history.

Centuries.
Continents.
Carnage.

Until — Snap.

A fracture.

A break.

John's mind — split.

The field vanished.

The fire, the altar and, more importantly, the demon.

Gone.

He lay twitching beside the open box on the cold church floor.

Eyes wide.

Mouth frozen.

Silent.

# Chapter 10: MEET THE NEW BOSS, SAME AS THE OLD

1

Maya pulled into Evelyn's driveway around 12:35 a.m.

In the back seat, Matt stirred and gently nudged Evelyn awake, whispering something Maya couldn't hear.

She didn't know why it annoyed her.
But it did.

Just like it annoyed her that they were now completely out of money after the detour to Rome.

She grabbed the black book from the passenger seat.
The leather gave off a comforting warmth.
It whispered again—Latin, yes, but self-translating.
Like it was *teaching* her.
*Training* her.

And God help her, it thrilled her more than any English Lit seminar ever had.

She stepped out of the car; the book tucked under her arm as if it belonged there.
She didn't look back.

"Matt," she said over her shoulder, "take Sleeping

Beauty up to her room. Then meet me at that bar we passed—Hubert something. I need a beer. And we need to talk about money."

She didn't wait for a reply.
Didn't need to.

Matt nodded—barely—then helped Evelyn out of the car, quietly praying her mother wasn't still awake to see them stumbling into the house at nearly 1 a.m.

---

Maya walked into the bar.

Nearly empty—no surprise for a town this small at this hour.
Despite that, every eye turned toward her as she crossed the room.

*New girl. Alone.*
*Wearing confidence like a tailored coat.*

The place smelled of old beer and older stories.
She liked that.

She slid onto a stool at the polished oak bar.

A woman of about her age approached—tired eyes, zero bullshit in her posture.

"What'll it be?"

Maya flashed a well-practiced smile.

"Two beers. Whatever's on tap. My friend's right behind me."

The bartender nodded and walked away.
Maya exhaled.

*If it had been a guy, I might've gotten the beers for free.*
But not tonight.
Tonight, drinks were going on the old Visa Gold.

Tomorrow, if the gods of eBay were kind, she'd sell a few of the rare books she'd snagged from the store.

The bartender returned, placing two cold bottles on the bar.

"No charge," she said.
"Owner says drinks are on him tonight."

Maya followed her glance to the far end of the bar.

A man in his mid-to-late fifties lifted his glass toward her.
Slightly overweight. Receding hairline. Tan that came from a booth, not the sun.
Trying too hard to relive his glory days.

She gave him a smile like polished brass.

"Thanks, sweetie. Go Sox."

Her Boston accent thickened just enough to sting.

He grinned as if she'd kissed his ego on the mouth.

Maya took a long drink, letting the beer wash down her throat.
One hand rested on the black book beside her—casually, like a lover.

---

After a beer and a half, Matt walked in.

He looked like hell.
Tired. Pale.

He saw her.

Saw the book—still beside her like it *belonged* there.

He sat down next to her, eyes avoiding hers.

"You get one for me?" he asked dryly.

"Here."

She slid the second beer toward him.

"You're welcome."

He took a sip and coughed.

"So...we're broke?"

She smiled. That smile that usually got her out of parking tickets and into VIP lounges.

"I spent everything on the book," she said lightly. "But don't worry. I'll flip those first editions, and we'll be fine. This place? Drinks are on the house. You worry too much, Matt."

Her hand drifted to his shoulder.

He let out a sharp laugh—flat, humorless.

"You don't worry at all. You haven't been yourself since you touched that thing."

He glanced at the book. Then at her.

"It's in your head. It's changing you."

Maya tilted her head. The smile cooled, but didn't fade.

"That isn't fair," she whispered.

Her fingers traced the back of his neck.

The book whispered too.

*Control him. Bind him.*

"This is what you've always wanted, isn't it?"
Her breath brushed his ear.

Matt tensed.

"Maya... Please. Stop. You're not... This isn't you."

She leaned closer. Pressed her body against his.

"Does it matter?" she breathed.
"Why or how?"

She kissed the side of his neck slowly and deliberate.

"I've seen how you look at me, Matt. You don't have
to lie."

Her hand slid down his chest. Paused at his belt.

"Maya."
His voice cracked.
"Please."

But he didn't move.
Didn't pull away.

She smiled.

But it didn't reach her eyes.

And in those eyes — something old.
Something hollow.

Something *not* hers.

---

Then she kissed him.

Hard.
Possessive.

A kiss that didn't *belong* to her.
That didn't belong to either of them.

It tasted like fire and ash and wrongness.

And somewhere—deep beneath it—Maya was screaming.

*Not out loud.*
*Not in any way Matt could hear.*

But inside—she was pounding at the walls of her own body.
Clawing to be free.

*This isn't me.*
*This isn't us.*
*Please, Matt. Please...*

But no one heard her.

And the book didn't care.

In that moment, she *knew* — something between them had broken.
*Gone.*
*Changed.*
*Stolen.*

A bloom of white-hot pain tore through her skull — but her body didn't flinch.

Her lips stayed on his.

And Matt...

Matt still hadn't pulled away.

2

Amanda stepped into the bar, just planning to grab her takeout.

She spotted them immediately—the two kids from her phone.
Locked in a kiss by the jukebox.
Though from where she stood, only one of them looked like they actually *wanted* it.

A flicker of something—close to hate—tightened in her chest.
Gone before she could name it.

She passed them without a word, straight to the bar where her order already waited.

"Hey, Sharen," Amanda said casually, nodding to the bartender. "I see you've got a pair of lovebirds tonight."

As she spoke, the guy pulled back—staggered, really.
Pale-faced, wide-eyed.
He muttered something—Amanda caught just the edge:

*"You're not you."*

Then he turned and stormed out of the bar, nearly knocking over a stool on the way.

The girl just stood there.
Frozen.

Amanda watched her for a moment and thought, *Huh.*
Then: *First rejection? That'll sting.*

She handed over her credit card without missing a beat.

"Get used to it, honey," she muttered under her breath.
"Happens more and more as you get older."

Maya looked over at her and offered one of *those* smiles—too polished, too practiced.
The kind that pissed Amanda off on instinct.

She smiled back anyway.
Tight. Polished. Poisoned.

"Thanks for buying that book, sweetheart. Maybe now my dimwit husband's one step closer to selling that bookstore."

Her voice dripped sugar and venom.

Maya's smile didn't budge.
She picked up her beer and the black book and crossed the room, heels clicking like punctuation.

"Have we met?" she asked brightly.

"No, sweetie," Amanda replied, turning to face her.
"But Ed—*my husband*—sold you that book. And a few others. So thanks for dinner."

She tapped the takeout bag pointedly.

Maya's smile dimmed, just slightly.

"Oh. *Ed.* The cute store owner."

Amanda's jaw tightened at the word *cute.*

"He *can* be cute," she said coolly.
"When he wants to be. Which is hardly ever."

She turned to leave, brushing Maya's shoulder as she passed.

That's when the voice came.

Smooth. Sultry. Cruel.

"Then maybe you should fuck him better."

Amanda froze.

So did the bar.

She turned—slow, deliberate—heat rising in her cheeks.

"How the *hell* would you know how I fuck my husband?"

Maya stood there—beer in one hand, the book in the other.
Still smiling. Too sweet. Too *innocent*.

The kind of smile that said: *What, me? I surely didn't fuck his brains out…yet.*

She was daring Amanda to swing.

And it was working.

Amanda took a step forward, gripping the bag.

"If you ever touch him—"

"I won't," Maya cut in lightly.
"Though if I did? Just know—he'd let me. In a heartbeat. And afterward?"
She leaned in, voice low and wicked.
"He'd feel so bad, he'd tell you himself."

Amanda's fists clenched at her sides.

"What makes you think you know us?" she snapped. "For all you know, we're *happily in love*."

Maya tilted her head.

The smile stayed.
But her eyes?

Her eyes said: *Bullshit.*

"Happy, huh?" she said softly.
"Is that why you're picking up a meal for one at 1:30 in the morning?"

Amanda flinched—barely.

Maya didn't stop.

"Do you even know where Ed is right now? Probably still at the bookstore you hate. The one that bought you that shiny red car. The one that paid for the food in your hand." Her voice dropped.
"The one that—fun fact—killed his father. And will kill him too."

Amanda's breath caught.

"Because of *you*."

Amanda's mouth opened—but no sound came.

"Oh," Maya added. "Did I say the quiet part out loud?"

She set her beer down.
Not the book.

The book *pulsed* in her hand.

Amanda's breath hitched.

*How did she know all that?*

Unless Ed told her…

"You should leave him," Maya said, voice like velvet-wrapped steel.
"Get in your fancy car. Drive south. Find someone who actually makes you *feel* something. Because we both know it's not Ed."

Amanda's face flushed red, but her feet stayed planted.

"It hasn't been for a long time, has it?" Maya's voice turned bitter. Precise.
"You fantasize about other men. Every time you let him climb on top of you—which, let's be honest, is rare. And when you do, it's not for the sex."

She stepped closer.

"And it sure as hell isn't for the love."

Then, gently:

"So tell me, Amanda—if it's not the money, and it's not the man—*why the fuck are you still with him?*"

That did it.

Amanda swung—hard.

Her fist slammed into Maya's stomach with a thick, wet *thud.*

Maya doubled over, gasping.

Amanda followed with a second strike, this time to the back of the head.

Maya dropped like a stone.

Amanda didn't stop.

She kicked her—once in the ribs. Then again. And again.

Each blow louder than the last.

"Why do I stay with him?" Amanda hissed. "*Fuck you*, that's why, you smug little bitch."

She spat on her.

Then turned, snatched her takeout, and walked out the door.

Calm.
Too calm.

Like the violence had burned the poison out of her.

---

What no one heard—what *couldn't* be heard—was the sound of Maya's low, ragged laugh from the floor.

Blood on her teeth.

And the black book glowing softly beside her.

3

Ed sat dozing in his chair when a soft, almost polite knock stirred him awake.

He blinked, groggy, and looked toward the front window.

A figure stood silhouetted beneath the streetlight— clutching her side, the other hand wrapped tightly around a black book.

Maya.

He rose to his feet, joints cracking in protest, and moved to the door.

When he opened it, she gave him a weak smile.
One corner of her mouth was swelling.
A smear of blood marked her temple.

"Can I come in?" she asked, her voice low.

Ed stepped aside automatically.

"Yeah…of course. What happened?"

Maya limped past him, her breath hitching once, then again, before collapsing into the nearest reading chair like a marionette with cut strings.

"Your wife," she said, cradling the book like a wounded animal.
"She attacked me."

Ed's face went still.

"What?"

"At that bar—Hubert House, or whatever you call it. I was just trying to have a beer. Talk to a friend. And she…"
She winced.
"She hit me. Then kicked me. In front of everyone."

Ed didn't know what to say.

The room felt colder all at once.

The hum of the overhead lights sharpened.
Outside, a dog barked once. Then silence.

Maya looked up at him—eyes glassy, but alert.

"I didn't hit her back," she added, as if that mattered. "I just walked away. Thought maybe…I'd be safe here."

Ed knelt beside her, concern etched deep into the lines around his mouth.

"Why did she?" he asked quietly.

Maya sniffed and dabbed at the corner of her eye.

"I don't know. One minute I'm sitting there with my beer, and the next—she's accusing me of…taking advantage. Of not having paid enough for the book."

Her voice caught in her throat.

"I'll pay more, Ed. If that's what it was—I didn't mean to cause problems."

Wordlessly, Ed stood and walked to the counter. He opened the drawer beneath the register and retrieved the first-aid kit.

His hands moved with surprising precision—like muscle memory from some other life.

"You did nothing wrong," he said, voice tight. "That's the last straw with her. I mean it."

He returned to her side and opened the tin box: gauze, ointment, bandages.

Maya extended her hands, then hesitated.

"Um… Could you?" she asked, voice small. "I can't see what she did. Probably for the best."

Ed blinked, then gave a soft smile.

"Yeah. Sorry. I wasn't thinking."

He leaned in.

The bookstore was so quiet he could hear the wind brushing against the old glass.
So quiet, Maya's heartbeat—steady, slow—seemed to sync with the faint hum from the black book in her lap.

A glow shimmered faintly beneath its leather surface. Like ink blooming in water.

Ed dabbed ointment just above her brow.
Her skin was warm. Smooth.

His fingers lingered just a moment longer than they needed to.

"I can see why she'd be jealous," Maya murmured, eyes locked on his.

Ed froze—just for a second.

Color flushed to his cheeks as he carefully placed the tiny bandage over the cut Amanda never gave her.

"There," he whispered.
"That should help."

Maya felt the shimmer of heat again—not just from his touch.

The book stirred in her lap.

It wasn't speaking in words anymore.
It didn't need to.

But inside her mind, curling like smoke, it whispered:

*"He can help… not just with your wounds… with everything."*

4

"What the hell was that, Maya?" he muttered into the empty night.

No answer. Just a dog barking—farther away this time.

He threw a wild punch into the air.
It didn't help.

His head was spinning. None of it made sense. Not the kiss. Not the way she looked at him—like someone else was behind her eyes.
Like it wasn't really her at all.

He knew she didn't mean it.
That's what made it worse.

He dropped onto the curb, elbows on his knees, fingers dragging through his hair.
His breath stuttered in his chest.

The street was silent.
Like the whole town was holding its breath.

The tears came.
He tried to stop them, but they broke through—hot and shameful.
His eyes burned.

A single car crept by at the far end of the block.
Headlights flickered across shuttered homes.
Then vanished.

He didn't look up.

The night settled around him like a blanket pulled too tight.

He was alone.

And that might have been the worst part of all.

---

"Matt?"

A small voice.
Off in the distance.

Evelyn.

He knew it anywhere.

Of course, she showed up now.
Right when he was falling apart.

"Yeah," he said, voice thick with tears and snot.

She approached cautiously.
Like he might bite.
Like he's something broken.

"What the hell are you doing out here? And why are you screaming?"

"Oh…that?" He wiped his face on his sleeve, cheeks flushing.
"Sorry. It's just…Maya."

Evelyn exhaled through her nose—quiet, but sharp.

She didn't say anything right away.
Just sat down beside him with that look.

The one that made him feel like she already knew everything.

Then—just a gentle nudge from her shoulder.

"Want to talk about it?"

Matt looked at her for a long beat.
Then exhaled.

"You don't like Maya, do you?"

Her eyes widened—just slightly.
The question caught her off guard.

"You don't beat around the bush, do you, Matthew?"

She gave him that faint, lopsided smile.

Then, more carefully:

"No, Matt. I don't. She takes advantage of you. I think the second you both graduate, she'll vanish. And it won't be because *you* stopped trying."

She paused.

"Every time you talk to her, it's like she puts a spell on you. And I don't get it. Yeah, she's drop-dead hot. Hell, if she wanted, I'd jump into bed with her too."

That hung in the air. Too long.

Then she added, quieter:

"But, sweetie... Come on. She's using you. Everyone sees it."

Matt stared at her, unsure.

Not sure whether to defend Maya.

Not sure whether to be mad at Evelyn.

Or at Maya.
Or at himself.

Eventually, he just lowered his head.
The tears returned.

His voice was small. Cracked.

"Why do people just use me?"

His shoulders shook.

Evelyn said nothing at first.

She just wrapped her arms around him.

Her breath brushed his neck—warm and steady.
Anchoring him.

Then, softly—so soft he almost didn't hear it:

"I won't."

She pressed a kiss onto his cheek.
Not rushed.
Not loaded.
Just…real.

And in that moment, something shifted.

For the first time in forever,
Matt knew what it felt like to be seen.
To be held.
To be cared for.

Actually cared for.

# Chapter 11: MILK & MADNESS

1

Captain Webb pulled up the long, rutted path to the Millard farm, his patrol car kicking up clouds of dust that hung heavy in the scorching morning air.

He parked.

Let the engine idle for a moment—its soft ticking the only sound.

Something was wrong.

Very wrong.

No animals.
No chickens scratching in the dirt.
No cows lowing.
No dogs barking.

Just silence.

Too complete, too deliberate.

Even the air tasted off.
Copper. Ozone. Burnt pennies and the electric tingle of a storm that wasn't coming.

Webb swallowed.

The hair at the base of his skull stood straight up.

He'd learned to trust those little warnings.
They'd kept him breathing longer than luck ever had.

He reached across to grab his hat—only then realizing his other hand was already resting on the butt of his service weapon.

He stepped out of the car.

The door creaked shut behind him.
Gravel crunched beneath his boots as he moved toward the house—slow, steady, deliberate.
Like a man approaching a sleeping bear.

He climbed onto the porch.
The old wood groaned underfoot.

Then raised his fist.

Knocked.

Waited.

Nothing.

Knocked again—harder this time.

Still nothing.

With a sharp breath, Webb stepped off the porch and began circling the house, boots crunching on the dry dirt, muttering under his breath. He was just about to announce himself again when something caught his eye:

A window—left open.

Thin white curtain, fluttering in the breeze like a ghost's breath.

He moved toward it.
Meaning only to call inside.
Just to make sure. But then he saw.

And he would wish—God, how he would wish—he

hadn't.

Captain Leon Webb, veteran of the New York State Troopers, a man who'd seen car wrecks, murder-suicides, overdoses, abuse...staggered back.

He turned.

Doubled over.

And vomited black coffee onto the porch steps.

Because what waited behind that curtain—what was nailed to the wall—used to be Alice Millard.

What remained of her.

Upside down.
Naked.
Her body nailed like a crucifixion painting gone mad.
Her skin flayed open.
Insides spilling out like grotesque garland, intestines roping down like festive hell.
Flies crawled in and out of her, like she was part of the house now.

Webb's breath hitched.
His vision blurred.

And then he saw it.

Scrawled across the floor beneath her.
In her blood.

*This pleases the book, so this pleases me.*

Webb wiped his mouth with the back of his hand, his legs shaking.

Then he looked up—thank Christ—and spotted a

telephone line running into the farmhouse.

That meant he was going in.

Into that goddamn house.

His stomach threatened to revolt again, but he held it down.

He stood tall.

Drew his service weapon.

Just in case.

Stanley was probably long gone.

But maybe not.

Webb reached the front door.
Tried the handle.

Unlocked.

It swung open easily.

And the smell hit him like a punch to the face.

Rot. Iron. Decay.

He gagged—then shoved himself forward into the house.

2

Father Patrick stepped out of his private office—and froze.

John lay curled on the floor, pale and drenched in sweat.

"John!" he gasped, rushing to his side.

As he knelt, his eyes fell on the open box…and the black book, now resting on the altar like it belonged there.

It didn't. It shouldn't.

Nothing about it felt right in the house of God.

But first: John.

"Come, my friend. Let's get you some fresh air."

Sliding his arms beneath him, Father Patrick hoisted John to his feet. The younger man swayed—still in shock—but stumbled along beside him, out the chapel doors and into the fading light.

Behind them, the book waited.

---

Father Patrick set John down gently on the bottom step.

Then turned back toward the chapel.

His jaw clenched.

This was God's house.

His to protect.

And now, he would defend it.

He stepped back inside.

A sick, echoing laughter spilled forth—rolling through the sanctuary…or maybe just inside his head.

He couldn't tell anymore.

*"The Lord is faithful, and He will strengthen you and protect*

*you from the evil one!"*

Patrick shouted the verse at the top of his lungs, crossing himself as he advanced. The air grew heavy, thick—like wading through deep water.

His steps slowed.

The laughter stopped.

*"How dare you presume to fight me, Priest?"*

The voice boomed in his skull—sharp, searing. He winced, staggered.

But did not stop.

*"Behold, I have given you authority to tread on serpents and scorpions, and over all the power of the enemy—and nothing shall hurt you!"*

He cried the words like a war cry.

A deep pain flared in his chest—hot, stabbing, spreading.

*"Stop now, or you will meet your God sooner than you like."*

The book's voice was cruel. Close.

Patrick's voice cracked, but he pressed forward.

*"So do not fear, for I am with you,"* he rasped.

*"Do not be dismayed, for I am your God. I will strengthen you and help you; I will uphold you with my righteous right hand."*

His trembling hand closed around the black book.

Pain surged.

His chest.
His arm.

Now his jaw.

But he held on.

With a cry, he slammed the book back into the box.

Snapped it shut.

His vision blurred. The room swam.

There—on the floor. The lock.

Shaking, he fitted it in place.

Click.

The book fell silent.

Patrick made the sign of the cross over the box, voice hoarse but defiant:

*"The images of their gods you are to burn in the fire. Do not covet the silver and gold on them… For it is detestable to the Lord your God."*

His knees buckled.

He collapsed forward, pressing his crucifix against the lid.

*"For our struggle is not against flesh and blood,"* he whispered, *"but against the rulers…against the authorities…against the powers of this dark world…and against the spiritual forces of evil in the heavenly realms."*

He crossed the box one last time.

Then fell still.

Silence.

John's mind went quiet.

It was the first time he had noticed the breeze on his face. The light. The world outside.

Wrong.

He turned.

And ran back into the church.

Father Patrick lay motionless on the stone floor, slumped in front of the locked box.

He had undone everything John had unleashed.

And died for it.

John stood frozen. The weight of it all crashed down.

This was his fault.

That meant it was also his responsibility.

He stepped forward.

The box sat silent—no hum, no heat, no pressure in his skull. Its power was gone. Or maybe…

Sleeping.

John knelt. Picked it up.

Held it close.

Then, he walked out of the church without another word.

---

Down the darkened street he walked, toward the construction site.

With the new bookstore going up—the basement wasn't

sealed yet.

It would do.

And with luck, no one would ever find this cursed thing again.

3

Stanley had made a few anonymous calls to Albany, warning of bombs in government buildings.

There were no bombs, of course.

But it felt good—messing with the suits, watching them squirm from a distance.

The book had gone quiet.

That scared him.

It meant he was on his own now.

But he still knew what it wanted. He'd heard its instructions enough to know them by heart.

He would follow the plan.
Word for word.
Step by bloody step.

---

The buildings would fall—one by one.

And if people went with them?

So be it.

---

He walked toward downtown.

His eyes weren't glassy anymore. Not corrupted. Not haunted.

Just insane.

---

God—there must have been *eight hundred* of them.

Out in the fields.
Clashing with the law.
Stopping milk trucks.
Choking on tear gas.
Fighting.

He wanted to run to them—throw himself into the chaos.

But not yet.

There were bigger things to handle now.

Still, he smiled wide.

Not with madness this time—but with pride.

The mob?

No.

He had built an army.

And they were ready to fight Albany—for their families.
For their farms.

It was with that thought—his army rising behind him—that Stanley slipped back into the woods, heading toward the high school.

About five minutes in, a sheriff's deputy happened upon him.

Bad luck—for both of them.

Stanley usually avoided this kind of thing. He wasn't careless.

But it seemed he was becoming a bit of a celebrity.

"Stop right there," the deputy called, hand on his belt. Sweat soaked his uniform.

Stanley didn't turn around.

He set the bag down. The shotgun still in his hand.

"Hot one today, isn't it?" he asked, casual.

"Yeah… What's in the bag?" the deputy asked, stepping forward. He looked down.

Stanley watched.

The man's hand dropped toward the bag.

Eyes off Stanley.

Gun forgotten.

Now or never.

Stanley spun.

Brought the shotgun up.

Fired.

In an instant, everything the deputy ever was—or would be—vanished in a red mist.

His head came apart with a wet roar, spraying Stanley, the bag, and the trees in brain, hair, and shredded skin.

Stanley exhaled.

Picked up his bag.

Wiped his face clean.

And kept walking.

4

John reached the construction site—what was supposed to be a bookstore, or something close to it.

Thankfully, no one was around.

He slipped inside the unfinished shell. The air was sharp with the scent of pine boards, fresh paint, and sawdust. Tools lay scattered across sawhorses, and sunlight filtered through plastic-covered windows.

It smelled like a fresh start.

Which made it worse.

His chest ached at the thought of bringing this cursed thing into a place so clean, so unburdened. But there was nowhere else.

He couldn't risk Stanley finding out he still had the book.

He found the narrow basement door and eased behind it, careful not to let it creak.

The stairs groaned anyway beneath his weight.

Down he went.

Deeper into the basement.
Deeper into the dark.

---

He pulled out his Zippo—a gift from his wife—and flicked it to life.

The flame wavered in the still, cold air, casting long shadows against stone and dirt.

Just enough light to see where the cursed thing would go.

John set the box gently on the dirt floor. His eyes scanned the room for a tool.
Something to help him work behind the wall.

Then he saw it—a small shovel, leaning against a bucket of nails like it had been waiting for him.

---

It would be hard work.
But it would do.

He moved to a freshly mortared section of the cellar wall and began chipping away with the shovel's edge.
Mortar flaked.
Stone shifted.

Eventually, he carved a space large enough to fit the box.

Or rather—his book.

When had he started calling it his?

It didn't matter.
He shoved the thought aside and kept going, clearing stone and earth by hand now, carving a crude hollow into the wall's foundation.

A small grave.

---

When the space was ready, he slid the box inside.

Its weight was unnatural in his arms—heavier than wood and ink should be.

Then, stone by stone, he sealed it up.

He found a half-used bucket of mortar. Smoothed it over the cracks. Covered his work like a man burying a body.

When he finished, he stepped back.

Crossed himself.

The flame on his Zippo flickered.

---

That was all it took.

John turned.

And bolted.

Up the stairs.
Heart hammering.
Darkness pressed close behind him.

5

Stanley had made it downtown.

And he knew exactly what needed to go first.

The book hadn't told him to do it—but he'd always hated that damn gazebo in the middle of Main Street. Couldn't say why. It just...pissed him off.

He walked toward it. Then he picked up speed.

His fingers slipped into the canvas bag slung over his shoulder, closing around a few sticks of dynamite. Cold. Solid. Comforting.

As he walked, a strange, crystalline thought broke through the noise in his skull—clearer than anything he'd had in days:

*If there were a God, why am I getting away with this?*
*If there were a God, wouldn't someone have stopped me by now?*
*Wouldn't there have been a bolt from the sky?*

The gazebo loomed closer—pristine and white, its little plaque catching the sunlight:

*Dedicated to All Those Who Never Returned from the Great War*

"Yeah," he muttered, kneeling. "I'm sure they're real appreciative of this outdoor sitting area while their bones rot in some grave in France."

The anger flared. Hot and real.

He struck a match—clean, fast, like it had been waiting—and touched it to the fuse.

It hissed, catching fire as if it *wanted* to burn.

Stanley rolled the stick of dynamite beneath the

floorboards of the gazebo, then grabbed his bag and ran—feet pounding against the street—aiming for the cover of the nearest building.

Behind him, the fuse snaked toward its target like a devil's finger.

Ticking down toward whatever came next.

He saw the flash first—then the BOOM.

The blast wave hit a second later, lifting his coat and slamming into his chest. Splintered white-painted wood rained down across Main Street. His ears rang. One was bleeding.

He didn't care.

That fucking gazebo was gone.

Smoke curled from the crater in the center of the square. Storefront windows had blown out from the force—glass glittered across the pavement like crushed ice. Somewhere nearby, a screen door slammed open.

A man stepped out confused, half-dressed.

Stanley raised his shotgun and fired. Missed—too far.

Didn't matter.

The message was obvious.

The man bolted back inside.

---

Beneath the future bookstore…

Deep in its dark, makeshift tomb, the book sat fuming.

Not at its new home—it found that lovely.

No, it fumed at the *disruption*.

It reflected on the path that led here—the long and stupid path.

Then—BOOM.

The earth trembled. A chunk of stone—one that might've fallen eventually—gave way and crashed into the box.

It cracked.

Not much. Just a hairline fracture.

But it was enough.

Not enough to free it completely.
Not enough for full control.

But...*enough*.

It reached out.

It found John. (*He would pay later.*)
It found Stanley.

And—oh — it found someone *new*.

Leon Webb.

*Delicious.*

It couldn't control them.
Not yet.

But it could whisper.
And it would.

Up on the street...

Stanley was still running—elated, breathless. He pumped a fist into the air, triumphant.

Then—a voice hissed in his mind. Low. Cold.

"Wasteful."

Stanley stopped mid-step.

His chest sank.

The triumph drained from his face.

It had been watching.

It had been testing.

And he had failed.

# Chapter 12: WE BRING GOOD THINGS TO LIFE

1

E d brought out the bottle of Jim Beam he kept behind the counter—for slow nights. Lately, that was *most* nights.

His third bottle this month.

He handed it to Maya, then rolled over in an old wheeled chair to sit beside her.

Maya raised one perfect eyebrow as she accepted the bottle.

"Trying to loosen me up with booze, Mr. Rodrick?"

Her tone was sweet—*too* sweet.

That carefully practiced innocence.

The kind she probably used on older men with something she wanted.

And damn if it didn't work.

Ed felt the flush creep up his neck. Warm.

Unwelcome.

"I, uh…figured you might need it," he stammered.

*Smooth.*

Maya smiled, and still holding his gaze, brought the

bottle to her lips.

She drank.
A long pull for someone so young.

The book dulled her gag reflex, but the burn still hit her throat like fire. Her eyes watered slightly—glassier now in the dim light.

She passed the bottle back.

"Few girls your age drink bourbon like that," Ed said, taking a swig of his own.
Familiar warmth settled in his chest—too familiar. Too heavy.

Maya smiled again. Slower this time.

"I'm not like a lot of other girls, Ed," she said, voice low and deliberate. "I thought you'd figured that out by now."

She reached for the bottle again. Another sip.
The book glowed faintly beside her, as if it were watching.

And smiling.

"I'm piecing that together," Ed said, handing it back.

Maya leaned forward, elbows on her knees.
Casual posture. But nothing about it felt casual.

Her shirt dipped—just enough.

Ed's eyes flicked downward.
Quick. Involuntary.

But she caught it.

Her grin curved slowly—knowing.
Like a cat that had already closed the door behind the mouse.

The store was quiet. *Too* quiet.
Only the cooler hummed. Old floorboards creaked.

Her voice dropped—low, smooth, coated in
something rich and ancient.

"Why don't you give me a tour of your little shop?"
She tilted her head. "I'd love to see *all* of it."

The bottle in his hand suddenly felt heavier.
He swallowed.

Outside, the wind shifted.
A sign banged once against the window—distant, hollow.

He heard it in his head:
A chorus of voices urged him to stop.
To *think*.

Amanda was still his wife.
Even if she hated him.
Even if he didn't remember the last time she touched him like
she meant it.

But...

"A tour?" he repeated, barely recognizing his own
voice.

Maya's smile widened.
Her fingers brushed against his knee—featherlight.
Deliberate.

She nodded.

Beside her, the book pulsed—like it was breathing.

Ed stood.

Took her hand.

Helped her up.

A sudden darkness fell over the store.

Or maybe it was just *him*.

But he led her anyway.

2

Maya liked Ed—but not like that.

So when the book first *suggested* it — no.
When it *demanded* it — she said no.

And it punished her.

By the time he returned with the bourbon, her refusal
was already ash and static.
The pain had hollowed her out.
The book, satisfied, had slithered back into its patient
watchfulness.

So she smiled.
She laughed.
She touched his knee.

*Men are simple creatures*, she thought bitterly.
The thought made the book purr.

She hated that too.

Now, Ed's larger, calloused hand wrapped around
hers, leading her deeper into the shop.
Old paper and pine lingered in the air, yet something felt
off—like rot beneath candle wax.

The book was pleased.
And—God help her—so was she.

Just for a second.

That was the worst part.

He led her past dusty stacks and mismatched chairs,
through a narrow hallway into the back office.
The overhead light buzzed.
Somewhere above, a floorboard creaked—though no one else
was home.

She clutched the book tighter.

It pulsed again.

Not glowing. Not hot.
Just...aware.
*Hungry.*

How long until thought becomes impossible?
She wondered.

*As long as you serve, my pet,* it whispered.
Its voice: silk and smoke and rotting teeth.

Maya shuddered.
A full-body flinch she couldn't suppress.

Ed mistook it for nerves.

"My God, are you...?" he asked, hand rubbing the
back of his neck, voice already cracking. "Listen—I don't
want to pressure you. In fact, this is a bad idea. We should
just...call it a night, don't you think?"

She *wished* he were right.
Wished it *were* that simple.

But it wasn't.

Not for her.

Not anymore.

Behind her, the door clicked shut.

She placed a hand against it—steadying herself. Gathering what little remained of who she used to be.

"No, Ed," she whispered.

She set the book on the desk.
Pulled her shirt over her head.
Her skin prickled in the cold air—not from the temperature.
From something else.
*Something that wasn't hers.*

"I don't think we should call it a night."

She smiled as she spoke—softly. Almost lovingly.

But the smile didn't reach her eyes.

If Ed had noticed that—*really* noticed—things might have gone differently.

Then she crossed the room.
Not seductively.

Mechanically.

Like someone playing a part they never auditioned for.
Like a marionette in her own skin.

The book pulsed again behind her.

*Approval.*

Ed stood frozen—somewhere between guilt and

longing.
Somewhere between who he was and what he wanted.

    She reached him. Took his hand.
Lifted it to her waist.
Then to her back.

    Guided his arms around her like it was *his* idea.

    Then she kissed him.

    Hard.
Possessive.

    She didn't want it.

    She didn't mean it.

    Inside, she was screaming.

    But the scream had nowhere to go.

    The book had built a wall inside her—a clean, glass barrier that reflected every moment she let it win.

    And outside, in the real world,
her hand pulled him closer
as she deepened the kiss.

3

    Evelyn held Matt's hand, their fingers interlaced as they walked beneath the soft glow of Boonville's streetlamps. He was talking about his hometown—leisurely mornings, nosy neighbors, a kind of small-town charm that felt familiar in every detail.

She listened. Smiled. Laughed at his dumb stories. And with every crooked grin and every wandering anecdote, she felt it: the slow, quiet collapse of the stone wall she'd spent years building around her heart.

It couldn't be love.
Not yet.
But the path *looked* like love.
And that terrified her.

So she stopped him.
Right in the middle of a ridiculous story about getting locked in a barn.

"Matt," she said, her voice steady, flat. "You're going back to Boston, right?"

Matt stopped.
"Yeah…unless Maya sells the car to buy a haunted Victorian or something," he joked.

But it didn't land.

Evelyn stood beneath the next streetlamp, arms crossed, her face unreadable.

"Because I like you," she said simply and clearly. "And I'm pretty sure you like me too. That's just…the plain truth of it."

She shifted her weight, suddenly uncomfortable in her own skin.

"And I need to know what we're doing. What *this* is. Because, Matt… I've been hurt. A lot. My whole life, really. And my mother—crazy as she is—was right about one thing."

Her voice tightened.

"I'm not some roadside attraction you and Maya can visit, smile at, and leave behind when you're full and bored. I'm not saying that's what you're doing—I just…"
She trailed off. Let out a soft, bitter laugh.

"I've been down this road before. Both metaphorically and literally. And I just…I need to know if I'm imagining this."

She looked up at him, eyes shimmering but dry.

"Do you even see me that way? Or am I just…some girl who'd be prettier if she wore makeup? Someone who'd be more appealing if she tried harder to be conventionally attractive?"

Her voice cracked. But she didn't cry.

Matt looked at her—really *looked*.
And for a moment, Evelyn swore the earth stopped spinning.

Then he spoke.

"No, Eve. I'm not using you."

His voice was low. Steady. Real.

"I have to go back to Boston. But only to finish school. That's it. I don't *live* there. Not really."

He stepped closer and took her hands in his. They were warm. A little clammy. Human.

"You're right. Whatever *this* is…I feel it too. It's real. And I would never ask you to change who you are. Because from what I've seen?"
He smiled.

"I like who you are."

Evelyn blinked. Unsure what to say.

Matt gave her a sheepish smile.

"I know this probably feels like some poorly written romance novel gone sideways," he added. "Which, yeah…fair. I *am* an English Lit major."

That got a genuine laugh out of her.

"I can't promise you forever," he said. "I can't even promise a happy ending. But I *can* promise I'm not here to use you. I'm here because you make me happy. And I'd really like the chance to make *you* happy too."

Then, with no fanfare, he lifted her hand and kissed it.
Simple. Honest.
It was the sincerest thing anyone had ever done for her.

Evelyn let out a breath she hadn't realized she'd been holding. Then she pulled him into a tight hug.

No hesitation.

She buried her face in his chest, and this time, when the tears came, they weren't from fear or heartbreak or exhaustion.

They were from something else.

Hope.

She looked up.
His hand brushed away a tear with his thumb—soft and steady, like she might vanish if he touched her too hard.

And for the briefest moment, Evelyn forgot who she

was.
Forgot the armor.
The cynicism.
The years of flinching first.

He cradled her face.
Carefully. Deliberately.

When he bent down to kiss her, it wasn't greedy or rushed.
It was reverent.

Something from one of his many books.

Later, she'd think of it as the best kiss of her life.

In that quiet instant, her mind went completely blank.

Her arms wrapped around his neck, pulling him closer.

For the first time in a long, long time—Evelyn felt chosen.
Desired.
Safe.

4

Ed lay on the old, scratchy couch in his office, his mind racing.

He kept replaying it—every second.
And if she weren't still curled against him now, softly snoring, nude and warm, her body pressed along his like a missing puzzle piece, he might've convinced himself it never happened.

He *should've* felt like a king.
A titan.

But he didn't.

From the first kiss to that final, breathless collapse, it hadn't felt like something he *chose*.
It felt like something taken.

Something…orchestrated.

Like he was just along for the ride.

And worst of all—like someone had been watching.
Maybe *still* was.

Even so, his arm curled around her on instinct.
She nuzzled deeper into his chest, sighing softly.

That sigh was the only thing that felt *real*.

Then came the voice.

Deep. Mocking. Familiar.

"Isn't that sweet?"

Ed's head snapped up.

The office was dark.
But not completely.

On the desk, the black book *glowed*—faint and ember-like.

"Yes, me," the voice said again, closer now.
Inside him.

Ed didn't respond.

He didn't have to.

Because the memories came crashing in.

A childhood of whispers.
Years of torment.
A mind worn thin by shadowy manipulations.

The book.

It had been there all along—twisting him, testing him.

Until one day, he'd finally *screamed* at it.

Told it to *fuck off.*

And somehow…
It had.

Or so he thought.

"Get out of my fucking head!"

He hurled the words in his mind like hammers—hoping they'd break the book's grip, crush the tether it had rewoven through him.

But it was no use.

Maya had reattached the cable.

The book had reclaimed him.
And this time…
There would be no escape.

"We had this talk once," it said, smooth as silk.
Then came a chuckle.
"And I listened. Doesn't mean I *completely* obeyed."

The weariness hit like a drug.

Sudden.
Suffocating.

His limbs grew heavy.

His eyelids, heavier still.

This was the book's doing.

It *always* was.

He tried to resist, to think through the fog:

*Stop this. I... Please... I...*

He yawned. Long and involuntary.

Maya stirred beside him, one arm draped over his chest.

"Shhh, sweetie," the book cooed—syrupy and low. "You need your rest. Tomorrow's a *big* day...for both of you."

His eyes slipped shut.
The weight was too great.

He could still feel her against him.
Still hear her breath.

Then came the hum.
Low. Strange. Faint.

*Love is the sweetest thing...*

The book's song.

Back again.

Ed slipped under.

And the dark came to collect him.

5

Dreams took Ed at first.
The usual kind.

Flying over downtown.
Asking out that pretty girl in high school—what was her name again?
He didn't remember. It didn't matter.

The images drifted like dandelion seeds through his mind: harmless, sweet.

But then the book started playing its games.

The tone shifted.
Dream became a memory.
Fiction, nonfiction.

He was six again—barefoot on the cool dirt floor of the bookstore basement.
His father, Charles, and several friends were there, replacing the old stone foundation with fresh concrete blocks.
Laughing. Sweating. Working.

Until they *found* it.

Grinning, one of the men called out,

"Looks like you've struck gold down here."
handing Ed's dad a shovel.

Charles stepped closer, curious. The others gave him space.

The box was buried shallowly in the soil.
Time had darkened the wood, blackened it like something cooked too long over a fire—but otherwise? It was *perfect*.

Unharmed.
Untouched.

Untouched *by time*.

Ed watched as his father crouched and pulled the box free from its little grave. A nearby stone—once resting on top—tumbled backward with a dull *thud*.

The lid had cracked.
Just a single line, like a fracture through glass.

But the rest of the box looked…*new*.

Too new.

Charles turned it over in his hands, his brows drawing tight.

"The top's cracked," he murmured. "But it looks new. Like it was made yesterday."

His voice trembled at the edges—not with excitement. With something colder.

Without looking at Ed, he said,

"Fetch me a rag."

Ed ran to the toolbox, grabbed one, and bolted back. His eyes never left the box.
Neither did anyone else's.

Charles wiped away the dirt, revealing brass and black oak beneath. The box gleamed as if it had been waiting.

Then he examined the lock.

"I hate to ruin something this nice," he muttered, "but I doubt any locksmith can get it open without a drill."

He pressed the edge of a flathead screwdriver into the lock and twisted hard.

### *CLICK.*

The sharp snap echoed through the basement.

The lock gave way.

Charles set the screwdriver down and opened the lid.

Ed stepped closer, standing beside him, peering down.

Inside—resting in red velvet—was a black leather book. Ancient. Pristine.

Charles lifted it out, turning it in his hands.

"It's warm," he said, almost to himself.

He placed it gently on the floor beside the box.

That's when everything tilted.

Time stopped.
The world froze.

Only Ed moved now.

And the book...*snapped open.*

A voice slid through the stillness. Deep. Amused.

"This is when I started the cancer, Eddy."

A soft, mock-gentle chuckle.

"No real reason. Your dad saved me. I could've let him live for years—brought in crowds, attention to your shitty little store. But he destroyed my box."

A pause.

"And what about you? You were always *good* to me."

The dream shifted again.

Now Ed was nine. Cleaning the book. Polishing its cover. Whispering to it. Listening.

"You forgot our chats," it said.
"Back when you were small. When you still loved me."

The dream twisted again.

Ed at twelve. Then fourteen. Then seventeen.

The book was *always* there.

Watching.
Whispering.
Feeding.

Until the day he fought back.

Last shift.

Teenage Ed stood alone in the basement, hands shaking.
A pocketknife in one fist.
A chained-up dog snarled in the corner.

Tears streamed down his face.

"*No! Get out of my head!*"

Then—*darkness.*

Everything fell away.

Only a single, blinding white light remained.

And Ed stood before it.

A man again.

Then came the voice—*one last time.*

"You don't get to refuse me anymore, Ed. What I did to your father? That was child's play. What I'll do to *you*—to *her*—to *all of them* if you don't listen now?"

A beat. Almost tender.

"That's for later."

And then—like a lullaby:

"Sleep, my sweet baby boy."

The light winked out.

And mercifully...
Ed's dreams ended.

# CHAPTER 13: NEW DAY, NEW PROBLEMS

1

The book wanted something *big* this time. It had waited ninety-three years patiently, festering, for the right opening, and it wouldn't squander the moment on petty murders or whispered infidelities.

No.

This time, it would be *biblical.*

The book was watching. And waiting.

Then came Maya.

Flawless.

Smart. Charismatic. Magnetic.

Even without its help, men flocked to her. Men adored her; men *needed* her.

Oh yes, *Maya Cartar* would do.

*Congresswoman Cartar… Maybe Senator Cartar, who knows?*

It liked the sound of that.

She would need the right image. A tragic backstory. A noble love. Something to make the public lean forward and sigh:

"She's been through so much…and despite that, she

rose."

A husband, perhaps.
Older. Weathered.
Kind.
Broken.
A man whose wife had died.

If the book had lips, it would smile.

Everything was aligning.

The higher Maya climbed, the deeper it could reach.
The deeper it reached, the closer it came to waking *Him*.
The True Being.
The start.
Every holy book spoke of the end times... The book pulsed.
*Well, let's give the people what they want.*

Giddy with anticipation, the book vibrated.

A new day.
A new vessel.
This will be an additional problem for the world.

Nothing could contain it.

It went to work.

---

Deep inside her mind—where thoughts dissolve into dreams—it stirred the fragments of Maya that still resisted. Just enough to hold a conversation.

*"Maya, dear,"* it cooed.
*"Time to wake up. You've got a very busy life ahead of you."*

She stirred within herself—not in body, but in

thought. Groggy. Confused.

"What do you want?" she muttered, exhausted.

*"Just a conversation,"* it purred.
*"A courtesy. To keep you informed. No surprises. No resistance. Therefore, management becomes unnecessary."*

That last word landed like a trapdoor in her chest.

"What do you mean, 'management'? What plan? Am I still asleep? Wait... Am I still *lying on Ed?*"

A long pause. The sound of silk sliding over steel.

*"So many questions already handled—or rather, punished. I thought we had made that clear. The plan is simple:* **you rise***. They follow. And in the end?* **They burn.***"*

*"You don't have to worry about it. I'm adaptable. You can be my willing puppet—or my unwilling one. Either works for me."*

Another pause.

A knowing warmth curled into its voice.

*"Yes...you're still lying on your future husband. Your affectionate nuzzling is* **endearing***. Almost convincing."*

Maya's inner voice *screamed.*

But she couldn't move.
Couldn't speak.
She had control only of her ears.
Her body curled up in a bed that no longer felt safe.

Her own breathing was the only sound she could claim.

*"No need for dramatics, my dear,"* the book murmured. "Screaming changes nothing."

It paused.
Savored.

*"If we pull this off,* **The One** *will reward us both. Even dear Eddy down there."*

A flicker of cruel amusement.

*"Perhaps your friend Matt and his new little lover too—if they cooperate. Though I rather doubt they will."*

Something *cold* slithered deeper into Maya's thoughts. She tried to brace herself, but it was too late.

*"That's fine,"* the book purred.
*"You don't need him anymore. You have Ed. Ed* **has** *you."*

A sick weight settled on those words—final and absolute.

*"I've arranged everything. The next phase will be...messy. But with your go-get-'em attitude? That's something I* **adore.***"*

It chuckled.
Low.
Wet.
Mirthless.

*"What's the current expression?"*
It rifled through her memories as if it were flipping through a magazine.
She could feel it—sticky and invasive.

Her skin crawled.

*"Ah. Yes. That's the one. Fuck around and find out."*

The voice laughed—rich with malice, dripping with affection.

Then it whispered:

*"Maya, please continue. It's time to decide."*

2

Matt woke alone in the queen-size bed to a soft knock at the door.
Still half-asleep, he shuffled over and opened it.

Evelyn stood there, holding two plates of breakfast. She gave him the once-over, her cheeks coloring.

"Nice boxers," she said, brushing past him like she owned the place.

"Uh…thanks."
Matt realized too late that he was underdressed. He shut the door and reached for his pants.

Over her shoulder, Evelyn called, "Don't get dressed on my account. In fact, remove more clothing."

Matt froze halfway through buttoning.
He looked at her, trying to gauge whether she was serious.

For a beat, he considered it.

Then remembered her mother was probably downstairs—and decided against gambling with his already garbage luck.
He tugged on his pants.

Evelyn gave a mock sigh, then sat down with her plate.
"Come eat then," she said, with a trace of suppressed

frustration.

Matt sat next to her, stealing a glance at her face.

"Were you serious?" he asked.

Evelyn didn't look up. She took a bite of her eggs and smirked.
"Perhaps you'll never know."

Matt laughed and leaned closer, his hand resting on her thigh.

"Eve, if I thought you meant it—and your mom didn't own a shotgun—I'd have already thrown you onto that bed. No hesitation."

The blush hit him halfway through the sentence.
But he finished it anyway.

Evelyn turned toward him, eyebrows raised—impressed, maybe.
Then she leaned in and kissed him. Slow. Sweet.

She laughed softly as she pulled back.
"God, you're lucky you're cute."

Matt laughed too, and for a moment, everything *felt right*.
Whatever this was with Evelyn—it was easy. Natural.
They *fit*.

And best of all?

Maya wasn't anywhere near it.

He hated how good that felt. Really, he did.

But she brought it on herself.

His gaze drifted. Eyes glazed.

A quarter tank of gas.
Four hours to Boston—assuming no traffic.

He didn't know how he was getting back.

"Hey... where did you go?"

Evelyn's voice broke through the fog. She was watching him carefully.

Matt blinked and forced a smile.
"Oh, nowhere, I guess."

Evelyn raised a skeptical eyebrow. That look that saw straight through people.

"Matt, I've known you—what—three days? And even I know that was BS."

Matt sighed, shoulders sagging under the weight of everything.

"Thanks to our fearless leader, I've got no way back to Boston."

He stared down at his plate—cold eggs and no direction.

She hadn't come home last night.
Which wasn't like her.
Despite the arguments, Maya always came back.

Because in her mind, *nothing was ever her fault.*

Evelyn's expression softened.
"Well...maybe she met someone at the bar after you left. You did say the drinks were free."

Matt hesitated.
Minefield.

Defend Maya? He'd look like he still cared.
Don't defend her? He'd sound heartless.

Lose-lose.

"That's not really her style," he said, guarded.
"Even in Boston, she never did the random hookup thing."

He took a bite, trying to look unaffected.

Evelyn didn't push. Not quite.
But her voice was quiet. Intentional.

"Then where is she?"

Matt had no answer.

She knew it.

She was watching—measuring him.
Maybe not even consciously.
Just testing what Maya still meant to him.

And what did she mean now?

Everything changed the moment Maya kissed him.
No—not kissed. *Cornered him.*

Came at him like some low-rent scene from a bad
adult movie.
Why?

Because she blew his money?

She always blew his money.
That wasn't new.

But *this* was different.

She crossed the line.

And now...

Nothing felt the same.

And Evelyn was right.

Where the hell was she?

Matt's voice cracked when he finally said it:
"I don't know, Eve."

He looked towards the door.
Hoping—*praying*—for that familiar smile to return.
For Maya to walk in, books in hand, carrying some ludicrous
excuse and half a story.

Something ridiculous.
Something so *Maya* it would be both infuriating and oddly
reassuring.

But the door didn't open.

Instead, Evelyn reached out and placed her hand on
his knee.
A gentle squeeze.

In that moment, Matt understood:
She wasn't competing with Maya.
She wasn't jealous.
She *saw him*—and still stayed.

At least for now.

3

Ed's eyes opened slowly, blinking against the morning
light filtering through the narrow window—and the harsh
buzz of the fluorescent bulb flickering overhead.

The office smelled of paper, dust, and old regrets.

Maya was gone—thank Christ.
But he was still lying there, naked as the day he was born.

He sat up, bracing for the usual ache in his back or the throb behind his eyes.

Nothing.

No pain. No stiffness. Just...stillness.

After the night he'd had, he should've felt used up.
Worn out.
But his body felt loose. Limber.
As if someone had scrubbed every ache from it.

It wasn't comforting.

He got to his feet and found his clothes in the dim light, dressing in silence.
The couch creaked under his weight. The sound echoed like guilt in the too-quiet room.

He needed to go home—shower, shave, find clean clothes. Hopefully dodge Amanda on the way.

He didn't want to think about what came after that.

DING.
The bell above the front door rang.

Ed froze.

Had he forgotten to lock it? Jesus. What if someone had walked in earlier—while they were — His thoughts spun as he turned toward the doorway.

Maya stepped inside, holding two coffees.
Already smiling.

"Hey, sleepyhead," she said, like they'd done this a dozen times before. Like this was normal.

She offered one cup.

Ed's hand trembled slightly as he took it. The blood drained from his face.

And then came a whisper—not hers.

*"I told you I had plans, Eddy."*

The book.

He tried to ignore it. Really, he did.

"Thanks," he managed, raising the cup to his nose. The smell of coffee grounded him. Barely.

"You didn't have to."

"You're welcome." Maya breezed over and sat in his chair. "I didn't know what you drink, so... I hope you like it black."

"Black is fine," he said, still studying her. Looking for the strings.

"Maya... why are you here?"

As soon as he said it, he wished he could take it back.

Her smile faltered—the mask dropped too fast.

"I didn't realize you didn't want me around... after you had your way with me."
Her voice wasn't sharp, just flat. Icy.

She stood and began collecting her things—quickly, clinically.

"Maya, wait," Ed said, stepping forward, coffee

forgotten.

"That's not what I meant. I just—"

He hesitated.

"I figured you'd be with your friends. Not…here. With me."

Even he didn't buy it.

Maya searched his face. For what, he couldn't say. An apology? Guilt? Weakness?

"Look, I'm sorry. Don't go," he said—and for better or worse, he meant it.

She paused. "You sure? I don't want to get you in trouble."

There was a warning buried in the sweetness. He ignored it.

"Actually," he said, trying for casual, "you need money, and I need someone to watch the store while I run home and clean up. So how about I hire you? Hour. Two tops."

Maya's grin returned—playful, sharp.

"If your wife walks in and sees me behind that counter, I hope the ER's open."

"She's in Syracuse," he said, remembering that she wanted to haggle in person with their poor realtor. "House stuff. She won't be back until late."

Maya slung her bag over her shoulder—carefully. Like it carried something precious.

"Why don't I just ride with you?" she asked, breezy as

ever.

Ed hesitated.

He thought of Amanda. Her shampoo still clung to the towels at the house.
Her voice, echoing in the empty rooms.

He thought about the book.

Its hum—always present—just under the surface.

Finally, he sighed.
"Okay. Fine. But maybe let your friends know you're alive?"

"Sure, boss."
She winked and stepped through the door ahead of him.

As she passed, the bag bumped her hip.

Ed didn't look.

He didn't need to.

The air shifted when it moved—like the room itself held its breath.

---

They reached Ed's truck—his dad's old F-150.
Once black, now mostly rust and road salt.
It groaned as Ed unlocked the doors and climbed in.

Maya slid in beside him, buckling her seatbelt without a word.
The cab smelled of stale pine air freshener and faint engine oil.

He turned the key.

The truck coughed, then rumbled awake.

The engine ran, and the AC worked. That's all Ed ever needed.

Amanda's car note swallowed most of his paycheck anyway.

As they backed out of the lot, it felt less like leaving—and more like fleeing a crime scene.

"So," Maya said, side-eyeing him. "Wanna talk about it?"

"About what?" Ed asked, glancing over.

"The book's plan for us."

Her tone was light. But it had teeth.

"Because if I'm gonna be the next Mrs. Maya Rodrick, you're at least buying me dinner—or fucking me in a bed."

She smiled.

But it wasn't a gift.

It was a blade.

The truck swerved slightly.

Ed's mind filled with last night—skin, sweat, silence. The bed. The way she said it. She meant to rattle him.

It worked.

Then the voice arrived—slick and sudden.

*"Clever, clever Eddy. Brightest in your class. Of course, it helped to have me whispering the answers, didn't it?"*

Ed gripped the wheel tighter.

*"Let's skip the nostalgia. Don't get clever with me. You saw what happened to Maya. This can be easy…or very easy. Just cough if you understand."*

*"She thinks you're on the same leash. Think you've lost your will. That's cute."*

*"Once she earns it, maybe I'll give some of it back. Some. But if you make me... I'll take more."*

Ed's throat was dry. His father's face flickered in the mirror—bloated. Gray.

He coughed. Once. Loud.

The book laughed.

*"Good boy."*

"Hello?"
Maya waved a hand in front of his face.
"Still with us, Captain Sunshine?"

"Yeah—sorry," he said. "Zoned out."

He turned off onto a narrow dirt road.
Maple trees lined either side, pale green leaves casting shadows on the gravel.

At the end of the drive sat a white colonial with black shutters and a red door.
A cherry tree bloomed defiantly in the yard.

It looked like a postcard.
It felt like a lie.

"As for the book," Ed said as he parked, "I don't know its full plan.
Just that it's obsessed with the idea of you and me being together.
It always played matchmaker. Even back when I was a kid."

He got out.

"Coming?"

Maya stepped out, staring at the house.

"I can see your wife did the decorating," she muttered.
"No way you're this stylish."

"You'd be right," he replied with a dry chuckle.
"Make yourself at home. I'm gonna grab a shower."

---

Inside, he climbed the stairs two at a time.

In the bathroom, he stripped out of his stale clothes, resisting the urge to burn them.
They hit the hamper like dead skin.

He turned the knob.

The pipes screamed.

Hot water hissed.

He stepped into the spray.

Let the scald burn away what he couldn't name.

4

Maya heard the shower start upstairs.
The book whispered.

She clenched her fists.
Not again.

But what she wanted—and what was going to happen—were two very different things.

She glanced up the stairs.
For one fragile second, she let herself hope.
Hope that the book might change its mind.
That it might offer a reprieve.

It didn't.
It never would.

So, she climbed.

One step at a time.

The sound of water grew louder with each footfall,
steam curling down the staircase like the breath of something
ancient and waiting.

At the top, she paused.

This place—his place—looked like a dream someone
once told her she could have.
Bookshelves built into the hallway walls stood full.
Paperbacks, hardcovers.
Some she recognized.
Others were yellowing, worn, and well-loved.

This was Amanda's house.
Ed's life.

But she was the one walking through it now.

Her fingers brushed the spines—part apology, part
warning.

She undressed slowly, her clothes falling behind her in
quiet stages.
A breadcrumb trail she wasn't sure anyone should follow.

This time felt different.
That made it worse.

Because she liked Ed.
Not the way the book wanted her to.
Not the way it twisted affection into performance.

But in some quiet, human way.
And part of her wanted this.

That was the cruelest trick of all.

She reached the bathroom door.
Steam curled out like smoke. Her skin prickled.

Her hand hovered over the handle.

Inside, water hissed. The room was a fog of heat and memory.

She opened the door.

"Ed," she said, soft, her voice almost lost to the spray.
"I need to wash up too."

Before he could answer, she stepped into the fog.

The glass door shut behind her with a whisper.

A hush of finality.

The steam clouded everything.
Even her guilt.

5

Amanda drove like a bat out of hell.
But honestly, that was just her usual speed—especially on the Thruway.

Her Tesla carved through traffic without hesitation, tires humming on the pavement like a promise. She barely registered the angry horns or the blur of cars in her mirrors. Her mind was still back in Syracuse. Back with that smug, underqualified realtor.

"Four hundred thousand?" she scoffed aloud. "Not on your goddamn life."

Her house was worth *at least* $575,000. And not a penny less.
He'd promised to work his magic. Find the right buyer. Maybe if she tossed in that crusty old bookstore as a "bonus."
The thought made her grin.

Ed, watching his little kingdom get sold out from under him…

She chuckled and glanced down at the console. Ninety minutes to Boonville, the screen said.
She figured she could shave that to just over an hour—maybe less, if traffic didn't screw her.

Her foot pressed harder on the accelerator. The Tesla surged forward—smooth, silent, a bullet made of money.

All Amanda wanted was a hot shower, a warm bed, and something mindless to stream—Netflix or Hulu, preferably something she *knew* would piss Ed off.

Assuming he even came home tonight.

He was probably sulking in some budget hotel, pulling his usual martyr act.
All because she *dared* threaten him with divorce.

And what of it?

She had every right to be angry.

"Keep the store," he'd said.
To *hell* with that damn bookstore.

Her jaw clenched. She swerved past a lumbering school bus full of high school baseball players, barely missing the side mirror.

"It's my life too, Ed!" she snapped at the windshield. "You ever think about that? No, it was always you. Or your dad. Never me."

Her knuckles whitened on the wheel.
"Well, guess what?" she hissed.
"From now on, it's about me. Amanda. No one else."

Goddamn him for making her feel this way.

It wasn't fair.
*None* of this was how it was supposed to go.

She was supposed to leave this backwater part of the state.
Leave the sad people. The insignificant life.
Start over—better.

Her thoughts drifted—and she almost didn't see the car swerve in front of her.

She slammed on the brakes.

The Tesla's tires screamed, rubber clawing at asphalt. The rear end fishtailed—but the system corrected. Compensated for her panic. Her speed. Her fury.

Somehow, she didn't crash.

But her hands trembled against the wheel.

"FUCKING ED!" she roared, voice raw.

As she steadied the wheel, the car dashboard flickered. Just for a moment, the screen went black—then blinked back to life.

Her phone buzzed once in the cupholder.

One notification.

Unknown number: *You're almost home.*

# Chapter 14: HOMECOMINGS

1

After breakfast, Evelyn could tell Matt's mind was still somewhere else—still with Maya. It clung to his face like fog. He tried to hide it, but it lingered.

She let the silence stretch, then gently offered, "Let's go check the bookstore. Maybe she went back there."

Matt blinked out of his haze.
"Yeah…yeah, that makes sense."
He pushed back his chair.
"If she's book hunting, she'd tune out the rest of the world."

He stood, stretching.
"You ready?"

Evelyn gave a soft smile, then grabbed the empty plates.
"I'll meet you at the car in ten."

She slipped out of the room and headed downstairs. The creaky old staircase groaned beneath her—a warning bell with every step.

In the kitchen, Miranda stood by the sink.
Face blotchy. Eyes sharp with too much rage and too little reflection.
One hand gripped a chipped coffee mug like it was an anchor. The other cradled a smoldering cigarette. The

morning air was crisp, too clean for the bitterness that filled the room.

Evelyn didn't need to see her face to know what was coming.

"Hey, Mom," she whispered, setting the plates in the sink.

Miranda raised one graying eyebrow, voice low and rough:
"Delivering breakfast for the guests now?"

Steam rose from the mug. Birds chirped outside. Somewhere in the distance, a leaf blower hummed—a spring morning trying to pretend everything was fine.

"No. Just him," Evelyn replied, back still turned.

She turned then, her jaw set. The message was obvious: *back off.*

But Miranda wasn't finished.

A dry, humorless laugh. Yellowed teeth.
"Him? The college kid from the third floor? How many times do I have to say it, Eve? We don't mix with the damn guests."

Evelyn's fingers curled into fists.

Her throat tightened.
Years of silence. Sacrifice. Shame.
It boiled beneath her skin, hot and rising.

"We've just talked," she said evenly.
"But even if we hadn't… I'm an adult. So is he. And if I wanted to sleep with him, that's my decision. Not yours."

Her cheeks flushed—not with embarrassment, but

with anger.

And Miranda, as always, struck the match:

"As long as you live in my house—"

That was it.

Evelyn snapped.

Her voice dropped—cold, controlled, lethal.

"You cannot be serious."

Miranda flinched. Just for a second.

Evelyn stepped closer.

"I gave up my life for you. My dreams, my education, and my *future!*"
She jabbed a finger toward the ceiling.
"And you want to throw this tired line at me like I'm some teenager sneaking out?"

Her voice trembled—not from weakness, but rage.

"You begged me to stay. Begged me to help keep this place running."
She leaned in.

"You don't get to pull the *'my house, my rules'* card now, Mom."

She took a breath—slow, steady.

The words came out like venom.

"You're right. This is your house. So find someone else to sweep the goddamn driveway and haul luggage up those fucking stairs—because it will never be me again."

She shoved past Miranda, who stood frozen. Silent.

The full weight of what she'd just lost sank in behind her eyes.

But Evelyn didn't turn back. She didn't give her the satisfaction of a glance.

She pushed through the screen door.
The rusty hinges screamed, but she didn't slow down.

Outside, the morning air hit her like a splash of cold water—bright, clean, alive.
Freedom. Sharp as citrus.

Matt was waiting by the car. He straightened when he saw her. Evelyn said nothing. She just climbed into the passenger seat and slammed the door behind her.

Matt glanced toward the porch.
Miranda didn't follow.

Maybe she was still in the kitchen, choking on her bitterness.

He turned the key, and the engine rumbled to life. They pulled away from the house. Gravel crunched under the tires.

And for the first time in her life, Evelyn felt something new stirring in her chest.

Not fear. Not guilt.

Freedom.

And for once, it felt like it belonged to her.

2

Maya lay naked next to Ed again—this time in his bed.

If last night was a mistake, this was a betrayal. The kind that doesn't wash out. That stains the sheets no matter how many times you change them. The kind that lingers in the walls.

Ed sat up slowly, his body heavier than it should've been.

This was the bed he once shared with Amanda.

Where they'd made love once—maybe a lifetime ago—back when they were happy. More recently, it was where they'd slept in bitter silence, backs turned, resentment thick in the dark.

He rubbed his face with both hands, as if he could scrub away what he'd done.

But the guilt clung like sweat.

The room tilted slightly. He stood unsteadily and made his way to the bathroom, gripping the sink to steady himself. Each breath came too hard. Too fast. He felt *everything*—every choice, every failure—pressing against his ribs like a second skeleton.

The faucet groaned as he turned it on. Cold water splashed against his face.

When he looked up…

It wasn't his own reflection staring back.

It was his father's.

Charles Rodrick. Not the man he wanted to

remember—but the version hollowed out by cancer. Gaunt cheeks. Dull eyes. Skin like wax. Soul already halfway gone.

One of the dead the book left behind.
Not dead enough to rest.
Just alive enough…to suffer.

Ed's throat tightened. Grief flared sharp and sudden, like it was new again.

Then he blinked.

And his own face returned.

Not much better.

Years of late nights, alcohol, and regret had carved him into something lean and tired. A man sliding into the same grave, one poor decision at a time.

He exhaled, grabbed a towel, and dried his face.

Then he went back to the bedroom.

Maya was sitting up now, knees drawn to her chest, the blanket clutched around her like armor. She looked wrecked—but not in the way he expected. Not ashamed. Not seductive.

Just…broken.

Like she was trying to stitch herself back together and couldn't remember how.

Ed crossed the room and pulled one of Amanda's old silk robes from the closet. He handed it to her.

"I take it that wasn't your idea," he said.

Maya stared at the robe. Took it slowly. Her expression shifted—no mask, no performance. Just something raw.

"Thanks," she whispered.

Whether it was for the robe or the fact he hadn't looked at her like she was a monster—he couldn't tell.

She didn't answer his question.

Or maybe she couldn't.

And Ed didn't push.

"I'm gonna get dressed. Head downstairs, make some lunch," he said, voice low and distant—too casual after what they'd just done.

She nodded silently.

He gestured toward the closet.
"Some of Amanda's old clothes are in there. If you don't want to wear yesterday's... up to you."

Another nod. Slower this time.

Without another word, Ed turned and left. His footsteps on the stairs were almost soundless.

He didn't look back.

---

Downstairs, the house felt unnervingly still. Like it was watching.

Ed moved through the kitchen on autopilot—bread, peanut butter, jelly. He made two sandwiches with practiced hands. Familiar motions. Normal sounds.

But nothing felt normal.

He sat at the oversized dining room table. The one

Amanda insisted on for "entertaining guests."

They rarely had any.

Silence pressed around him like insulation. Too quiet. Too close.

Then: footsteps on the stairs.

He looked up.

And froze.

Maya was descending slowly, barefoot, yesterday's clothes folded neatly in one hand. In the other, she tugged at the hem of a yellow sundress—Amanda's. A dress Amanda hadn't worn in years.

It fit Maya awkwardly. A little too short. A little too tight across the chest.

But somehow, it still worked. Too well.

The light from the window caught her hair just right, making the moment feel unreal. Like a memory that didn't belong to him.

She paused on the steps and met his gaze.

"What?" she asked, cautious.
"Something wrong?"

Ed blinked. Shook his head.
"No, you, uh…you look amazing."

Maya gave a small, unreadable smile.

He gestured to the plate in front of him.
"Made you a sandwich if you want it."

She nodded and came down, the dress swaying gently

at her knees.

And in that moment—barefoot in Amanda's sundress, carrying folded clothes like a guest who stayed too long—she didn't look like someone passing through.

She looked like she *belonged*.

And that terrified him more than anything.

3

Maya descended the stairs slowly, barefoot and quiet.

She saw Ed watching her.

Men looked at her like that all the time—she was used to it. But this...

This was different.

There was something in his eyes she didn't recognize.

Not lust.

Not conquest.

Affection.

It caught her off guard. Even in the tight, shadowy corner of her mind where she still lived—still resisted—she felt her heart twitch. A reflex, like a muscle moved by surprise.

Why did that affect her?

She didn't know. Maybe because no one had ever looked at her like that *after*.
Not *after* they got what they wanted from her.

And Ed had.

Twice now.

Though, in fairness, he hadn't exactly *wanted* it—not in the usual way.

Maya couldn't recall a straight man ever refusing an open invitation. But Ed hadn't sought it out. He hadn't pushed. Not really.

And now, here he was.

Just *looking* at her.

If she'd had full control—*proper* control—she might've said, *Stop it. Don't be stupid, don't fall for this, and for fuck's sake don't look at me like that. This is a dangerous game we're playing.*

Because it was.

She could see the path laid out before them—and it didn't end well.

Not for him.

Not for her.

Flames, eventually.

But he'd argue, wouldn't he?

Say it wasn't like that. That they were *both* in this now. That he *cared*.

And the worst part?

She might believe him.

Because—God help her—somewhere, buried beneath everything the book had hollowed out and hijacked, something inside Maya was starting to…*like* him.

And she *definitely* liked the way he was looking at her now.

But she didn't have control.

So it didn't matter what she thought. Or felt. Or feared.

It didn't matter that she liked the quiet way he handed her the robe. Or how he never once flinched when the book flexed its power around them.

None of it mattered.

Still, the little things were piling up—becoming something *dangerous*.

She told herself to stop. *Don't do this again. Don't be stupid.*

It was Professor Halstead all over again. Different man, same mistake.

She tried to file it away under "another older-man phase."

But even she didn't believe that.

Not really.

The book answered for her before she had a chance to argue.

She didn't even care what it said anymore. It was like watching a movie she couldn't pause.

Cut to: the kitchen.

She walked in and sat beside Ed as if it were the most

natural thing in the world.

She heard her voice—her own voice—say: "So, PB and J?"

She still hadn't gotten used to that. Hearing herself speak like that—like someone had memorized her voice and was puppeting it from the inside.

Ed answered. Asked how she was feeling.

Genuine concern. Casual affection.

Maya didn't respond.

Not *her*.

The real Maya was screaming into a pillow inside her mind.

She'd started calling her imposter Maya B.

Short for *Maya Bitch*. Or *Maya Book*. Take your pick.

It helped. Like giving the monster under your bed a name.

If the *real* Maya had answered, she'd have said something like:

*Thanks for the above-average sex, Ed. Also, I think I might be developing actual feelings for you, which is…a problem, considering you're married. And live four hours away. And, oh yeah—I owe the U.S. government $125,000 in student loans. I have no idea what I'm doing with my life or where I'm going.*

Yes, that would've spoiled the mood.

But Maya B?

She just smiled, picked up half a sandwich, and kept

playing the part.

Maya listened as the conversation unfolded—line by predictable line.

The book pawed through her memories, stitching together its best impersonation of her. Like a cover band playing her greatest hits.

The words were hers.

The tone, the inflections—close enough.

But not *her*.

Not really.

Still, Ed was smart. On some level, he knew.

She could see it—the way he leaned in just slightly, believing despite himself.

The way he *wanted* to believe.

Now and then, the book slipped.

Dropped a line too flat. Smiled too soon.

And in that brief breath of space, Maya surged through.

A sentence here. A word there.

Tiny sparks of herself cutting through the static.

It probably freaked Ed the hell out—this strange, stuttering possession of the girl beside him.

But maybe—*hopefully*—he heard her. Just enough.

Just enough to hope.

It gave *her* hope, at least.

The book either hadn't noticed she was meddling...

Or it didn't care.

Which, in some ways, was worse.

4

Matt and Evelyn pulled up in front of the bookstore.

Closed.

Not just locked—lights off, shades drawn, sign flipped.

Closed-closed.

Evelyn stared through the windshield, her brow creasing.

"That's...weird," she muttered. "Really weird."

Matt glanced over. "Weird how?"

She didn't answer immediately. Her eyes stayed on the darkened storefront, mouth tight.

"That store's open every day," she said. "Christmas, New Year's...even the days his parents died, the store was always open."

Matt shifted in his seat. "So...what? You wanna check on him?"

Evelyn gave him a sharp look.

"First, Ed's not a stranger. I've known him my whole life. Second...he only lives five minutes away."

Matt blinked. "Okay. But we're just gonna roll up and say, 'Hey, you good, bro?'"

Her voice sharpened—still raw from her fight with her mother.

"Where I come from, that's exactly what you do."

Then, softer, "Didn't you grow up in a small town? Don't you check on your people?"

Matt raised both hands in surrender. "Fair enough. Which way?"

She pointed forward. "Down Main, right on Schuyler, then Moose River Road. I'll show you the driveway."

As he backed out onto the street, Evelyn leaned against the window, eyes scanning the passing shops and houses.

Something about the closed store didn't just feel odd—it felt *wrong*.

Not *slept in* wrong.
Not *got the flu* wrong.

Wrong, like something had slipped out of place and couldn't be put back.

---

They turned onto Main. Traffic picked up—pickup trucks, minivans, people with nowhere to be in a hurry to get there.

Boonville blurred past.

It always pulled on a strange, aching part of Evelyn that couldn't quite let go of the place. Not even when it hurt.

It wasn't anything special—just familiar. A town stuck between what it used to be and what it never became. Full of half-shuttered shops and people aging too fast.

The old were bitter.

The young were hopeful—and growing bitter by the year.

Upstate New York had a way of dragging the truth out of people.
Sometimes their best. More often than not, their worst.

Evelyn had seen both.

Too many around here delighted in watching others fall—not out of cruelty, but because it made their own misery feel smaller.

She wondered if Ed had learned that too.

---

They drove in silence as the town gave way to woods. Houses thinned. Streetlights vanished. The canopy above grew thicker, darker.

The deeper they went, the worse Evelyn felt.

"Matt," she whispered, "what if we find something out there...something bad?"

He kept his eyes forward.

"Well...we call the police, I guess."

He didn't sound convinced.

The trees blurred past her window.

"I don't know, Eve," he added. "This whole

thing…feels off."

---

The pavement turned to packed dirt.

Evelyn sat up straighter.

"There," she said, pointing.

A narrow road veered off to the right—less a driveway, and more a forgotten trail.

"That's it. That's his."

Matt turned onto it. The tires crunched over gravel and dead leaves. Dust billowed behind them, rising like smoke.

As they rounded the last bend, the house appeared— a white colonial, still and quiet. Black shutters. A cherry tree in bloom.

And in the driveway, hunched like a tired animal, sat Ed's rust-bitten F-150.

"That's Ed's truck," Evelyn said, already unbuckling.

The car dinged in protest, but she didn't wait.

Before Matt even shifted into park, she was out, boots thudding up the porch steps. She raised her hand and knocked—hard.

The sound echoed.

Once.

Twice.

No answer.

She knocked again—louder.

The door creaked.

Slow.

Reluctant.

Like it didn't want to open.

Or like whoever was behind it didn't want to be seen.

"Ed?" Evelyn called, voice suddenly small. "Are you okay?"

It was the right question.

Just not the right person.

It wasn't Ed who opened the door.

It was Maya.

Barefoot.

Wearing a sundress that fit too tight—like it wasn't hers.

And smiling.

Smiling as if someone had just invited them to brunch.

Like nothing was wrong.

Like *this* was how the morning was supposed to go.

Evelyn's mouth parted, but no sound came out.

Matt froze, one foot still on the stair, as a chill ran down his spine.

"Hey, guys," Maya said, too sweet. "You're just in time."

5

Traffic had crawled to a stop near Canastota—because of course it had. It was construction season on the Thruway, which, in Upstate New York, meant *every* season.

Still, Amanda was determined to make it back to Boonville before dinner. She just needed to hit the Verona exit. After that, it would be smooth sailing all the way north.

She drummed her fingers on the steering wheel and glanced at the ETA on the console.

Delayed. Again.

Her jaw clenched.

In the sterile silence of the Tesla's cabin, her mind wandered back to her blow-up with Ed. She'd been furious—righteous, even—but now?

Now it just felt... *messy*.

Maybe she owed him an apology.

Not for the argument, of course. She still wasn't keeping that godforsaken bookstore, and they sure as hell weren't staying in that dead-end town. But maybe—*just maybe*—she could've handled it better. Been a little less of a bitch. A little more... *gracious*?

Or—she thought with a smirk—he might run off and shack up with some twenty-something tart just to spite her.

Amanda actually laughed at the idea.

Ed? Please.

He was dependable. Dull. Aging in that slow, gray

way men do when they stop trying. He couldn't pull that kind of thing off.

…Could he?

Her smirk faltered.

Something prickled in the back of her mind—a quiet chill beneath her collar.

She brushed it off. Nerves. Paranoia. Stupid.

The traffic thinned.

She checked the map. The area had no reported cops.

Good.

Her foot eased down, and the Tesla surged forward— sleek, smooth, and silent.

In seconds, she was doing ninety.

Her happy place.
Where everything was under control.
Where she didn't have to feel *anything* at all.

Without warning, her phone rang, and her mother's voice boomed through the Tesla's speakers.

"Hello, sweetheart, how did your meeting go?"

Amanda sighed. "Hey, Mom. It went fine—though the bastard is trying to lowball us for a quick sale. Says the place is only worth $450,000. Can you believe that shit?"

"Well, he *is* the expert. And it's not like you have a mortgage on the house. Charles left it to you, remember? It's all profit. Maybe a quick sale is just what you two need."

Amanda hadn't looked at it that way.

Fast would be better. It would give Ed less time to bitch, moan, or change his mind. And if they *ever* sold the damn bookstore...the house and the store combined might push them over a million.

She'd always wanted to see that many zeros.

"Okay," she said. "But I'm telling him $500,000. I still think $450,000 is way too low for all the work I put into that place after his father died."

The thought of Charles dying in that house still made her skin crawl.

"It's your decision, of course," her mother replied. "Have you two decided where you want to move? You know, there are plenty of nice places near us in Florida. That way, when you have that baby, we'll get to see the little one more often."

Amanda cringed.

She hadn't timed it, but her mother *never* failed to mention a baby.

What could she say?
*Sure, Mom. Ed and I will crank out a kid to save our marriage. Hopefully, the little shit keeps him tethered to me for eighteen years.*

Did she even *want* him tethered anymore?

That question had crept in—and lately, it wasn't going away.

The answer used to be yes. No doubt. One hundred percent.

Now?

Now there were doubts.

"No, we haven't," she replied. "But Saint Augustine is on the shortlist."

"Very good, sweetie. I'll keep an eye out for listings. Tell Ed we say hello. Daddy wanted to say hi too, but you know him—had to make his tee time."

Amanda knew, alright. His love of golf nearly rivaled his love of cheating.

Not that she'd ever tell either of them.

She'd seen him sneak women into the house more than once while her mother was out "running errands."

"Okay, Mom."

"Love you guys, talk to you la—"

Amanda hung up before she could finish. She'd had enough of the *Stepford Wives* routine her mother had adopted to keep her father happy.

---

The Verona exit appeared up ahead.

She took it fast—but the Tesla handled it like a dream.

*All roads lead to Boonville now*, she thought.

And that damned bookstore.

She told herself it was just business. Sell. Cut ties. Move on.

But the place had roots—messy, tangled ones.

She could still smell the old wooden shelves and fresh coffee. Still hear the creak of the back door no matter how many times they fixed it.

Charles had loved that creak. Said it gave the place *character*.

She used to laugh at that.

Now, it made her angry.

He'd left her the house, the store, the *memories*—wrapped in obligations she never asked for.

Selling it felt like a betrayal.
Keeping it felt like drowning.

And Ed?

He just wanted out. Out of Boonville. Out of the small-town gravity.

Maybe...out of *them* too.

She gripped the wheel tighter.

She blew through a red light. Nearly clipped a truck. A horn blared.

She didn't even notice.

The fight played again in her mind.

"We are *not* keeping the store, Ed."

---

Boonville wasn't home anymore.

But it was the last thread still tethering her to whatever came before.

And she wasn't ready to let it go.

Not yet.

# Chapter 15: HELLO EDWARD

1

Ed saw Maya open the door, and everything slowed to a crawl.

He wanted to yell, *"Don't do it!"*

But something told him that would only make it worse.

The can of worms was open now.
It was time to deal with the fallout—insert whatever cliché you wanted.

---

He heard Maya's voice:

"Hi guys, come on in."

*Guys...* not *Amanda.*

No yelling.
So, not Amanda.
Of course not—why would *his wife* knock?

---

Ed dropped onto the kitchen stool, his mind spinning.

When Evelyn and Matt stepped inside, they looked just as stunned as he felt.

"Um... Hey," Ed stammered. "Can I get you something to drink?"

Evelyn stared at Maya.

Then at Ed.

Then Maya again.

"Did you… Are you two…" She trailed off. "Tell me you aren't, Ed."

Matt didn't say a word. He stared at the floor, shoulders slumped.

Ed suddenly wondered just how deep Matt's feelings for Maya really went.

He turned to Evelyn, searching for the right words— but he never got the chance.

Maya stepped beside him and slid her arm around his waist.

The message was unmistakable:

*Yes, we are.*

*No, you don't get to know more than that.*

---

Ed met Evelyn's eyes. He waited.

"I guess I'll take that drink," Evelyn said coolly, settling onto the stool beside him.

Her gaze never left Maya.

"Your new friend and I need to have a heart-to-heart, I think."

"Oh. Okay."

Ed stood quickly.

"Beer okay?"

Maya let go of him slowly, peeling herself from the moment like it still clung to her.

"Perfect," Evelyn replied, still not glancing at Ed.

Then, a knife wrapped in velvet:

"Say, Maya—want one? You've sampled everything else he has to offer."

Maya smiled—cool, sharp, knowing.

"I'd love one, sweetie. Thanks."

She slid into Ed's chair as if it were hers by right.
Legs crossed. Eyes locked on Evelyn.

"I love girl talk."

Matt moved closer to Evelyn, leaned in, whispered something low.
Ed caught only a scrap:

"Now's not the time to defend her."

Whatever followed was for Evelyn alone.

---

Ed didn't ask.
He just walked into the kitchen and came back with four cold beers—bottled, simple, no ceremony.

He handed them out like peace offerings.

Maya took hers in silence.
Evelyn didn't acknowledge him at all.

Then Evelyn spoke. "Why don't you boys fuck off for a bit?"
She didn't even look at them.
"Take a walk. I'm sure Matt's got some questions for you too, Ed."

Ed didn't argue.

He handed Matt a bottle and nodded toward the front door.

"Come on."

---

Outside, the late afternoon air was cool and still. The sky had turned dull pewter, streaked with slow-moving clouds.

"Storm's coming," Ed muttered, squinting upward.

Matt took a sip and stepped off the porch.

"Good. Maybe it'll wash the bullshit off the place."

Ed let out a dry chuckle and followed. Their boots crunched along the gravel path edging the yard.

Old lilacs leaned over the fence line, blooms browning and soft at the edges.

The house loomed behind them—quiet, waiting.

---

"So," Matt said finally, breaking the silence. "Wanna tell me what the hell's going on?"

Ed didn't answer right away.

But that was okay.

The sky hadn't finished darkening yet.

2

Evelyn stared at Maya, rage simmering under her skin.

"So just what the fuck is going on here, Maya?"

Her voice cracked like a whip—low, cold, lethal.

"You *do* know he's married, right?" she hissed, the beer clutched like a live grenade.
"Or does that not matter in *Maya's world*, where men are just—what? Toys? Tools?"

Maya didn't blink.
Didn't flinch.

"I'm perfectly aware of Ed's unfortunate marital arrangement," she said coolly, folding her arms.
"But using Ed? That's unfair. I've never used him…"

She leaned in, smile too sharp to be kind.

"Unless you count how many times he's brought me to — well. No need to be crass."

That smile. *That* Maya smile.

It made Evelyn's teeth grind.
Her eyes flicked toward the chair—and there it was.

The book.

That goddamn book.

---

Before she even realized it, she was holding it.

The leather was warm.

Not just warm—soothing.
Familiar.
Comforting.

*"Good, Evelyn,"* the voice cooed inside her skull.
Soft. Deep. Intimate.
*"That's good. Just relax now."*

The world narrowed to a point.

*"I want you to set me on the counter,"* it whispered.
*"Ask Maya to show you the correct page. You can do that, can't you? I promise…you'll never feel pain again. Never."*

Her hands moved on their own.

She set the book on the kitchen island and opened it halfway.
The spine sighed like an old door.

---

Maya stepped beside her, calm as candlelight.
She turned the page, tapped it with one manicured nail.

"Read this, Eve," she whispered.

Evelyn's lips parted.

Her voice sounded far away, not quite her own:

*"Clavis numquam fuit sanguis… sed voluntas."*

*The key was never blood… but will.*

A low rumble of thunder stirred far in the distance —
a breath from something older than storms.

"Good girl," Maya murmured, brushing a strand of Evelyn's hair behind her ear.

She turned another page.

"Now read this, sweetie."

And Evelyn did.

*The Rite of Unveiling:*

*"Per velamen carnis, undique viscus quaero..."*

**Through the veil of flesh, I seek the gaze that sears...**

*"Visus meus non deficiat; ut veritati testimonium perhibeam sub veritate..."*

**Let my sight be unmade, that I may witness the truth beneath truth...**

*"Vexillifer Lucis, Custos Oculi Qui Foris Videt; aperi me..."*

**O Bearer of the Unlight, Keeper of the Eye That Sees Without—open me...**

*"Non ad salutem... sed ad denudationem..."*

**Not for salvation... but for unveiling...**

*"Lumina detrahe minora; nisi inane relinquere..."*

**Strip these lesser eyes; leave only void...**

*"Lux falsa uratur. Figura post figuram reveletur..."*

**Let the false light be burned away. Let the shape behind the shape be revealed...**

*"Visionem meam praebeo; pro claritate..."*

**I offer my vision in exchange for clarity...**

*"Nomen meum offero; in commutatione ad cognoscendum..."*

**I offer my name in exchange for knowing...**

*"Me praebeo..."*

**I offer myself...**

*"Fiat. Fiat."*

**So be it.**

The kitchen lights flickered.
Once.
Twice.

Then everything settled.

Evelyn blinked.

She looked around the room—calm, serene.
The tension in her jaw was gone.
Her grip had softened.

She gently closed the book.

No shaking hands.

No fury.

She couldn't quite remember why she'd been so angry a moment ago.

3

Ed and Matt stepped back into the house, and immediately everything felt wrong.

The change was subtle, but undeniable. The air had weight now. That eerie, invisible pressure that settles before a thunderstorm.

In the kitchen, Maya and Evelyn were laughing.

Clinking dishes.
Garlic and butter are on the stove.
Cooking. Together.

The same two women who, less than an hour ago, had looked ready to draw blood.

Ed stopped cold.

Matt thumped off his boots, frowning.

"So…you two kissed and made up?"

Without looking up from the pot, Maya replied smoothly:

"I know you'd love to see that show."

Matt flushed. Crimson.
Ed side-eyed him.
Yeah. That one landed.

Evelyn, noticing Matt's discomfort—and maybe indulging it—walked over and hugged him, planting a quick kiss on his cheek.

Matt tensed.
Only for a second.
But it was there.

Ed saw it.
Maya did too.

No one said a word.

Then Ed saw it.

The book.

Open.
Resting on the kitchen counter like a cookbook.

Like it *belonged* there.

Like it hadn't whispered death into his father's veins.

Like it wasn't the most dangerous thing in the house.

He stepped toward it, reaching to close it.

---

The voice came instantly.
Familiar.
Silk over ice.

*"Don't you dare, Eddy. The girls want me to be open. I want to be open. Let's leave well enough alone, shall we? We're having such a nice, balanced relationship: You don't fuck with me—I don't fuck with you."*

As if to underline its threat, the lights flickered.
Once.
Twice.

Ed's hand hovered just above the page.

Then pulled back.

---

Maya looked up.

For the briefest second, something real flickered behind her eyes.

Panic?
Fatigue?
Maybe even pleading?

He couldn't tell.

Evelyn had returned to the stove.
She was humming softly now. A melody he couldn't place—but one that stuck like a thorn in his mind.

Matt said nothing.

Ed just watched the book, thinking:

*What did it take from Evelyn to make her hum like that?*

---

"Eve, are you feeling okay?" Ed asked, inching closer. "How's your head?"

Evelyn didn't answer right away.
She just kept humming the same odd little tune.
Something about it sounded...wrong.
Old. Off.

Matt tilted his head.

"Wait—is that the song from the car? That old creepy one?"

Evelyn's voice cut through—calm, flat. Final.

"It's not creepy. And my head is fine, Ed."

The tone ended the conversation before it could start.

Ed heard it.
And let it go.

For now.

He walked to the fridge, grabbed two beers, and gave Matt a nod toward the living room.

---

The moment it clicked shut, Ed handed Matt a bottle.

"Matt," he said, settling onto the couch with a sigh. "How much do you know about the book?"

Matt twisted off the cap and took a drink.

"I know it's creepy as hell. I know it affects people.

Why?"

Ed took a long pull from his bottle and exhaled.

"It does more than affect people. It can control them. Make them do things they don't want to do. And if it wants to…"
He paused.
"…It can kill them."

That landed.

"From what I can tell, it has affected everyone but you," Ed said, looking at Matt.

Matt straightened.

"Wait…what do you mean *everyone but me?*"

Ed leaned forward, elbows on his knees.

"It's got its hooks in all of us—me, Maya, Evelyn. I'm guessing Amanda too. But you?"
He shook his head.
"Far as I can tell, you're untouched."

Matt blinked.

"No, that's not right. It's…it's tried. Back at the bookstore. It definitely tried."

Ed's eyes narrowed.

"And?"

Matt shrugged.

"I told it to fuck off. Not in those exact words—but yes. That was basically it."

Another sip.

"It hasn't bothered me since."

---

Ed leaned back slowly, staring.

A silence settled in the space between them—thick with unspoken truth.

"You told it no..." Ed murmured, testing the idea aloud.
"...And it stopped?"

Matt nodded, uncertain.

"Yeah. Why? You couldn't?"

Ed laughed.
Dry. Joyless.

"You think I didn't try?"

---

Outside, thunder rumbled—low and distant.

But inside, Ed understood:

The actual storm was already here.

4

Amanda saw the storm clouds coiling over Tug Hill, bruised purple and low against the horizon.

Almost home.

She was just outside Rome now, coasting north on Route 46—this route was better: fewer cars, more trees, and less of New York's urban rot clawing at the edges.

Ed better be home. And dinner better be on the damn table.

Her grip tightened on the wheel as she replayed the day in her head: that smug, underqualified realtor; her mother's usual passive-aggressive commentary; and the near miss with some jackass who had cut her off without signaling. Her fingernails clicked against the wheel—fast, sharp. She hadn't realized until now that she'd been driving in *total silence* for over an hour.

She tapped the steering-wheel controls.

SiriusXM. 90s on 9.
Comfort food for a fraying mood.

Nothing.

Just static.

"Ed pays you bastards enough—" she snapped, then froze.

The static faded.

And something else bled through.

Not the 90s.

Not even the right century.

*"Love is the sweetest thing...*
*What else on earth could ever bring...*
*Such happiness to everything..."*

"...As love's old story."

"What the fuck?" Amanda whispered.

The song wavered slightly, warped as if it were crawling from the grooves of a dusty record player. Hearing it over the Tesla's immaculate sound system only made it worse. Wrong. Off.

She jabbed the touchscreen.
Nothing.
No volume change…no mute…no app swap.

The display didn't even acknowledge her touch.

She tried the wheel controls again—dead.

*"Love is the strangest thing…"*

The volume crept higher, not suddenly—intentionally.

Her pulse spiked. She pressed harder, swiping, mashing buttons. Desperation building. Nothing worked.

Then—the screen flickered.

A glitch.

Something looking back.

Amanda's foot pressed harder on the gas unconsciously. The Tesla surged forward.

Delta Lake blurred by on her left.
The trees leaned inward as if they were listening.

The song played on.

*"It's the only thing that matters in this world to me…"*

A bitter, metallic taste bloomed on her tongue. Blood, maybe. Or fear.

The Tesla drifted across the double yellow.

Its autopilot gently corrected, guiding her back between the lines—calm, obedient.

But this wasn't a malfunction.

This was something else.

Tesla engineers hadn't accounted for a sentient, malevolent book with a 1930s playlist.

And the music—God, the music—was swelling.

*"Love is the sweetest thing…"*

Amanda didn't see the speedometer ticking upward.

120.
135.
145.

She'd been flooring it.
Didn't even notice.

Her gaze remained fixed on the screen. Her fingers kept stabbing uselessly at the controls.

The Tesla did as it was told.

---

She never saw the truck.

Not until it was far, far too late.

---

A lifted F-350, belching smoke from twin stacks, barreled toward her from the opposite lane.
Its driver—drunk, red-faced—mid-sentence to no one in particular:

"Seatbelts are for—"

The Tesla hit 145.

He never finished.

The impact wasn't metal-on-metal.
It was steel through *flesh*.
A violent collapse of tinfoil, horsepower, and hubris.

Amanda's car spun, fishtailed—rear panel crunched
by the impact as the Ford clipped it again, this time squarely.

The drunk flew through his windshield like a rag doll.

Amanda didn't scream.
Didn't even blink.

Just gripped the wheel.

And the Tesla rolled.

Once.
Twice.
Then again.

Metal shrieked. Windows exploded outward. The final
collision came as the car slammed sideways into a utility pole
just outside the state park entrance.

Everything went black.

---

Silence settled over the wreck.
No sirens yet.
No voices.

Just the faint, flickering crackle of a speaker half-
dead...

*"...as love's old story..."*

The music skipped.

And died.

5

Matt set five plates on the table.

One for each person.

He worked in silence, the rhythmic placement of forks and napkins oddly soothing. Ed had told him Amanda would be home soon—loud, uncomfortable, inevitable. Like pulling off a Band-Aid that had long since grown into the wound.

He placed the last plate and turned just in time to see Evelyn quietly pick one up.

"Eve…what are you doing?"

She smiled—soft, strange. Not quite *her*.

"We only need four, silly."

Matt frowned. "What about Ms. Rodrick? Ed's wife?"

Evelyn turned toward him slowly. Her movements were graceful, gentle—but her eyes…
Her eyes weren't there.

"She won't be joining us, Matt."

There was no malice. No sarcasm. Just flat, emotionless finality.

His stomach clenched.

He didn't want to ask. But he had to.

"Why not, Eve?"

She leaned in close, pressing her cheek to his. Her breath was warm, oddly childlike. She whispered it like a lover's secret:

"Because she is delayed, silly. And the book says…don't wait up."

A pause.

"It was pretty clear on that."

She kissed his cheek—soft, casual—and then walked back to the kitchen, humming some tuneless, implausible melody.

Matt stood there frozen.

The overhead light buzzed louder than it should.

His fingers trembled on the edge of the plate still in his hand.

He had to tell Ed. Right now.

Matt found Ed on the couch, jabbing buttons on the remote like it owed him money.

"The fucking book's messing with the TV," Ed muttered, tossing the remote into the armchair. He looked up and saw Matt's expression.

"What's up?"

Matt hesitated in the doorway, then crossed the room and sat opposite him.

"You should probably sit down," he said softly.

Ed raised an eyebrow, glancing at himself. "Already am."

"Okay... Well, you're about to wish you weren't."

Matt leaned forward, voice low.

"Evelyn just told me Amanda's not coming back tonight. She said the book 'delayed' her somehow. Her exact words were: *Don't wait up.*"

He let the weight of it hang.

Ed didn't respond. He didn't blink. He just...stared.

His mouth opened, then closed again.

And then —

"Dinner's ready!" Maya's voice called from the kitchen.

"Come on, boys!" Evelyn added, cheerful as ever. "Before it gets cold."

Ed stood.

Just like that.

Calm. Silent. Glassy-eyed.

Matt blinked. Then followed.

---

In the dining room, Ed sat down as if it were any other night. Maya beside him, smiling like a hostess. Evelyn across from her, still humming that eerie tune.

Matt followed suit, but he could feel it—wrongness curling through the air like smoke.

And there it was.

The book.

Sitting open on the kitchen counter, its pages spread like an invitation.

Ed looked at it. Hard.

But didn't move.

Didn't speak.

Didn't breathe for a second.

Matt knew he'd heard him.

He just wasn't reacting.

Or maybe—he couldn't afford to.

---

And that's when the voice slithered into Matt's skull again. Cold silk on his mind.

*"Oh, Matt,"* it purred, oily and amused.
*"It's simple. I can only influence people I've touched. I can't just mess with a Joe Thompson in Indiana. But if I've touched you? If you let me in..."*

A shadow-smile in his head.

*"...Then we're bonded. And from there? Oh, the wonderful things I can do. Both good... ...and bad."*

Matt's jaw tensed. His neck prickled.

*"So maybe don't talk shit about me behind my back with Ed again."*

Then, a sudden shift in tone—a mocking *child's voice*:

*"I...have feelings too..."*

Matt nearly gagged.

Then the voice darkened again. Whispering, intimate and lethal:

*"Seriously though, Matt. Just read me sometime. I could make all of this so much easier for you."*

Matt looked around the room. Evelyn passed him a beer with a warm smile, as if nothing was wrong. But Amanda was missing. And Evelyn?

She was fine with it.

What did that say about what the book had made her?

What did it say about what he might become...if he gave in?

"Thanks, Eve," he murmured.

He took the beer.

And the voice chuckled, soft and amused, curling back around his thoughts like ivy.

*"Wouldn't it be nice... ...to stop being the only sane one in the room?"*

# Chapter 16: A BIG DAM PROBLEM

1

Stanley crouched just outside Boonville's town hall, sweat beading along his brow in the thick, humid summer air.
The book whispered again—soft and sinuous, curling through his thoughts like smoke.

*"Forget Boonville, Stanley. It's not the right stage. Not yet."*

The voice had changed. Quieter now. Distant. As if pacing the halls of some deeper, unseen corridor in his mind.

Stanley frowned.
"What about the dynamite?" he whispered. "The entire plan—"

*"The plan has evolved. There's a dam north of Rome. Delta Lake spillway. You know the one."*

He did. He'd visited once, years ago. Quiet. Serene. It held back half the valley.

*"Blow it. Millions of gallons. Downhill. Fast. Glorious."*

Stanley flinched.
Rome? He liked Rome. The old general store. That diner he hit on Sundays. Families lived there. Kids.

"That's…a lot," he murmured, nausea blooming in his gut. "I have nothing against Rome."

*"But I do. And you love me, don't you, Stanley?"*

The voice shifted again. No longer the harsh masculine growl it had once used—now soft, maternal, coaxing. It had adapted. It had learned him.
It knew the holes no parent, no god, had ever bothered to fill.

*"It's okay to hesitate. That's human. But trust me, my love—do this, and I'll make sure you're never alone again."*

A part of him—the part that was still Stanley—shivered.
But the other part?
The part that had been hollowed out and filled in by the book?
That part nodded.

"Are you okay?" he asked the air. Habit. Reflex. A ghost of prayer from back when those still meant something.

*"I'm exactly where I need to be, darling,"* the book purred. *"Don't worry about me. Just keep going. Your reward's waiting."*

Stanley stood.
The dynamite—still zipped inside the weathered canvas bag—lay buried in the brush behind town hall. He retrieved it, slung it over one shoulder, grabbed the shotgun, and started walking.

The dam was thirty minutes by car.
But the road?
Too many eyes.

So he walked.
Through the trees.
Into the dark.

Somewhere in the distance, a dog barked—sharp, angry, like it wanted to chase the night back into the woods.

Stanley didn't blame it.
Part of him wanted to bark too.

But there was no turning back now.
Not after everything.
Not after what the book had shown him.

He would see it through.
For the book.
For The One.
For whatever was left of himself.

2

Captain Webb waited as long as he could stand it—
which wasn't long at all.

The damn sheriff was taking his sweet fucking time,
and Webb knew it. Probably didn't believe him. Two dead
bodies. Livestock torn to shreds like something out of a
nightmare.

Hell, Webb didn't want to believe it either.
But he'd seen it. With his own eyes.

He checked his pocket watch.
9:30 p.m.

The moon had just crested the tree line, throwing
silver light across the yard. The Millards didn't have
electricity, so Webb had strung up a few lanterns. They
flickered in the wind like nervous eyes.

He'd already radioed for backup—told Trooper Davis
to haul ass over—but they were still recovering from that riot

with four hundred pissed-off farm boys.

No one was available. Not tonight.

"Fuck," Webb muttered.

He didn't want to leave the scene—not for a second—but Stanley was still out there. Doing God knew what. Planning worse.

And no one but Webb seemed to believe it.

---

At last, an Oneida County Sheriff's cruiser pulled into the yard, spitting dust and gravel.

A deputy stepped out—kid looked all of twelve—but Webb didn't care. He was off the porch and in his face before the boots even hit dirt.

"Secure the scene," Webb snapped. "Nothing goes in or out until it's photographed. Understand?"

The kid blinked.
"Um—"

"'Um' isn't an answer. It's, 'Yes, sir,' or, 'Understood.' That's it. Your job's simple—sit your ass here and keep everyone out. Got it?"

The kid stiffened. Like someone had yanked his spine into place.

"Yes, sir."

Webb nodded once. "Good."

He grabbed his hat off the porch railing and climbed into his cruiser. The engine groaned to life. As he backed down the gravel drive, a knot tightened in his chest.

If Stanley got too much of a head start...

They were all in for a hell of a night.

---

He turned onto the county road, heading toward the Jenkins dairy farm—just in case Stanley had made another stop.

The heat had finally broken, but the air was still thick.

Cool and muggy, his mother used to say.
Didn't matter.

What mattered now was finding Stanley Millard before he left more bodies in his wake.

That's when Webb saw it.

A horse.

Standing dead still on the shoulder, just barely in the sweep of his high beams. Like something out of a fever dream.

He slowed. Pulled over about a hundred feet back. His gut twisted.

"Now what the hell is this..." he muttered, stepping out. He tugged his hat into place and unholstered his sidearm.

He wasn't playing anymore.

"Stanley Millard!" he called, voice sharp. "This is Captain Webb of the New York State Troopers! If you're out here—show yourself! Hands up! Don't make this worse!"

Silence.

Webb crept forward, muzzle low but ready.
The closer he got, the clearer the horror became.

The horse was dead—its skull half-gone, blasted apart.

A man lay crumpled beside it. A milk can spilled near his outstretched hand. One shot to the chest. Gone.

Webb's stomach clenched.
Jesus.

Then—movement.

A few feet away, nearly swallowed by blood, dirt, and insects—another man.
Tied to a tree. Barely conscious.

Webb rushed forward. Holstered his weapon. Pulled out his folding knife. One slash.

The man collapsed into his arms—fever-hot, barely breathing.

Joshua Miller.

"Hang in there," Webb muttered, hefting him into a fireman's carry. He staggered back to the car and laid Miller across the back seat.

Then, he lunged for the radio.

"Dispatch, this is Webb. I need backup—two units — immediately. County Route 74, just past the Jenkins' place. One confirmed dead. One critical. I don't give a damn what else is happening—get someone here. Now."

A long pause.

Then static. A crackled voice.

He didn't wait.

He slammed the door. Locked it.
And stood in the middle of the road.
Breath misted in the cool night air.

Waiting.

Waiting to pass the torch.

So he could go hunt Stanley Millard in the dark.

---

Twenty minutes later, headlights pierced the trees.
Two patrol cars pulled in. Webb was out of his cruiser before
the engines stopped.

He looked calm.
Stone-faced, precise.
But inside?

A storm.

"Trooper Sherwood," he barked, pointing to the
backseat.
"This man needs immediate transport. Rome Hospital or
Murphy Memorial. He's been tied to a tree for hours. No
stops. No detours. Got it?"

"Yes, sir," Sherwood replied, already moving.

Webb turned to the second car. A fresh-faced trooper
stepped out—uniform crisp, boots too clean.

"Name?" Webb asked.

"Trooper Hoskins, sir. Troop D—Sylvan Beach."

Webb nodded. "Didn't know you boys made it this far north. Appreciate it."

Hoskins smiled, proud.

"Here's your job," Webb continued. "Secure this scene. No civilians. No press. At first light, sweep the area—tight. This is a secondary crime scene. We'll need photos. Don't touch the body. Understood?"

"Yes, sir."

Webb liked him.

"Good man."

They loaded Joshua Miller into the backseat. Just before Sherwood climbed in, he turned.

"Sir, you should know—there was an explosion in Boonville this afternoon. Gazebo's gone. Left a crater. Some poor bastard stepped outside and got shot at. No ID yet...but it could be your guy."

Webb froze.

Explosives. Public target. Witnesses eliminated.

Stanley wasn't spiraling.

He had a mission.

"Jesus Christ."

Sherwood gave a grim nod and shut the door.

Webb turned toward the road. Boonville.

He climbed into his cruiser.
Dropped his hat on the passenger seat.
Threw the gearshift forward.

Gravel sprayed behind him as the tires bit into the road.

His headlights cut across the shredded horse. The crumpled body. The blood.

He didn't look back.

3

John Westcott thought he was done.

He'd sealed the book in a box. He had the box blessed by the priest. Buried it in consecrated ground.

So why was he halfway through his fifth glass of whiskey when it spoke again—soft, but unmistakably there?

The voice curled through his mind like smoke.

*"Johnny boy…you didn't think you were rid of me that easy, did you?"*

John flinched so hard he slammed his knee against the table, knocking over his glass. Whiskey sloshed onto the worn wood, glinting amber in the bar's dim light.

*"Don't bother answering,"* the voice purred. *"I've got a job for you."*

John's breath caught in his throat.

*"First, you're going to go home, get that revolver of yours—load it—and pray I don't make you put it in your mouth."*

A pause. Then a little chuckle, like silk catching on a nail.

*"After that…head to Delta Lake Dam. Stanley might need backup. If he gets cold feet, well—you won't."*

John's hands shook as he picked up the glass, what was left of it. He drained it, but most of the whiskey soaked his shirt.

Then he stood slowly.

The bar was quiet. The world outside, still quieter.

John Westcott walked out into the night.

Headed home.

To get his gun.

Just like the book wanted.

God help him—just like the book wanted.

---

John stumbled through his house, rummaging for the old ammunition, each step unsteady on the warped floorboards.

He shouldn't have crossed the damned thing. He knew that now.

The priest would still be alive. Hell, maybe *he* wouldn't even be on its radar.

But it was too late for maybes.

He found the dusty box of .38 cartridges in a kitchen drawer buried under expired coupons and cigarette lighters. He grabbed it and a half-finished bottle of whiskey from the counter. The ammo went into one pocket, the bottle into the other. He took a long drink—for luck; he told himself.

But in truth, he just wanted to forget tonight before it even began.

"Shit… Forgot to load you," he muttered, pulling the revolver from his pants pocket.

His finger curled instinctively around the trigger—
BANG.

The shot rang through the house like thunder. A perfect hole now marked the wooden floorboard. His ears roared. His heart galloped.

John froze. Then slowly looked down.

"Jesus," he breathes, patting himself. "Could've shot my dick off."

He laughed, a brittle, cracked thing. He shoved the loaded gun back into his pocket. Shook his head, still ringing, and stumbled out into the cool night air toward his beat-up car.

The night didn't care that he wasn't ready.

And neither did the book.

He walked over, gave the crank a few hard turns, and the battered old 1920 Model T sputtered to life with a wheezing cough.

Once behind the wheel, he backed out onto the road—clipping the edge of his lawn and nearly hitting a tree. Didn't matter. The car was ancient, the suspension shot, and the tires balding, but she still ran. And that meant he had no intention of replacing her soon.

The Ford groaned as he swerved gently down the road, weaving slightly from shoulder to shoulder. He wasn't going fast. Hell, he wasn't even going *straight*. But he was moving.

South, toward the dam.

That's where the book said to go.

He took another long pull from the bottle, its neck knocking against his teeth. Whiskey burned its way down, dulling his nerves and sharpening his fear into something manageable—something just shy of rage.

The trees leaned in overhead, the road narrowing like a funnel pulling him toward something he already regretted.

Nevertheless, the Model T chugged along.

Like him, it had no business still running.

4

Webb rolled into Boonville to find three locals standing around the crater like it had always been there—like the town hadn't just been attacked.

He parked, grabbed his hat, and stepped out, gravel crunching beneath his boots.

"Evening, folks," he said, slipping into dry charm. "Hell of a hole you've got here."

"Yeah, lovely, ain't it?" one man said, arms crossed. "That nutjob Stanley Millard did it. I saw him from my porch. When I came out to yell at him, the bastard shot at me— looked like a shotgun. Or something bigger. Big and loud, I know that much." He spat into the crater as if it had personally offended him.

A woman jumped in, gesturing toward her shattered windows and rattling off a list of damages.
Webb only half-listened—he already knew who needed his attention.

When she finished, he gave a polite nod. "Ma'am, I'll have a trooper come by to take your statement and get some photos."

Then he turned to the man. "Sir, mind stepping over to my car for a minute?"

The guy hesitated, then nodded and followed Webb over to the cruiser.

"What's your name?" Webb asked, flipping open a notepad and pulling a pencil from his shirt pocket.

"Tim Warwick," the man said, suddenly less sure of himself. "Am I in trouble?"

"No, sir. Just trying to stop a man before he does something worse than this."
Webb's voice stayed calm but clipped. "What else did you see? Did you catch where he went?"

Tim glanced off toward town hall.
"I might've…followed him. A little."

Webb didn't blink. "Why?"

"I was pissed. The last guy who shot at me was a German in France. And I'll be damned if—" He caught himself.

Webb's expression stayed flat. "Tim, I'm going to level with you. That explosion and your busted window? That was just the opening act. Stanley has hurt people tonight. Bad. If you know where he's headed, I need to know now. This isn't mischief. This is lives-on-the-line stuff."

Tim swallowed hard, eyes twitching.

"He was talking to himself. Arguing with someone who wasn't there—different voices. Creeped me the hell out."

"What was he saying?"

"Said something about Delta Dam. Said he was gonna blow it up. I didn't think fireworks could do that kind of damage, though."

Webb's stomach dropped. He glanced back at the crater.

That wasn't fireworks. He knew it. And judging by the look in Tim's eyes, so did he.

"When did this happen?"

"An hour…maybe an hour and a half ago." Tim looked up at the town clock, hands twitching.

Webb didn't respond right away. He just nodded once.

"All right. Thanks, Tim. You're good to go." Tim let out a breath and walked off.

Webb climbed into his cruiser, slammed the door, and jammed it into reverse. Gravel spat from his tires as he spun around and floored it toward Delta Dam.

There couldn't be much time left.

And if he didn't catch Stanley in time…

There wouldn't be much of anything left at all.

5

Stanley Millard's entire body ached. His knees were shot, his back was screaming, and his breath whistled out of him like it was trying to quit. Sweat ran in steady rivulets down his spine, his shirt soaked through. Burrs clung to his pants, thorns had sliced his arms, and something had bitten him behind the ear so many times it now throbbed with its own pulse. This was Oneida County in summer—feral, overgrown, and completely unforgiving. Especially to the man who had no business being out here.

But then, through the break in the trees, he saw it: Delta Lake. And stretched across its black waters like a scar on God's face was the dam.

Stanley stopped and leaned against a tree, panting. His heart thudded hard, like it was trying to warn him. But the warning had come years too late.

He remembered the day they'd finished the thing— back when they said it would save lives, manage floods, protect farmland. He also remembered the homes it swallowed whole. A village erased by progress, every clapboard house and picket fence buried under a creeping tide. They called it "relocation." Stanley remembered it as a drowning.

Maybe if he leveled it, the people could come back. Or maybe it'd just be another mess someone else had to clean up. It didn't matter anymore.

He trudged forward, deep in his thoughts, and never saw the root until it snagged his boot. He went down hard, pitching headlong through the brush and tumbling ass-over-elbows down a muddy slope. He landed in a shallow ditch with a bone-jarring thump and lay there for a moment, stunned.

Nothing broken. He'd take it.

Then he saw the shotgun.

It lay several feet away, its barrel bent like a question mark—snapped sideways after striking a tree during his fall. Stanley stared at it for a long moment, then swore.

"Goddamn piece of shit!"

He hurled it into the woods, watching it vanish into the undergrowth. He liked that shotgun. It had weight. History. It had *meant* something.

But the bag… The bag was still with him.

He looked down and patted the canvas satchel at his side. Still zipped. Still heavy. Inside, the dynamite waited—twenty red wax-paper sticks like sleeping devils. The matches, dry and safe, were tucked in the side pouch. That was the part that mattered.

The plan wasn't dead.

Not yet.

He got up, wiped blood from a cut on his cheek, and began moving again—shoulders squared now, boots thudding over the gravel path that curved toward the dam. The moon slipped out from behind the trees like a shy child, lighting the way. Somewhere behind him, a whippoorwill called once, then fell silent.

As he neared the chain-link fence by the pump house, he didn't notice the rusted-out Model T tucked just off the road—or the shape slumped in the driver's seat, motionless under the moonlight. Even if he had, it wouldn't have mattered.

He was past caring.

Stanley was on a mission. The kind of mission that no one thanks you for. The kind you're remembered for with candlelight vigils and news coverage, if you're lucky—or just whispers and nightmares, if you're not.

He rattled the pump-house door. Locked. Of course, it was. Blowing it open would draw attention—noise, light, questions. He needed quiet.

He moved instead to the concrete catwalk along the upstream side of the dam. Mist from the spillway rose to meet him, chilling his sweat-slicked skin. For the first time all night, he felt alive.

Then the voice came back.

"You need to hurry," it said, soft and low, like a whisper spoken just behind his ear. A voice made of silk and teeth.

Stan flinched. He would never get used to that voice. It didn't come from inside his head—it came from just outside it. Like someone pacing the edge of his sanity.

He kept walking.

At the farthest point he could safely reach—just above the roaring water—he knelt. The concrete was slick beneath his knees. The moonlight silvered the surface. He pulled off the bag and unzipped it slowly, as if it were something sacred. Twenty sticks of dynamite. He lined them up in neat rows, whispering a soft count as he worked.

"Delta Village drowned under this thing," he muttered. "Guess it's only fair it goes down too."

The book purred in his mind. Pleased.

He tied the fuses the way he'd been taught in the war—steady, precise, just like back in the trenches. Funny the things a man carries with him. He coiled the main fuse up the walkway, tucking it under the edge of a drainage grating, just far enough to give himself time to run.

Then came the voice.

"Stanley Millard! Don't move another muscle or I will shoot!"

It came from the far side of the dam, crisp and hard and full of authority.

Stan froze. He didn't turn around.

"I don't know who that is," he said flatly, dumbly.

"Right. Don't move all the same."

Footsteps. Crunching gravel. Getting closer.

Then—gunfire. Five shots in quick succession, wild and fast, from somewhere behind them. Not the first man.

Stan dropped to the ground. Rolled toward the dynamite. Heard a grunt—someone hit. Then another shot, cleaner. Quieter. Aimed.

The man in front—whoever had shouted the

warning—hit the deck, groaning in pain.

"Holy shit, I think I hit him, oh shit… I'm bleeding," someone slurred from the direction of the road.

Stanley's eyes found the matches lying in the dirt, just inches from his fingers. He snatched them up and surged to his feet.

This wasn't a mission anymore.

It was the finale.

A funeral.

A fuck-you to every person who doubted him, and to the world that forgot Delta Village.

He sprinted toward the explosives.

"Stanley!" the wounded voice shouted. "Don't— don't you fucking—!"

Too late.

Stanley Millard was already running toward the edge of the dam.

Toward the roaring water.

Toward the end.

# Chapter 17: THAT IS HER BOOKSHELF; THIS IS HER BED

1

Evelyn sat at the table, humming.

She liked to hum now. It soothed her. She didn't know why—only that it helped quiet the noise.

The book liked it too. Maya had once said it made her seem softer. More…helpful.

Matt, sitting beside her, was watching her strangely again. Like she'd done something wrong.

She tilted her head.

"All I said was Amanda wasn't coming. Why does that make everyone so tense? Something wrong, Matt?" she asked sweetly, folding her hands in her lap like a proper hostess.

He'd looked so stressed lately. The book said he was under pressure. She'd help with that later. He'd feel better once he was part of things.

Family made everything easier.

Matt blinked. "Um, no, sweetie. I just think…we're a little worried about Amanda, is all."

Sweet Matt. He was always thinking of others. He was always kindhearted.

The book was right to want him. To need him.

It was building a family. One to help Maya. To help them all.

Amanda had threatened that.
Amanda wasn't family.

The book had taken steps.
And Evelyn trusted the book.
The One always knew best.
Who was she to question it?

She took a bite of the food she and Maya had made—warm, familiar.
The house creaked softly around them, as if it were settling around the truth.

"Ed...are you okay?" she asked.

Ed looked up and smiled—or something close to it.

"I'm fine. Amanda's probably just running late."

Then he went back to eating. Like it was any other night.

Evelyn opened her mouth to respond, but Matt's hand gently closed around her knee. A silent squeeze. She glanced at him. He shook his head once.

So she stayed quiet.

She didn't understand why everyone was in such a strange mood. The food was good. The fire was ready. Amanda wasn't here.
Wasn't that good news?

After a few more bites, she couldn't take the silence anymore.

"So...what should we do after dinner?" she asked

brightly. Too brightly.

Everyone looked at her.
No one smiled.

Finally, Maya spoke, her tone calm and careful.

"Why don't we have a relaxing evening? Maybe a fire
out back, if the weather holds. If not, we'll stay in."
She reached over and patted Ed's thigh.

"That would be fine," Ed said—flat, distant. Eyes
locked on his plate.

Evelyn's smile faltered.

This wasn't how tonight was supposed to go.
It wasn't how the book said it would be.

She was supposed to be part of something. A family.
The kind she'd never had.

*"They'll come around,"* the book whispered in her mind,
silk on stone.
*"Just relax. Be patient. Ed's adjusting—his wife won't be joining him
for a while…if ever. He needs time. Matt is stubborn. Maya
is…Maya. Let her work on Ed. You focus on Matt."*

Evelyn nodded slightly, unaware she was doing it.

---

After dinner, Evelyn helped Matt clear the table while
Maya and Ed stepped out to prep the fire pit. The soft clink
of dishes echoed through the kitchen.

"I'm sorry if I've disappointed you," Evelyn said
softly, without turning.

Matt paused, then set a dish down harder than he

meant to.

"Eve...that right there is the problem. That's not you. That's not something you'd say."

She turned to face him, a plate trembling slightly in her hands.

"What do you mean?"

He held her gaze.

"You wouldn't care this much about having the perfect dinner. Or what activity comes next. You've never been that person. And now you're best friends with Maya? That's...weird, Eve."

He shook his head.

"You'd be worried about Amanda. You'd be asking questions. Not brushing her off like she was just inconvenient."

He took a breath.

"It's like everything you do now is...curated. Like you're performing happy. And it's freaking me out."

There was a pause. Not long.
Just long enough to notice the delay.
The glitch.

Then Evelyn's shoulders slumped. Her voice cracked.

"I...I don't even know how to respond to that, Matt. You know I fought with my mom. Maybe I just wanted one enjoyable meal with friends, okay? I'm tired of being the broken one. I just wanted to feel close to people. I thought you'd understand."

The tears came easily.
Real or not, even she couldn't tell anymore.

Which, in a twisted way, made it easier.

The book could take the wheel now—handle the manipulation, the molding, the lies that sounded like truths.

And deep down, buried under it all, some splinter of her hated it.
Hated what the book wanted.
Hated what she was becoming.

But she stepped closer to Matt anyway.

"I know I haven't been myself," she whispered, voice delicate as tissue. "Since that walk you took with Ed… I've been different. I know that."

She let the silence stretch. Then:

"Maya told me some things."
Her eyes searched his, rehearsed confusion blooming behind them.
"I've been processing, that's all."

She moved in closer.
Close enough to touch.

"Matt…have you really been trying to be with her for two years?" Her voice dipped—silk and venom.

"Because I thought I knew you.
But that's…stalker-level devotion, sweetie."

Her fingers rose to his jaw.
Gentle. Almost loving.

Like a lover.

Or a knife held backward.

She leaned in, slow and deliberate, and wrapped her arms around him.
Her head rested against his chest. She felt his heartbeat—fast, uncertain.

Then came the nail. Quiet. Precise.

"I'm just worried..." she whispered, voice shaking, "that I'll never live up to her."

A pause.

"That I'll never be *Maya* enough for you."

The tears followed—soft, just enough to glisten into his shirt.

And Matt... Matt pulled her close.

"That's not true..." he whispered, rubbing slow circles on her back. "You just need to be you, Eve. That's all I've ever wanted. You."

Evelyn looked up at him, eyes brimming.

But something behind them wasn't hers.
Not entirely.

*"Then take me upstairs and prove it."*

She leaned in, voice a breath.

*"No more games, Matt LaFord."*

For a second, he didn't move.
Didn't blink.

Then slowly, he took her hand.
And led her upstairs.

---

Somewhere on the breakfast nook table, unnoticed and unmoved,
the book lay open—pages fluttering in the draft as if it were breathing.
And smiling.

2

Maya watched in horror from her glass prison—as she'd taken to calling it—while Matt led Evelyn upstairs to do what guys do upstairs.

Meanwhile, down in her own body, near the fire pit, *Maya B* was busy trying to cheer Ed up with a rotating arsenal of bedroom tricks—some more successful than others. Maya wasn't sure if that was her doing or the book's.

She didn't care anymore.

She was just a passenger in this horror show now.

Something had happened to Ed's wife. Amanda.

Maya didn't need to be told who was responsible.

The book had offered her the same deal it gave Evelyn: bend or break.
Eve told it to go fuck itself.
Now she lived in a cage.
Evelyn didn't exist anymore—just Evelyn the puppet.

Maya wondered:
If something happened to the book, would Evelyn come back?

The brain was still there, right? Somewhere?

*"Why are you asking silly questions, girl?"*

The voice boomed from nowhere.
A loudspeaker materialized in the corner.

"It's a fair question, don't you think, Book? Or do you have a name?"

*"I do. And it's not yours to know."*

A pause.

*"As for your theory? Maybe if I'm destroyed, you and your friends regain control. Or maybe you become mindless husks. Who's to say?"*

The voice grew smug.

*"Best not to test it."*

"So…you don't even know."

*"How would I? No one has ever destroyed me, have they?"*

It hissed—mockery twisting every syllable.

*"Jesus, are you always this stupid, or is that a recent development? No wonder you owe $125,000 in student loans. I now have to figure out how to pay."*

Maya scowled.

"I'm not the first person to pick the wrong major in college."

*"Perhaps. But you kept going. You could've switched. What was the plan, genius? Get a degree, hate your job, drown under $200K in debt while building indie games no one plays? Because yes, game designers are just rolling in cash."*

Maya folded her arms, glaring at the speaker.

*"Oh, come on, dear, don't get pissy."*

Its tone softened—*sickeningly sweet.*

*"I saved you from that shitty life. No more ramen dinners and unpaid internships. Now…it'll be Congresswoman Cartar. Doesn't that sound better?"*

Maya hesitated.
She hated herself for it.
But a small part of her liked how that sounded.

"How?"

*"How what?"*

The book already sounded bored.

"How are you going to get a broke college student from Boston elected?
No job. No experience. No family.
And as you so *graciously* pointed out—$125,000 in debt."

The book chuckled. Dry. Knowing.

*"You think I'm going to supervillain-monologue my plan to you?"*

Maya opened her mouth—then stopped.

*Shit. I was thinking that.*

The book felt it.

*"Exactly,"* it purred.
*"Try to remember, genius: you don't get secret thoughts in here. Might as well say your shit out loud."*

Maya clenched her fists.

*"No, I will not tell you my plans,"* the book continued. *"But you'll get front-row seats. And if you're a good little prisoner?"*

Its tone shifted again. Silken, mocking.

*"Maybe I'll give you a bigger cage."*

A pause.

*"Instead of just controlling when Maya goes to the bathroom… maybe I'll let you decide what she eats. Maybe even what she wears."*

It sounded almost…*kind.*

*"See how generous I can be?"*

Then everything changed.

The walls moved.

The glass of her prison *shrieked* inward, collapsing on itself.
Her bed splintered into shards.
The desk cracked in half.
The chair exploded into debris.
The room shrank—smaller and smaller—until there was barely space for Maya to stand.
The air thinned.
Her ribs ached.

*"I can shrink it too."*

Now the voice was *inside her skull,* whispering behind her ears.

*"Understand?"*

Maya gasped, breathless.

"…Yes."

And just like that—the glass pulled back.
The walls expanded.

Her bed reformed. The desk. The chair.
A new shelf appeared, filled with unfamiliar books.

Her prison was slightly larger than before.

*"Good,"* the book said brightly, as if none of that had happened.

*"See? I can be nice. Or I can be an asshole. So let's not have any more what if the book dies thoughts, okay?"*

Silence.

The voice vanished.

3

Amanda came to slowly.

Everything hurt.
Her head was bleeding.
Her ribs screamed with every breath—at least one had to be broken.

But she was alive.

More than she could say for the poor bastard in the road.

He was in two pieces.
His upper half lay just a few feet away, intestines unspooled like red ropes, hands frozen mid-motion—as if he'd tried to push them back in.

Then came the smell.
Fuel. No—diesel.
Thick. Sharp.

Then she saw the flickering glow—orange and growing—dancing just ahead of her.
Fire.

Her car must've called for help.
Emergency responders should be on the way.

But no sirens. No flashing lights.

She fumbled for her seatbelt.
Credit to Tesla—the restraint popped loose, and she slid forward, not realizing the car wasn't upright.

Her body dropped sideways and slammed into the already-shattered glass.
She crawled out through the jagged frame.

Metal scorched her thigh as she passed over it, the searing pain ripping a scream from her lungs.
She rolled off the wreck and hit the blacktop hard. The pavement tore at her arms.
Her breath came in wet, ragged gasps.

Silence.

But the diesel stench was stronger now—sweet and sick, like rot.

She staggered to her feet.

Behind her, the wreckage groaned.
Flames licked along twisted steel.
Diesel leaked from the F-350.
Somewhere in the wreck was a lithium battery—ready to light

the sky.

Amanda didn't look back.
She hobbled away, favoring her right side, one hand pressed
to her ribs.

She passed the man's body. Didn't look down.
Just stared straight ahead as bile rose in her throat.

She needed help.
The town of Westernville wasn't far.

She could make it.
She had to.

Behind her, the Tesla caught fire in earnest.
The battery erupted in a *whoosh* of white flame.

Amanda didn't stop.

She just kept walking.

---

Then the sky opened up.

A thunderclap cracked overhead, shaking the air as
cold spring rain fell in sheets.
Amanda gasped at the sudden chill—her skin already raw
from the crash, now soaked and stinging.

The wind picked up, slicing sideways through the
trees and howling down the road.
Lightning split the sky—white fire across black.

It felt personal.
Like the world wasn't done trying to kill her.

But Amanda kept moving—limping down the road,
arms wrapped tight around herself, jaw clenched.

She could see the gas station ahead, its lights a blurry promise through the rain.

If she could just get there…find a phone…

She'd call Ed. Then the police.
Tell them what happened.

That the truck crossed the line.
That she wasn't speeding.

They'd believe her.
They had to.

Not that the other guy would give his version—unless they figured out how to bring people back from the dead.

Ed would fix this.
He always fixed things for her.

Why wouldn't he fix this?

*"Because you're a bitch now."*

The voice came softly.
Too sweet—the kind of sweetness that rots teeth.

It whispered just behind her ear, close enough to make her skin crawl.

Amanda stopped in the middle of the road and turned in a slow circle, convinced someone was there.

"So we had a fight," she snapped, talking to no one— or maybe to the owls, maybe God, maybe herself. "Couples have fights. He still loves me."

*"Ed deserves better, and you know it. You should walk in front of the next eighteen-wheeler that comes down this road. You killed that poor guy back there. And all you got was a broken rib. All because*

*you couldn't listen to the radio station you wanted."*

Each word struck like a slap.
Colder. Sharper. Meaner.

"I — He was in my lane!" she screamed, tears cutting through the dirt on her face.

*"Don't lie to me, Amanda. Lie to the cops. Lie to Ed. Hell, lie to yourself if it helps you sleep. But don't lie to me."*

Her breath hitched.
Her chest heaved.

"I'm not lying! And Ed doesn't deserve better," she shrieked, voice cracking.
"I'm the best he's ever gonna get!"

She looked up at the dark trees, eyes wild and shining, her words echoing into the branches as if they might argue back.

Only the wind answered.

*"What about that young little thing sniffing around?"*

If the voice had a face, Amanda was sure it would be smiling.

"Ed wouldn't dare..." she muttered.

But she wasn't sure anymore.

Two days ago, she knew the sky was blue.
Books didn't talk.
Ed Rodrick didn't cheat.

Now?

Well...the sky was *still* blue.

*"Hate to break it to you, sweetie,"* the voice cooed, *"but the sky isn't actually blue either."*

That was the last straw.

Amanda stopped walking and screamed at the top of her lungs:

**"SHUT THE FU—"**

She never finished.

She'd wandered into the middle of Route 46—right into a blind corner.

And like the book had once whispered:

Eighteen-wheelers do frequent that road.

4

*"It's done, Eddy. And before you start to fucking pout again, remember one thing—she wanted to tear everything you and your father built apart. Brick by brick. Book by book. And she would've done it, too, with that too-white smile of hers."*

The voice was honey—and something far more lethal.

Ed winced.

He knew what *it* meant.

And part of him—the part he didn't want to acknowledge—felt relieved.

He looked over at Maya, who stared into the small fire they'd built. Then down at his own hands, as if he'd murdered his wife.

Hadn't he?

He'd kept the book. Let it worm its way back into their lives. Let Maya into their bed…

*"Oh, stop the pity party. Jesus, Eddy. The holier-than-thou shit was old when you were ten—it's fossilized now. I'd have stopped you if you had ever seriously tried to get rid of me. I like you. We're soulmates, you and I."*

It chuckled at the last part.

*"Besides, you know she was going to leave your ass the second you hit Florida. One country club brunch and the right rich guy sniffs around—poof. There goes Amanda. And then what? Eddy, alone in a state he hates. No money. No prospects. No me. How long before you put a gun in your mouth?"*

Ed clenched his jaw.

"So you needed to kill her?" he asked silently, well-practiced in hiding these dialogues from Maya.

*"Big picture, Eddy, my sweet. Big picture. A dead wife plays better than a divorced one when you marry Maya right after she helps you through the 'tragedy.' So sad. So poetic. She'll be your rock. Your everything. You'll write about it in your book, I'm sure."*

Another laugh—soft, amused, serpentine.

"You can't be serious… Does Maya know? The *real* Maya?"

Silence. Perhaps a beat too long.
Like the book hadn't considered Ed might *care* what Maya thought.

*"Never mind her,"* it hissed, voice suddenly barbed wire and ice.

*"Don't try me, Ed. I won't hurt you or her—but I can hurt plenty of people along the way. Make no mistake."*

A pause. The tone coiled like a viper.

*"This can go one of two ways. You get to be Eddy—my favorite person on this shitty plane of existence. Or... ...you can be like her, staring into a flame because I told her to. And if I don't remind her to blink, she'll go blind. Or maybe I let Eve up there bite Matt's dick off. Would that suit?"*

Ed flinched, revolted by the image of *either* scenario.

*"Just play the game, Ed. Enjoy the ride. Why is that so fucking hard?"*

The voice twisted—bitter, disappointed.

*"Jesus. I could've treated you like Stanley..."*

"Who?" Ed asked cautiously.

*"Doesn't matter,"* the book snapped. *"Just a plaything I passed the time with."*

Another pause. Longer now. Then:

*"Now. Do we understand each other, Eddy? I don't want to take your free will."*

A pause.

*"But don't think for one second I can't."*

As if on cue, Ed's arm moved on its own. Slid around Maya. Pulled her close.

She leaned into him, warm and unaware.

The book chuckled—low and cruel.

*"Good boy."*

Deep down, Ed bristled at the invasion—of his mind,

of his body.
But there was little he could do now.

Less still that Maya could do.
Even if she *knew*.

And yet, as she nestled into him—soft and trusting—
God help him...

It felt right.

He didn't know anymore whether that feeling
belonged to *him*...

...or to the book.

Her arm wrapped around his waist.
She kissed his cheek and whispered something soft—
something sweet—about how *nice* this all was.

Ed sat there, staring into the fire, and realized — with
a slow, aching clarity — that he was starting not to care.
Not at this moment.
Not with her skin against his.
Not when it was easier to feel good than to fight.

And he wondered—not for the first time — how
many more moments like this it would take...

...before he belonged to her and the book
completely.

5

Matt lay there, Evelyn's skin warm against his, both of
them slightly breathless, slightly sweating.

He stared at the ceiling, heart still pounding—not from the sex, but from the gnawing feeling curling tighter in his gut.

It had been good.
But not *right*.

Not *her*.

She'd moved like she was reading from a script—some porn scene she thought he'd want. Every motion, every moan…too perfect. Too rehearsed.
She wasn't trying to enjoy it.
She was performing.

For him.

And that wasn't Eve.

He'd only known her a few days, but in that short time, she'd been fierce. Smart. Tough as hell. The kind of woman who made you work to keep up—not the kind to mold herself into what she thought a man wanted.

And that's when he knew.

The book had her.

She might be breathing and sleeping beside him, but whatever made Eve…*Eve*—was buried now.

Something else wore her like a skin.

His chest tightened.

He had to do something. Fast.

Matt slipped out of bed as quietly as he could. He gathered his clothes and tiptoed into the bathroom, locking the door behind him. Then he sat on the toilet lid, phone in hand, trying to slow his pulse.

He googled:

*Evil black book* — nothing, garbage. Demon fanfic and heavy metal album covers.

*Black Book Boonville* — A few TikToks from the bookstore launch. Some ghost-hunting nonsense.

Then—buried near the bottom—a hit.

A college essay.
"The Milk War: Oneida County's Forgotten Tragedy."

He tapped it.

A scanned photo loaded: a man in overalls, wild-eyed, clutching a black book that made Matt's stomach twist.

*Stanley Millard.*

The essay didn't mention the book by name, but described how "once-happy Stanley" snapped, killed people, caused chaos. The author blamed local corruption and dairy union politics.

But Matt could read between the lines.

The book did it. Just like now.

He searched again:
*Milk War 1933.*

More hits: articles, short documentaries, even a Reddit thread arguing about the body count.

Still, no mention of the book.

It had erased itself.

Then—another link.

A low-res YouTube video:

"John Westcott Tells a Tall Tale–1994 Interview,"
30 views. Thumbnail of an elderly man in a hospital bed.

Matt turned his volume down. Clicked on captions.
Pressed play.

The screen flickered.

The man's face appeared—frail, but sharp-eyed.

Matt's breath caught as he read the closed captions:

*A cursed black book.*
*How it drove Stanley Millard insane.*
*Why Westcott hadn't spoken to anyone in sixty years.*
*What really happened at the dam.*
*And—most importantly—how he got the book to stop.*
*At least for a while.*

Matt's whole body went stiff.

Like the room had shrunk.

He spent three more hours on Google, Bing, and
Reddit, and found two more videos, old newspaper articles,
and a prayer outline.

"Jesus Christ…" he muttered, snapping the phone
off. He stood—legs numb from sitting too long, heart
pounding in his ears.

He turned toward the door.

Eyes wild.

"I need to find a box."

# Chapter 18: WHAT'S IN THE BOX?

1

Evelyn woke with a start, the soft light of morning creeping through the window. Birdsong drifted in from outside—robins, maybe a mourning dove. A perfect spring morning, if not for one problem:

Matt was gone.

The spot beside her was cold.

Frowning, she rose from the bed without bothering to cover herself and padded barefoot into the hallway. No one would be up this early, she figured—and she was right.

She peeked into Ed's room. Maya lay draped over him, lightly snoring, hair spilled across the pillow like ink. Evelyn closed the door quietly and moved on.

Guest bathroom: empty.

Now with hands on her hips, she frowned deeper. *Fine. If he wanted to sneak off, let him.*

Still, she turned on the guest shower. The pipes groaned like old bones, sputtering cold before finally warming enough to step in.

She let the water run over her, rinsing away the night. But not the questions. Not the weight.

Today, she had to go back to her mother's house.

Pack. Close that chapter.
She wasn't living there again. Not after everything.

The steam thickened around her, but the ache in her chest clung tight. Some things didn't wash off.

After a long shower, Evelyn stepped out and wrapped herself in a thick white towel, twisting another into her damp red hair. The mirror was still fogged, her reflection distant, ghostly.

She made her way back to the guest room, steam trailing behind.

Her underwear from the night before was a no-go—crumpled and wet on the floor. Her jeans and shirt from yesterday would have to do. Maya's closet might've offered options, and Amanda's wardrobe was probably full of flowy, designer nonsense, but Evelyn was too short for those—and too proud to try.

*Jeans and a shirt are fine,* she told herself. *They're me.*

Right?

She paused, towel still in hand.

*Did Matt like that?*

She blinked. *Why does that matter? Why am I even thinking that?*

Still, the question lingered.

*I should ask him.*
*No—why?*
*Stop it.*
*I need to ask him.*

She shook her head as if she were trying to clear cobwebs and rubbed it hard with the towel. Then she got dressed—no bra, no clean underwear, just jeans and a stretched-out tee.

*It'll do. For now.*

Hum…just hum…

That always helped.

*The book liked the humming. So do I.*

"*Love is the sweetest thing…*" she sang under her breath, then let the melody slip back into a hum as she padded downstairs, still barefoot.

*Maybe making breakfast would bring Matt out of hiding.*

*Men think with two things,* her mother used to say. Time to test that theory.

*He hadn't had trouble thinking with the first one last night.*

She giggled at the memory—until she stepped into the kitchen.
And stopped.

Matt was already there.
Dressed. Coffee in hand.
Staring out the window.

"Matt!" Her face lit up as she hurried to him.

"Good morning, Eve."

His voice was flat.

She slowed.

"Did I do something again?" she asked, the warmth

already draining from her voice.

Matt sipped his coffee. "No. Why would you think that?"

She stepped closer, tentative. "You seem...off. Is it because I'm wearing the same clothes? I—I need to go get my things from my mom's—"

"It's not your clothes," Matt said, eyes still on his mug. "We can go later. If that's what the book wants."

She froze.
The words hit like a slap.

*If that's what the book wants.*

"You think me wanting you is the book?" Her voice cracked. Tears came fast.

Matt winced. "I...never said that."

"It feels like you're punishing me for something I can't control," she said, her voice rising. "Like you hold me to some impossible standard—and Maya gets a pass. Ed gets a pass. But not me."

"I didn't mean to—"

"No. You never do."

She stepped in now, voice trembling, face flushed.

"But every time you make these little comments, you rip my heart out."

And somewhere inside her head — the book laughed.

"You think it's controlling me all the time?" she snapped. "You think I'm just some fucking Eve-puppet for your amusement?"

Matt stared, guilt pooling in his chest.

"I'm sorry if I tried too hard last night. If I wanted it to be perfect," she said, voice breaking. "I've never had someone even remotely give a fuck about me, Matt. So, no— I don't know what I'm doing."

She turned and stormed out of the kitchen. Then out of the house.

Anyone watching would've seen a young woman on the verge of breaking.

Anyone *inside* her mind would've heard only a soft, tuneless hum.

And the book—laughing.

2

Ed woke to his cell phone buzzing on the nightstand. Morning light filtered in through the blinds.
Maya was sprawled beside him, one leg kicked half-free of the sheets.

He already knew what the call was about.

But that didn't mean he wanted to hear it.

Still, he answered.
"Hello." His voice was rough with sleep.
"…This is he."
Silence. Then a sharp inhale.

"My God. Is she—? I… Yes. Of course. I'll make the arrangements."

A pause.

"Was she depressed? I don't think so. She was upset about the store not selling. The house too. But…she walked into traffic?"

Another silence.

"I see. I didn't know…"

His hand trembled.

"Thank you."

He hung up. Sat on the edge of the bed. The room tilted. His stomach rolled.

*She walked into traffic.*

*Or… Did the book do this?*

*Too clean for you, huh?* the voice in his mind purred. *"Me? Little old me? Eddy, please. I would never harm her like that. I had cancer lined up—quick and tidy. Why would I send her onto the road? Too messy."*

Ed clenched his fists. "Why should I believe you?"

No answer. Just the whisper of silk sliding out of his mind again.

Behind him, Maya stirred.

"What's that, sweetie?"

He turned, and for a moment, he couldn't look at her. Finally:

"Amanda killed herself last night."

Maya sat up, the sheet clutched to her chest.

"I need to make some calls," Ed said. "Start planning. Probably best if you and Matt head back to Boston. Get back to class."

His voice cracked.

She moved closer, wrapping her arms around him from behind.
"Whatever you think is best. We'll just need some gas money. I hate asking—especially now."

"No, it's fine."

He stood, crossed the room, and lifted a painting from the wall. Behind it, a small safe.

"Amanda never knew the combination," he said with a dry, humorless laugh.
"Drove her crazy. This is the money my father left me—how I kept the business going."

He spun the dial. The lock clicked. The safe opened.

Bundles of cash. Two passports. Some jewelry.

He pulled out six hundred dollars—then hesitated. Reached in again. Pulled out a velvet pouch.

"My mother's necklace," he said. "I think she'd have liked you. She hated Amanda."

He shut the safe and replaced the painting.

Maya took the necklace as if it were sacred. Carefully, reverently, she clasped it around her neck. The pendant caught the morning light and scattered it across the room.

"I love it," she said, brushing her fingers over the stone.
"I'll wear it always."

Then she reached up and kissed him.

He kissed her back—just wanting to feel something

besides the dull ache in his chest. Pain. Guilt. Confusion.

Amanda was gone.
And all he could ask himself was:

*Did I miss something?*

Maya cupped his face in her hands.

"You know you couldn't have stopped it, right?" she said softly.

"I... Did I miss the signs?"
His voice cracked.
"Was there something I could've—?"

"Ed, listen to me."
Her tone was calm, unwavering.
"People who go through with this...they usually hide it. No notes. No warnings. No cries for help—because they don't want help."

She held his gaze, needing him to believe it.

Logically, he knew it was true.
But logic had nothing to do with the war inside him.

*What if we hadn't fought in the bookstore?*
*What if I'd sold it when she asked?*
*What if I'd just...been better?*

And then—like poison — *if you had a twelve-inch cock, you'd be in porn, Eddy. Enough with the poor-me shit—it bores me.*

The voice slithered behind his eyes like smoke.

*Also? Maya stays here. With you. Not Matt. Stop fucking up my plans.*

Ed winced. Maya either didn't notice...or was giving

him space to hide it.

He swallowed hard, blinking back tears. "Yeah…okay," he murmured.

And the book smiled.

"On second thought… maybe stay," Ed said. His voice was softer than expected.

Maya looked up, surprised. Then smiled. "I could switch to remote classes. Or just, you know…not finish. I hate the degree path anyway."

Ed nodded slowly, but his thoughts were racing.

He wanted her to stay. Needed her, maybe.

And that terrified him.

How easy it was to move on. How natural she felt beside him. How little he was really thinking about Amanda. How much he had *craved* Maya instead.

Was that *him*?

Or was it the *book*?

*Why do I have to take the blame all the time, Eddy? I'm not making you fall in love with her. You're doing that all by yourself. Though…I can't say I blame you. She's a trade-up, so to speak.*

*I'm not having this conversation*, Ed thought as he leaned in and kissed Maya's forehead.

Then he slipped into the bathroom. Closed the door.

*Oh, but I'm having it with you, Eddy.*

*Last I checked, I'm the one in charge…*

A pause.

*Hang on. I need to take care of something with Evelyn.*

And just like that, it was gone.

Silence.

Ed stood still. For the first time in what felt like years, it was *quiet* in his head. No pressure. No voice.

Just…stillness.

He took a shaky breath.
Cracked the door. Peeked out.

Maya sat on the bed, turning the necklace over in her hands. She looked peaceful. Untouched.

His heart ached at the sight of her.

And it was real.

The book wasn't there now. He *knew* it.

But he still wanted her.

Which meant…
*some part of this was him.*
His choice.
His weakness.

He stepped back into the bathroom. Turned on the faucet.

Let the water run.
Let it steam away the guilt—for now.

3

Matt caught up with Evelyn halfway down the driveway, breathless.

"Eve—please. Wait."

He reached out, gently resting a hand on her shoulder.

She turned.

Her face was blank. No anger. No sorrow. Just…nothing.

"Yes, Matt?" she asked.

That flat tone chilled him more than any storm ever could.

"Come back to the house, sweetie," he said, voice careful, calm.
"You don't look okay."

He could feel it now—rising in his chest like a sickness.
The thing he'd been trying not to name:
*Maybe Evelyn isn't in there anymore.*

"Okay," she said, nodding.
"Whatever you want, sweetie."

She turned and walked beside him, slipping her arm around his waist as if nothing had happened.
Like they were just coming in from a morning stroll—not returning from a fracture in reality.

It felt *wrong*.

Then, about ten feet from the porch, she stopped.

Went still.

Tensed.

And something shifted behind her eyes—like a switch being thrown.
The lights flickered. Came back on.

Her gaze rose to meet his.

"Matt?"

"Yes, Eve?" he said, his voice cracking.

"We should go back in," she murmured. "Get warm…"

"We will," he said. "But, Eve—"

"I don't like fighting with you," she whispered.

"I don't either."
He reached for her hand—and this time, she didn't flinch.

"I'm just…worried about you."

"Worried about me?" she echoed, her expression confused—like waking from a dream.

"I can't explain it," he said. "It's just a feeling. When you look at me… sometimes I think you're asking for help. Not with words. Just—your eyes."

He swallowed hard.

"I don't know what's happening. But something's not right. And I don't want to lose you, Eve. Not to *whatever this is.*"

Without warning, Evelyn threw her arms around him.

Tight. Real. *Hers.*

"No matter what happens right now," she whispered, "I want you to know—I care about you."

Matt froze for half a second, heart hammering.

"I care about you too," he whispered, hugging her back like it might keep her from slipping away.

And for a moment, he believed it might work.

But then—just like that—it was gone.

The warmth in her grip faded.
The light in her eyes dimmed.
And Evelyn…wasn't Evelyn anymore.

She smiled at him. Soft. Sweet.
Distant.

"Come in now, sweetheart," she said, cupping his cheek.
"Let me make you breakfast."

Matt's heart sank.

But he nodded.
And let her lead him inside.

4

Maya watched from her glass prison as Ed gave *her*— or the version of her—a diamond necklace.

Something twisted inside her when he kissed the imposter's forehead.

Why did he have to be so damn sweet to *her?*

She wanted to hate him. Hate all of this.
But with each passing hour, she knew she was falling deeper.
Not because of the book.
Not even despite it.
Because Ed…*actually saw her.* The real her.

They had things in common—books, stories, obscure references.
Sure, there was an age gap. But not that big.

"Stop justifying it," she muttered.

*"Why not justify it?"*
The voice slithered in over the speaker—too sweet to be anything but cruel.

"Because what's the point? You don't care what I think. You never should have."

*"You say that…and I just don't know, Maya. Do you even love me anymore?"*

Mocking. Mock sorrow. But sharp all the same.

Maya stared at the speaker, jaw slack.
"I…I don't even know how to respond to that."

The book's laugh echoed—low and rolling.
*"It's fine. I leave most people speechless."*

A pause.

*"And it's okay that you're developing feelings for our dear Eddy. He is for you too. All without my help. Isn't love just so special?"*

"…He is?"
God dammit. She sounded like a schoolgirl with a crush.

*"Yes, and — wait."*
The voice stopped.
*"I need to deal with Evelyn."*

And then…silence.

And something changed.

The glass cracked.

First, a spiderweb fracture in the corner. Then more—racing along the walls like lightning bolts.

Maya gasped.
She stepped forward, pressed her palm to the wall—and it *gave.*

She was *free.*

Her mind surged forward, reclaiming her body like a breath after drowning.
Maya B. stood in the way—vague, flickering, like a ghost.
But Maya didn't stop. She *moved through her* and took control.

Air touched her skin. *Real* air.
The sensation was intoxicating.

She reached for Ed's phone.

Then froze.

Who would she call? What would she say?

She needed a plan.

Her fingers hovered—then *something yanked her back.*

A hand clamped around her throat. Her body lifted, thrown.
Slammed back into the glass prison.

The walls rebuilt in an instant.

"Thanks for stopping by," said her voice. *Her* voice.

*"Naughty girl,"* the speaker hissed.

Maya crossed her arms, seething.
"Like you wouldn't have done the same damn thing."

*"Don't test me."*

The playfulness was gone now. What was left was *frost and venom.*

*"You don't get to take over. Or make phone calls."*

Maya sat on the edge of the bed, suddenly weak.
"I wasn't going to call anyone. What could I say? 'Hi, I'm a college student possessed by a sentient demon book'?"

She looked down.

"I just... I wanted to leave a message. For Ed, or Matt, something. *Anything.*"

A beat of silence.

*"How sweet,"* the voice said at last.
*"But they have their own problems. Ed's already conflicted. And Matt..."*

A pause.
Like a knife being chosen.

*"Just pray I keep him around."*

Maya's blood ran cold.

The idea of something happening to Matt—because of her—settled like *ice* in her gut.

"Don't hurt him."

"*You suddenly care about the guy?*"

The book's voice was syrupy-sweet. Mocking.

"*That's odd, Maya, because I've been through your brain. I didn't find many Matt means something to me files. Unless I check the people, I can use folder.*"

"That's not fair," she said—but it rang hollow.

Wasn't it though?

She *had* used him. Often.
She knew Matt would never call her on it—and maybe that was what hurt the most.

"*Don't be like that.*"
The voice tsked.

"*He's hardly innocent. Trying to buy his way into your pants. So what if you never planned on letting him in? You wouldn't be the first woman to lead a guy on. You won't be the last.*"

Maya lay back on the bed and stared at the ceiling.

"Can we talk about something else?"

"*Sure,*" the book replied smoothly.

"*What would you like to discuss?*"

"I don't know. Ways to *defeat* you? You know—asking for a friend."

She stared into the dark void above her.

A pause.

Then — "*Funny,*" the voice said.

"*I could make you watch yourself having a three-way with Evelyn and Ed if you keep up the snark. Maybe even ensure you feel every part."*

Maya didn't flinch.

"Punishment…or reward?" she said, eyes half-lidded.

The silence that followed?

Point, Maya.

5

Matt sat at the kitchen breakfast bar, staring at the black book where it lay on the counter like a fucking cookbook.

It felt like it was *smiling* at him. Mocking him.

He wanted to dump gasoline on it and light a match.

But that wouldn't work.
Not with *this* thing.

What he knew—or at least *hoped*, based on that old YouTube interview—was that a box worked.
A *blessed* box.

He didn't have one.
But maybe…maybe Ed's father had kept the original.
Wouldn't that make sense?
Men like that didn't throw away something like that.

Matt turned the thought about while finishing his breakfast, tuning out the sound of Evelyn humming that goddamn song.

It was burrowing into his skull.

He was starting to hate it.

Hate her humming.

Hated how *sweet* her voice sounded while she wasn't even *her* anymore.

"This was amazing, sweetheart. Thank you," he said, pushing back his chair.

"I'm going to take a walk. Burn off some of this food."

Evelyn didn't look up from the sink.
"Hmm. Okay. Wear a coat."

Matt paused.
Something in her tone—too casual. Too measured.

"Yep," he said. Then, he walked out of the kitchen.

But he didn't leave the house.

He moved quickly, quietly, down the hall.
He needed the basement.
If there *was* a box—*the* box—it had to be down there.

That's when he spotted a door that didn't quite fit.

Smaller than the others. Tucked awkwardly into the wall.

Anyone familiar with old Northeastern homes would know the type—basement doors were always an afterthought in houses like these. Back then, basements were for boilers and dirt, not drywall and dreams.

Still, Matt had a hunch.

Maybe Ed's dad modernized it, kept the original frame. It felt like the kind of weird, sentimental decision a guy obsessed with old books would make.

He stepped forward, reached for the small iron handle —

*"What're you doing, Matt?"*

The voice exploded in his skull.
Sharp. Sudden.
A hammer to the temples.

He winced, staggered—but didn't stop.

He yanked the door open.

Just a broom closet.

A mop, paint cans. Cobwebs.

"Looking for cleaning supplies?"
The book purred. *"Presentation matters, Matty."*

Matt slammed the door shut and spun around—and *froze.*

He wasn't in Ed's house anymore.

The hallway behind him was gone.
In its place: darkness, aged wood, and the heavy, oppressive *rot* of a place that hated him.

He blinked.
Rubbed his eyes.

Still there.

"Hello?" His voice cracked. "Eve? Ed? Maya?"

No answer.
Only the creak of warped floorboards underfoot.
He took one hesitant step forward. Then another.

A dim light flickered at the far end of the hall—weak and yellow.
Ahead, a wet sound.
*Rhythmic.*
*Wrong.*

He passed by a window.
Dusk—or dawn. Impossible to tell.
The light outside looked bruised, like the sky had been punched.

And the sound was closer now.

Matt turned the final corner—and saw him.

A farmer.

Gaunt, dead-eyed.

Standing in a room soaked in shadow—and something thicker.
A woman hung upside down from a meat hook, her hair brushing the floor.
He was carving her open.

Not fast.
Not angry.
Just...*working.*

Matt wanted to run.

But he couldn't.

The book wasn't going to let that happen.

And then, deep in his marrow, the voice returned.

*"See how nicely my Stanley worked for me, Matt?*
*Look how lovingly he opened his own wife—just because I asked."*

*"Imagine what I can make you do. To Evelyn. Or what I can make her do to you."*

*"The last man who tried to box me away didn't speak a word for sixty years. Just sobbed. Want to know why? Because of what I showed him."*

*"I killed the priest too. The one who blessed the box. Think you'll find another holy man dumb enough to die for a cursed book?"*

Matt screamed in his mind:

No.

But his body moved.

Step by step.

Toward the butchered woman.

Toward the knife.

No — and then his *hands* were helping.

Helping hold her. Helping part the flesh.

*"Feel that? That's what a human heart feels like, Matt. So the next time you go breaking Evelyn's? You'll know exactly what I'm coming for."*

It *laughed then.*

Not in the room.

Not in his ears.

Inside.

**"*FUCK YOU!*"** Matt roared, every nerve on fire.

The blood. The cruelty. The butchered woman.

None of it was real.

Not anymore.

This *wasn't* his life.

This wasn't *his* story.

Eyes clenched, he forced it out.

He pictured the kitchen. The breakfast bar.
Evelyn's *actual smile*—bright and imperfect.
The one she gave when she didn't know anyone was
watching.

And then—silence.

He opened his eyes.

The broom closet stood before him.
Just a mop. Just paint.

He let out a slow breath.
Turned around.

The warped hallway was gone.
Ed's house. Warm light. Real floorboards. Reality, restored.

But now, at the end of the hall, was a door he hadn't
noticed before—slightly ajar.
A faint draft whispered beneath it.

The basement.

Matt clenched his fists.

This time, he was going in by *choice*.

He moved. Slowly at first.
Each step a quiet dare.
But nothing happened.

No whispers.
No nightmares.

He reached the door. Flipped on the light.

The basement greeted him with cool, musty air—like a breath exhaled decades ago.

He'd assumed Ed's father had updated the space.

He hadn't.

But it wasn't in bad shape either. Built-in shelves lined the walls, cluttered with old life: tangled Christmas lights, rusted tools, ancient paint cans, boxes marked in fading marker.

Just a normal basement.

Mostly.

Then he saw it.

Tucked in the far corner, half-hidden behind a cracked cabinet — a wooden box.

Oak, lined with red velvet.
Dulled by time.

Matt's breath caught in his throat.

He stepped forward, slow, deliberate.

The box was *heavier* than it looked.
Not just physically—spiritually.
It felt like someone had built it to hold something holy.
And something damned.

He traced its lid, fingers pausing at a long, hairline crack—expertly repaired.

Someone had needed this box again.

Had cared for it.

Had believed in it…even after it failed.

Matt didn't know who had fixed it.

But in his gut?

He knew the repair probably cost Ed's father his life.

He shut the lid gently. Reverently.

This was it.

His only shot at saving them.

# Chapter 19: DE-O-WAIN-STA

1

"**S**tanley!"

"Don't—don't you fucking—!"

Webb's shout cracked across the dam as Stanley surged to his feet, a matchbook clenched in one trembling hand. He made a desperate break for the row of dynamite.

*He's going to blow himself up.*
The thought hit Webb like a gut punch.

Fueled by pain and fury, Webb scrambled up, blood slicing his side. His gun was in his hand. His hat—lost somewhere in the brush. He didn't have time to care.

He ran.

Even with a bullet lodged under his diaphragm, Webb was in better shape than Stanley—and he had something to lose.

As Stanley struck a match with shaking fingers, Webb slammed into him, driving him hard into the cold concrete of the dam.

The gun flew from Webb's hand.

Rookie fucking mistake.

But the matches flew from Stanley's too—that was the win.

Webb went for a quick pin, but Stanley twisted out of it.

Military training—just enough to be dangerous. He landed a solid punch to Webb's side, and the world went white. A flash of agony nearly dropped him.

Stanley's follow-up swing could've ended it.
But he slipped.

Webb saw his chance—ducked out of range —
CRACK, CRACK, CRACK!

Gunfire erupted from above.
Both men dove for cover, bullets sparking off the concrete. Webb's heart thundered. Whoever was shooting didn't seem to care who they hit.

Now the whole damn hill was a war zone.

"Who the fuck is shooting up there?!" Webb's voice echoed off the dam and the rock face, sharp as the rifle cracks.

"Um…me…sir… John. John Westcott." A slurred voice floated down from the road above. "You shot me…"

"I'll kill you if you shoot down here again, John!" Webb bellowed. "Right now I'll call it *help*—but one more shot in my direction and I'm assuming you're aiming for me!"

As he shouted, Webb spotted his handgun—twenty feet away, just beyond the concrete platform.

He moved.

So did Stanley.

Both men lunged.

Stanley was closer. Much closer.

He reached the pistol first.
Snatched it up.
Turned with a sick grin.

He raised the barrel.

CRACK!

Another shot from above. Stanley jerked as a bullet slammed into his shoulder. He staggered. The gun tumbled from his grip and splashed into the dark water below.

More gunfire from the road.

Webb had enough.

He charged.
Slammed into Stanley with everything he had left. The collision knocked the wind out of both men.

Stanley tried to break free, elbowing blindly—neither of them noticing how close they'd drifted.

Stanley stepped back.

There was nothing.

Just air.

He grabbed for Webb instinctively—fingernails digging into his jacket—and the two of them tumbled together over the edge, down ten feet into the cold, rushing backwater of the Mohawk River.

2

John Westcott watched from the roadside as the two men—the trooper and Stanley Millard—pitched into the black water below.
Their bodies vanished with a splash, swallowed by the churning maw of the Mohawk River.
Rain misted across the spillway like ghosts.

Slumped against the warm hood of his car, John couldn't move.
His leg was in ruins. Whiskey thick in his blood.
He stared at the water, waiting. For movement. For a survivor. For a miracle.

But no one surfaced.

That's when the voice came.

*"Get down there. Finish it."*

It slid through his skull like smoke under a door.

"I can't," John rasped, lips numb. "I'm shot…bad."

*"It's not a request."*

The voice didn't need to raise itself. It didn't have to.

Pain exploded behind his eyes—white-hot and blinding. His body convulsed, yanked upright like a marionette on broken strings.

He screamed.

Not from pain. From the *presence*.
Something cold curling beneath his ribs.

Still screaming, he stood.

The first step was a stumble.
The second—a collapse.

He tumbled down the muddy slope, roots and rocks ripping jagged lines across his arms. A sack of broken limbs.

He slammed into the side of the cruiser with a wet, meaty thud.

The breath left him. He tasted blood.
Rain hammered his face.

But still—he tried again.

Crawled half-conscious toward the base of the dam.
Each foot dragged through wet gravel.
His body gave out five feet from the dynamite.

There—he stopped.

A lighter in his shaking hand.

---

When they found him hours later, he was barely alive.
Muttering "no" over and over through cracked lips.

The young trooper from Sylvan Beach, Troop D,
would later write in his report:

*I've never seen an unconscious man with that much fear on his face.*

John Westcott lived for another sixty-five years.

He gave one interview.

He spoke to no one else.

The book made sure of that.

It whispered to him every night.

About his failure.
About the fire waiting for him.

About how close his thumb had come to flicking that lighter...

...and setting them all free.

3

Webb felt Stanley grab him—then the world tilted. A sickening weightlessness seized him, and in that heartbeat before the crash, he *knew*.

He took a breath—then another. One final lungful, just before they hit the water.

The impact stole everything. Light. Sound. Direction.

He tumbled. The spillway's undertow spun him like laundry in a basin, and Webb went still. Not panicking. Not yet. He let the current carry him, arms tucked, conserving energy.

That's what would keep him alive: stillness, patience.

Let the river do its work, and maybe he'd surface whole.

Let Stanley fight it. Let the bastard panic and waste his breath. Maybe they'd find his body bloated and face-down a mile downstream.

But then—something closed around his ankle.

Not a log. A hand.

Webb twisted, eyes stinging in the black water. Enough light filtered down to make out Stanley's face — pale, bloated, and smiling.

He was wedged into a submerged logjam, his body pinned, one arm free—wrapped tight around Webb's ankle.
He *could* let go.
But he wouldn't.

That smile said it all: he'd rather drag them both down than die alone.

Webb gritted his teeth, yanked his leg up as far as the current allowed—then drove his heel down.

Hard.

Crunch.

Something gave.
Stanley's grip slipped.

And the river seized Webb like a lover — yanked him away into the deep.

---

He didn't know how long the current carried him.

When he came to, he was coughing on a muddy bank, half a mile downstream where the Mohawk bent sharply left.

The sky above was dark velvet, pinned with stars.

He gasped, water and blood pouring from his mouth. His ribs ached. His side burned. His skin was raw.
But he was alive.

Somewhere upstream, dynamite still waited.
Somewhere upstream, Stanley Millard's corpse might still be

tangled in a log like driftwood with a grudge.

Webb didn't know if he'd stopped anything.
Maybe he'd just delayed it.
Maybe he'd die here, and someone else would finish what Stanley started.

The thought gnawed at him.

And with it came the familiar itch — a sliver behind the eyes. Like a splinter in the soul.

Then came the voice.

*"You probably think yourself a hero, don't you, Captain?"*

It wasn't spoken—but felt. A thought curled through his mind like smoke under a door.

Now that Stanley was dead and John unconscious, the book had time.

Focus.

---

"No…I don't," Webb rasped aloud—not to the voice, but to the owl perched in the pine above him.
It blinked once.
Judging.

*"Good,"* the voice hissed, pleased. *"Because you're going to die on this muddy riverbank. And I'll be the only one to keep you company. Just thought you should know."*

Webb coughed.

"If that's my fate…then so be it."

The stars stared back, cold and unblinking.

The river whispered beside him—soft, endless. And somewhere nearby, the owl crooned. Low. Hollow. Then silence.

Webb closed his eyes.

And listened.

To the night. The river. And the voice—sliding through his skull like a blade of ice.

And still, despite it all... Leon Webb smiled.

Because even now, *especially* now...

He still had the stars, and in his last moments on this earth, he thought of his wife holding his baby boy. He held onto that thought as long as he could until the cold and black surrounded him and pulled him under one last time.

4

TO: Boonville Daily Chronicle Editor

FROM: Emily Holtz
DATE: August 2, 1933

RE: Unrest in the North Country

Over the last 72 hours, the village of Boonville has become the epicenter of a violent and deeply troubling series of events.

What began as organized resistance among local farmers—part of the broader Milk Strike gripping the state— has spiraled into tragedy. Riots between striking farmers and law enforcement have left multiple people injured, two residents dead, one New York state trooper killed, and another individual currently missing. One man is in custody but remains uncooperative.

Most alarming, however, is a credible plot uncovered to destroy the Delta Lake Dam system—an act that would have endangered thousands of lives downstream.

The mayor's office declined to return our request for comment. Off-the-record sources within law enforcement and among the farming community speak of chaos, suppressed information, and fear.

As of this writing, a heavy presence of New York State troopers remains in and around Boonville and Rome, with ongoing efforts to locate a man named Stanley Millard, identified by several sources as a person of interest.

Though most farmers have returned to their fields for now, the tension remains high. Many believe this unrest is far from over.

During the height of the clash, between 400 and 600 farmers—some armed with axes, clubs, and firearms—blocked two dairy trucks on County Route 46. Tear gas was deployed. Troopers charged the crowd with clubs and nightsticks. Eyewitnesses described the scene as *a battlefield*. Eight farmers were hospitalized.

Boonville, a town once known for quiet hills and milk deliveries, has become a crucible of violence, secrecy, and fear.

—Emily Holtz

REPLY FROM: Mr. Keith McGrady, Editor-in-Chief, Boonville Daily Chronicle

Dear Ms. Holtz,

Thank you for your submission.

Our paper does not accept unsolicited independent reporting, particularly on matters as sensational and inflammatory as your attached piece. The New York State Police categorically denies several of the incidents you've described. There is no record of a "Stanley Millard" owning a farm in this region, nor any credible threat to the Delta Lake Dam.

Your article—if printed—would serve only to spread panic and misinformation. As you are surely aware, we have a responsibility to preserve order, not invite chaos.

Ms. Holtz, those who publish such provocative and unsubstantiated material can find themselves in unfortunate situations. I would hate to see a young woman fresh out of university stumble into such territory unnecessarily.

That said, we are currently hiring for a junior reporting position. If you're interested, please come and speak with me directly. Naturally, publication of the current story would be off the table.

Warm regards,

*Keith McGrady*
*Editor-in-chief*
*The Boonville Daily Chronicle*

# Chapter 20: WHAT'S OLD IS NEW AGAIN

1

Ed walked downstairs to see Matt sitting in the living room with that goddamn box, polishing it with fucking Pledge. The lemon kind.

*Well,* Ed thought, *wouldn't want the book to smell mold.*

Matt was hunched over the thing like it was a prized antique, rubbing slow, deliberate circles into the wood. Ed walked up behind him and put a hand on his shoulder—and Matt *nearly jumped out of his skin.*

"Easy," Ed said.

Matt blinked, looked up—pale, hollow-eyed—and gave a tight, manic smile. "Getting the book's prison ready."

He went right back to polishing.

Ed stared at him for a beat, then walked deeper into the room and dropped into the chair across from him. "Buddy, that's a risky thing to say out loud."

Matt just shrugged like someone who'd run out of fucks a while ago.

Ed sighed. "Okay, I know you can't—or won't—tell me your plan. But *please* tell me you have one. Something more than polishing the apocalypse away with a four-dollar bottle of lemon-scented optimism."

Matt didn't answer. Just smiled. Nodded.

Ed wished that gave him hope. It didn't.

It made him worry about Matt—worry in that deep-down, gut-sick way only men who've been chewed up by life *know* how to worry. Matt was still young enough to think he was invincible, still under the illusion that being the good guy meant things would work out. Ed had learned better. The world didn't care about your age. It would *hurt* you. It would *wreck* you.

Hell, Ed had just gotten off the phone with the funeral home.

Cremation. That's what it came to. There wasn't enough of Amanda left to bother with a casket.

That wasn't a call he ever imagined he'd have to make.

He still needed to call her mother. Jesus. What the hell would he even say?

Would they want to come stay at the house?

If they did, would Maya stay?

*So, Ms. Wilson, this is Maya Cartar—we were fucking the night your daughter threw herself in front of an eighteen-wheeler, but I'm sure it's totally unrelated. Anyway, can I take your jacket?*

He dropped his head into his hands.

Somewhere, he could feel the book laughing. Laughing at all of it. Delight soaked into every terrible thing it touched. It was always laughing.

And Ed knew he'd be the one cleaning up the mess. Just like the cats. All over again.

Ed stood up and left Matt to his polishing. The sharp scent of lemon Pledge clung to the air, crawling into his skull and sparking a headache—or maybe it was just the sight of Matt, hunched over that cursed box, slowly losing his mind.

Did it matter?
He wanted it not to.
God, he was tired.

Then he saw her.

Maya, standing in the kitchen, holding a mug of what looked like tea. The morning light hit her just right, and his heart—traitorous thing—gave a small, helpless tug.

Yeah.
She was pretty great.

And in the middle of all this horror, maybe—just maybe—she was his safe harbor.

Ed walked to the coffeepot, dropped in a K-cup, set a mug beneath it, and waited for the brew. "How are you ladies doing?" he asked casually, though he'd already clocked Evelyn standing at the sink when he walked in.

"We're just discussing what we're going to do about Matt," Evelyn said, not looking up.

Maya nodded slowly, sipping her tea.

"Matt? Why, what's wrong with Matt?" Ed asked, already knowing the answer. *The book knew. Hell, anyone with eyes—or a nose—knew.*

"He's being naughty," Evelyn said with a giggle.

"Might need to spank him later."

"Eve, gross," Maya said with a smirk. "I don't need to hear about your perverted sex life with my friend."

The humor was there, light and easy. But Ed could feel it—*that dangerous undertow.* The book was playing its games again. Warning him, maybe. Telling him to keep things under control, or it would.

"Well, kinky sex aside," Ed said, forcing a grin, "any other plans on the books? I've got to head into town…make the funeral arrangements. Probably best if you all stay close— here or nearby."

He hated how flat his voice sounded. Like he was discussing car repairs, not burying his wife.

"I need to get my things," Evelyn said, finally turning from the sink. "So does Maya. We can do that while you're handling your…wife."

Ed flinched but said nothing.

"We'll drag Matt along," Maya added casually. "Best we don't leave him to his own devices."

Ed chuckled, but it came out dry. Forced. The entire conversation had left him uneasy. He knew Matt wouldn't want to leave the house—he never did—but with Evelyn and Maya pushing, he'd give in. Two against one always won.

"Okay, well…play nice," he muttered, grabbing his coffee and heading for the door.

"Wait."

Maya's voice stopped him cold. She stepped forward quickly, almost knocking the mug out of his hand.

"I need a kiss goodbye," she said, trying for playful, but Ed caught the flicker of something else—worry?

He turned to face her. Smiled. Kissed her.

When he pulled back, her eyes searched his. "You'll come back tonight, right?"

"Yes," Ed said, eyebrows furrowing. "Why wouldn't I?"

"Oh, nothing. Never mind..." she said quickly and turned back to the sink like she hadn't just clutched at him like he was walking off to war.

Ed lingered a moment longer. "Okay, well... Call me if you need anything."

Silence. No response from either woman now. Just the faint hum of Evelyn's song and the smell of lemon Pledge drifting in from the living room.

Ed shook his head and walked out—intent on checking in with Matt one last time.

He found Matt still at the living room table, polishing the box like it was a prize-winning car. The wood gleamed now, rich and warm, catching the morning light like it had just come off a craftsman's bench.

"Looks pretty good for almost a hundred years old," Ed said, trying to sound casual.

Matt glanced up and smiled, proud. "Yeah. Hopefully, it'll do the trick."

He set the box down and stood, stretching. "Now I just need to figure out how to get the book in there."

He gestured toward the kitchen with his chin. "I'll deal with those two today."

Ed nodded, frowning. "Well, I've got to go into town. Make the arrangements. I can't...put it off any longer." His voice caught slightly. "I'm sure you'll be fine."

Matt looked at him carefully, then turned the box over in his hands. "What do you think? Looks brand-new now."

"Yeah." Ed stared at it a moment. "Just remember...it didn't work last time. Not really. It just slowed it down."

Not that he really knew. Hell, he didn't know much of anything anymore. Just that he had to drive into town.

Suddenly, his mind conjured it. The morgue. The stainless-steel table. Her mangled body was dumped like meat. Blood and whatever else pooling on the floor. With one side of her face gone, the other—God help him—was still recognizable. An eye dangling loose in its socket, turned just enough to *look at him.*

*"I know you're fucking her, Ed. In our bed..."*

Ed staggered back a step.

"Ed?" Matt asked, stepping closer. "You okay? You spaced out. You look like hell."

"Huh?" Ed blinked. "Yeah. Sorry. Just — I need to go."

He turned fast. "Be careful with all of that, Matt. Please."

Matt opened his mouth to say something else, but Ed

was already at the door, snatching the keys off the wall.

Amanda's voice echoed in his head as he closed the door behind him.

*"In our bed."*


2


Tom Waldner looked out the tall window of his office. Mr. Rodrick would arrive in twenty minutes to finalize the arrangements for his wife's funeral. A tragic thing, really—Amanda, so young, so vibrant.

He shuffled some paperwork on the mahogany desk, mentally preparing. He'd known Ed for years—handled both his parents' funerals. Ed wasn't as well-off now as he'd been back then, so Tom would need a different approach if he hoped to upsell.

*"House of Peace Funeral Home: where transparent pricing makes healing and meaningful services affordable for every family."* The slogan played through his head like a jingle, and he smiled.

Standing, he slipped into his black jacket. The navy tie—Ed's favorite color—was already in place. These details mattered. Most people didn't realize how much went into being a funeral director in a small town. You didn't just handle the dead—you had to *know* the living.

*"Of course, Ed, I understand. Amanda would want you to be frugal. But this…this is her last resting place."*

*"We also have urns—this one, solid silver. I remember Amanda always had a thing for that metal…"*

*"Celebration of Life? A modest fee, naturally. But don't worry about the numbers now. That's my job. You just focus on honoring your wife. We'll handle the rest—just like we did with your father."*

Tom descended the black maple staircase—original to the house, lovingly polished for over a century. The carpet runners were flawless, the wood gleamed, and the air smelled faintly of rosewater and lemon oil. The House of Peace was a time capsule, preserved from 1856, when his great-great-great-grandfather first built it and began the family trade of ushering the dead from this life to the next… and separating the grieving from their wallets with gentle, practiced hands..

---

Meanwhile, in the basement of the House of Peace, Sarah Wilson was striving to transfer the remnants of Ms. Rodrick into a temporary casket—or what was left of her, anyway. The truck had done a number on her body. Even though Sarah considered herself skilled, there was no way she could make Amanda presentable for a viewing. *This one was cremation or a closed casket—no in-between.*

She needed to know which. The protocols were different, and in New York State, that mattered. If something was fun, the state would regulate it. If you owned it, they'd tax it. Those were the only two rules you could set your watch by in this goddamn place.

She glanced at the clock. Ed Rodrick should be upstairs by now, sitting in the velvet-trimmed office with Mr. Waldner. Time to clean up and vanish. The boss didn't like her to be seen during viewings—probably liked the clients thinking he did all the work himself.

Not that Sarah cared. The pay was decent; the hours

were quiet, and the dead didn't talk back.

She closed the casket one last time and locked it, wiped her tools clean, and slipped into the tiny office tucked between the cold storage and the embalming sink. She'd barely pulled the door shut when she heard two sets of footsteps coming down the old stairs.

*Men with grief in their mouths, and sales pitches close behind.*

3

Matt drove in silence, the book stowed in the trunk and dread pulsing behind his ribs. Maya and Evelyn whispered and giggled in the back seat, their voices soft and syrupy, as if this were just a weekend road trip. But the air in the car was wrong—thick with something artificial, like perfume over rot.

He felt less like a driver and more like a hostage steering a getaway car.

"We should do some quick shopping while we're in town," he said, pulling into the nearly empty parking lot of the old Tops grocery store.

"What a *wonderful* idea, sweetie," Evelyn said with a brightness that scraped his nerves raw.

Maya gave him a small, slow smile in the rearview mirror—too calm, too confident.

Matt parked the car and stepped out into the gray mid-morning light; the sky was overcast like wet wool. The grocery store loomed ahead, outdated and washed out, its fluorescent sign buzzing faintly. He rounded the car as the women stepped out, Maya cradling the book like a fashion accessory. The cover shimmered ever so slightly—a heat haze that shouldn't exist.

"Does it have to go everywhere?" Matt asked, already knowing the answer.

"Matt, that's no way to talk about Evelyn," Maya joked, giving Eve a playful smack on the backside.

Evelyn squeaked, her cheeks turning red. "Stop it, Maya."

It was a scene straight from a bad porno, and Matt hated how obviously scripted it felt—like the book was feeding lines to its marionettes.

He forced a smile. Had to keep playing along.

Inside the store, the automatic doors whooshed open, letting out a breath of cold, lemon-scented air. The place was nearly empty, save for a lone cashier leaning on her elbows and a janitor mopping near the front coolers.

The lighting was harsh. Too bright. It made everything look staged, like they were walking onto a set, not into a store.

"Okay, essentials," Matt said, grabbing a basket. "Milk, eggs, bread—normal people's things."

"Oh, we're *very* normal," Maya said, her smile sharp now.

They passed down an aisle of canned soup. As Matt reached for a can, he noticed the janitor watching them—not directly, just out of the corner of his eye. His mop moved slower than it should. Almost…ritualistic. Then the man turned away, muttering to himself.

Matt gripped the basket tighter and moved on.

In the cereal aisle, a small child froze mid-step, staring at the book in Maya's hands. His mother noticed too late and yanked him away, murmuring, "Don't stare."

The book shimmered again—like oil on water, like heat rising from a corpse.

"Matt?" Evelyn had slipped her arm around his waist. "You're being quiet."

"I'm thinking," he said, managing not to pull away.

"About putting us both in that box?" Maya asked sweetly.

Matt's stomach twisted. Her tone was light, almost flirtatious, but her eyes never blinked.

"What?" Matt's eyes widened, not sure she had said what he thought she had said.

"Are you thinking about getting us both in bed?" Maya giggled.

"I… No, just wondering what kind of coffee to get," he lied. He knew she said box, and now the other image played in his mind as well. The cart slowed for a moment.

The fluorescent light above them buzzed louder for a moment—then popped. A single bulb going out.

Matt flinched. Evelyn giggled.

"Oops. Power surge…maybe," Maya said, still smiling.

They moved on, their cart half-full. Matt glanced at Maya's hands. The book no longer shimmered. It pulsed, and he thought he could hear it humming, a vibration too low for human ears.

The book needed to go into the box. He just needed time, some distance, and a moment.

Instead, he pushed the cart toward the checkout, pretending everything was fine, all while the air in the store thickened around him like smoke—and the book drank it in.

Matt pushed the cart up to the register, heart thudding a little too hard in his chest. The cashier, a college-age girl with a pleasant smile and a half-grown-out pink streak in her hair, gave him the usual nod. Then her gaze flicked to Maya—and the book she cradled in her arms.

"That's a weird book," she said, her tone casual, fingers beginning to flick the groceries over the scanner.

Matt's pulse kicked up a notch.

"Oh, sweetie…" Maya purred, running a hand slowly over the cover, "you have *no* idea."

Matt's stomach twisted.

He wanted to scream. Wanted to snatch the book from her hands and hurl it across the store, wanted to shout: *You like it? Take it! It's yours now!*

Instead, he faked a smile that barely held together and tried to focus on the task—item, belt, item, belt.

"Eighty-four seventy-two," the girl chirped. "Do you need bags?"

"Yes, please," Matt replied, forcing calm into his

voice.

She handed him the paper bags. He packed the items with care, methodically. Cereal. Milk. Bananas. Toothpaste.

Then, just as he reached for the bread—he froze.

A sound. A soft *thud-thud-thud*, rhythmic, growing louder.

He looked up.

A human head was rolling down the conveyor belt. Hair matted. Skin pale. A trail of slick, black-red blood followed in its wake, smearing across the plastic rollers.

Matt couldn't move. The world tilted around him. Sound fell away into a low, suffocating hum. His vision tunneled.

The head slowed.

It came to a gentle stop right in front of him. Its eyes stared up, cloudy and lifeless. Its mouth hung open as if it had just let out a last gasp.

Then— It winked.

Matt didn't scream. Didn't collapse.

He just…left. For a little while.
The book took over.

Maya's arm slid gently around his waist. Evelyn paid for the groceries. The cashier never even looked twice.

They walked out together like three friends on a weekend errand.
A young man, pale and dazed, flanked by two beautiful women—one carrying a book that pulsed faintly in her hands.

It looked normal.

Until the groceries went into the back seat.
And Matt climbed into the trunk.

He didn't speak. Didn't protest.

He just curled up—knees to chest, thumb in his
mouth—like a child trying to disappear.

Evelyn leaned in, brushed a strand of hair from his
forehead, and kissed his cheek—sweet, almost maternal.

Then she closed the lid.
Gently.

Like tucking him in for a nap.

4

Ed sat across from Tom Waldner in the dim hush of
the House of Peace's consultation room. The wood-paneled
walls and antique furnishings were designed to feel
comforting, but to Ed, they felt like a coffin dressed up in
Sunday clothes.

Tom's voice droned on gently, warm and rehearsed.
A velvet sledgehammer. "This package includes the viewing,
cremation, the floral display, and the life montage slideshow.
I'll personally ensure everything's handled smoothly, Ed. You
won't have to lift a finger."

Ed nodded absently. He wasn't even sure what he was
agreeing to anymore. His mind was drifting—back to the
house, to Maya, to her asking, *"You'll be home tonight, right?"*
like it wasn't a foregone conclusion. That had stuck with him.

It still clung like a splinter under his skin.

Tom's smile grew with each nod. Professional. Polished. A hint of *"Thanks for the down payment on that bass boat"* beneath the sorrowful sheen.

Well, Amanda always liked a show. He kind of owed her that, didn't he?

The thought hit like a gut-punch. For the first time since the call, Ed actually *missed* her. Not the bitter arguments, not the icy distance—but the quiet familiarity of her presence. The way she used to sing to herself in the kitchen when she thought he wasn't listening. Her laughter—loud, unabashed—was reserved for stupid reality shows.

Grief caught him off guard.

Tom noticed. Of course he did.

"Here you go, Ed." A crisp box of tissues slid across the polished oak desk.

Ed took one, not even realizing his eyes were wet.

"As I was saying," Tom continued, softer now, "my staff and I will take care of *everything*. Your package covers the lot. Just send me a list of attending family members, and we'll coordinate their travel and lodging. You focus on saying goodbye."

Tom placed a hand on his shoulder with the practiced gentleness of someone who'd done this hundreds of times.

Ed swallowed. "Thank you, Tom. That…makes this easier."

But what he *thought* was: *This is going to bankrupt me.*

He stood up, shook Tom's hand—warm,
professional, too rehearsed—and walked out on legs that
didn't quite feel like his. Rubbery. Too long, like stilts made
of old bone. He moved through the front doors of the House
of Peace on autopilot, grateful for the numbness.
Grief was heavy, but shock floated. Shock let you coast. He
just wanted the day to end. Hell, he wanted the *month* to end.
Maybe the year too. Outside, the light hit him like a slap—too
bright, too golden for the kind of morning where you pick
out a cremation urn for your wife.
His wife…*Amanda*. Her name felt unfamiliar now, like
something he was supposed to care about but didn't
recognize anymore.
*Dead names*, he thought, then immediately hated himself for
the wordplay. Then something caught the corner of his eye.

Matt's car. The thing rolled slowly past him, as if it
belonged to a dream he wasn't a part of. The girls were
inside—just the girls. Maya was at the window, laughing.
Evelyn beside her, grinning.
Their faces lit up in that weightless way young people had,
like they'd never known what it meant to run out of time.

They didn't see him. They didn't *need* to see him.

For a second, it felt like watching a scene from
someone else's life. A movie he didn't audition for, let alone
get cast in. Then the car rounded the corner and was gone—
just like that.

Like it was never there at all.

What held his attention after the fact—and what
worried him the more it settled in—was a simple absence:
*Where was Matt?*

As the car had rolled by, at first, he'd just clocked the smiles. The girls, with the book probably nestled between them like some purring cat. But the more he thought about it—the slower the moment replayed behind his eyes—the more wrong it felt.

Matt should've been driving... Would have been driving. He was the one who wouldn't shut up about keeping it locked down, keeping it safe. Not to mention, Matt was the one polishing that old box like it was the goddamn Ark of the Covenant.

So where the hell was he?

A breeze moved through the parking lot, warm but unwelcoming, like a sigh from something old and patient. Ed didn't like the way it made him feel.
Didn't like the fact that he'd seen the car, seen their faces, *and hadn't noticed until now* that something was missing.

A chill climbed his spine—not cold, but slow and knowing.

5

Miranda Callahan sat in her kitchen, fingers curled around a chipped mug of lukewarm coffee, her eyes fixed on the window. The backyard beyond was still, cloaked in the flat gray light of an overcast afternoon.

It had been a full day since her fight with Evelyn. Too long.
The girl should've come home by now, tail between her legs, ready to apologize for her tone—for the backtalk, the

attitude, the *utter disrespect*.

Miranda seethed quietly.

She blamed *those damn Boston kids*. She didn't know their names—didn't care to—but she knew *them*. Knew the type. Self-important, smug. Kids who thought student loans and therapy lingo made them better than the people who scraped by for real.

And to top it off?

Their credit card got declined last night.

She had run it early, sure—but what of it? She'd intended to square up with that girl when she came crawling back. Put a little pressure on. Maybe Eve would learn a thing or two about responsibility.

As if summoned by her righteous fury, her phone buzzed. A Ring notification.

She tapped the screen, expecting a delivery or a squirrel.

No.

*Evelyn.*

Smiling.

With *her*. That *girl*—red hair like some kind of cheap wine, laughing like she owned the place.

Thick as thieves.

Miranda's jaw clenched. Her grip on the mug tightened.

The sound of their laughter through the camera made her stomach twist. All that *giggling*. As if nothing had happened. As if *she*—Miranda—was the villain in all of this.

Without a word, she stood. Moved to the stairs. Her bare feet made no sound on the linoleum, but her heartbeat thundered in her ears like drums.

Up the back steps.

She'd catch them in the act. Have her say. And this time?
*They would listen.*

She waited for twenty minutes but, after hearing a bunch of noise downstairs, she headed that way to see what was going on and to give them a piece of her mind.

6

Matt's eyes blinked open to darkness.

Not just dark—*wrong*. Thick. Humid.

And he couldn't move.

His arms were held behind the back of a chair, his wrists pressing against something sharp and unforgiving. Plastic? Zip ties?

The air was musty. Damp. Mold and rust mixed with the scent of something older, rotting. A basement. Definitely. But not Ed's.

Ed had an oil furnace, he remembered—he'd seen it when hunting for the box. This one had a cast-iron boiler straight out of the 1930s, groaning like it still remembered the war. The walls were fieldstone, sweating behind peeling stucco. The floor beneath him was dirt. Uneven. Cold.

This had to be the Airbnb.

*How the hell did I get here?*

His mind thrashed back through memory. To the store. The cashier. The head on the belt.

He tugged at the restraints uselessly. They were tight. Professional, almost. Then — laughter.

It drifted down the stairs toward him.

The overhead light snapped on with a harsh click, searing into his retinas. He squinted. Blinked.

Two figures stood in front of him like a nightmare play unfolding in real time.

Maya, in a white dress with a crimson sash, held *the book* against her hip like it belonged there. Evelyn stood just behind her, dressed in black, a long kitchen knife dangling from her hand as if it were part of her arm.

Matt swallowed the scream building in his throat.

"Going out on the town?" he tried. Light. Joking. It came out weak. Afraid.

Maya stepped forward, her voice detached and cold as winter ice.
"That depends on you, Matt. We can go out, get drinks, maybe even have that three-way you've been daydreaming about."

She tilted her head.

"But the box bullshit ends. The book knows everything."

Matt's mouth went dry. "Why would you help me if—? Oh." His eyes narrowed. "You want me to read you."

He didn't say *it*. He said *you*. Just to see if Maya flinched.

She didn't. She smiled—but it didn't touch her eyes. She turned and set the book gently on a side table, like tucking a baby in for the night.

Then Evelyn stepped forward.

Knife in hand.

"Eve...you don't have to do this." His voice cracked.

She leaned close, her breath warm against his cheek. "It's not the voices that scare me anymore," she whispered. "What scares me is what happens if they stop."

The knife came down in a blink—fast and brutal— plunging into his thigh with a sick *crunch*. The blade hit bone. Snapped off.

Matt screamed, his world going white.

Blood spread across his jeans like a flower blooming in time-lapse.

"The book says pain will make you better," Evelyn murmured, kissing his brow with twisted affection as she pressed a folded towel against the wound like it was just another scraped knee. "It will *purify* you."

Then the voice returned. Not from her.

*From inside his head.*

Soft at first. Then louder.

*"I can speak through them,"* it hissed, *"or to you...like this.*

*Which do you prefer?"*

"Like this," Matt thought bitterly—and suddenly the world stopped.

Literally.

Evelyn and Maya froze mid-motion. Eyes open. Bodies upright. But utterly still. Like mannequins in a wax museum.

"Jesus Christ."

*"Yes, creepy, isn't it?"* the voice said. *"Don't worry. They're paused. Won't hear a thing. The world could implode and all they'd hear is my favorite song on repeat."*

A familiar melody crept into his skull—soft and sweet and awful.
*Love is the sweetest thing...*

Matt gritted his teeth. "Let me guess. That's your lullaby?"

The voice chuckled. *"What can I say? I have taste."*

"What do you want from me?"

*"To stay out of my way,"* the book said. *"I can't control you, not really. Just like that cop—Webb. You're immune to me, Matt. That makes you dangerous."*

The voice dropped lower. *"So here's the deal. Stay out of it...and you live. Push, and you'll end up like Captain Webb. Or worse. Burned out from the inside. You know how creative I can get."*

Matt didn't answer. He was watching the floor.

More specifically, the edge of something poking up from the dirt.

The broken half of the knife.

*"You're stalling,"* the book hissed.

"No," Matt whispered, tilting the chair. "Just…repositioning."

With a breath and a shove, he threw his weight forward—the chair crashed down hard on the basement floor.

Pain flared in his leg, white-hot. But he didn't care.

He was just close enough now to reach the blade.

Rocking the chair back and forth, Matt edged himself closer to the broken blade, his body trembling from blood loss and adrenaline.

Closer. Just a little…*closer.*

He lunged, grabbing the knife with his bound hand. The jagged metal bit deep into his palm, slicing through skin and muscle. He didn't care. He barely felt it.

He sawed furiously at the first zip tie. The plastic strained, then—*snap.*

Footsteps.

Maya stirred. Her head jerked slightly. The trance breaking.

"Shit—"

She reached him just as the last strand gave. Matt surged forward and drove his fist into her face.

A sickening *crack* rang through the basement as cartilage shattered.

Maya crumpled, shrieking, blood pouring from her nose as she fell back against the wall, screaming and clutching her face.

Matt spun, hand bleeding, adrenaline surging, and hacked through the ties at his ankles.

One. Two. *Free.*

He stood—his injured leg screaming in agony.

Then Evelyn was on him, a blur of black and pale skin.

They crashed to the floor, but Matt had the weight. He shoved her off, raw strength overriding pain.

She stumbled backward—into the boiler.

Her head connected with the iron tank with a sickening *crack*, like a hammer on a melon.

She dropped, twitching.

No time to check.

Matt turned, found the book still perched on its table like it *belonged* here. Like it was *watching.*

"Not today, you bastard."

He grabbed it with his good hand—burning, almost. Cold and hot all at once—like static, like dry ice—and limped toward the stairs.

Blood dripped from his fingertips.

The girls didn't move.

Yet.

He didn't look back.

At the top of the stairs stood Miranda Callahan—solid, middle-aged, and entirely in the way.

Even in perfect health, Matt wouldn't have been able to get around her easily. Winded, bleeding, and dragging a leg, he stood no chance.

"Where do you think *you're* going, buddy?" she snapped, hands on her hips. "That credit card you gave me was declined, and now I find you *creeping around in my damn basement?*" She smiled when she said it, like this was all still fixable. Like a scolding could unwind everything he'd just survived.

Her eyes flicked to the book clutched to his chest.

Matt moved, fast as he could—but she was faster than she looked.

She reached for it.

"Don't—"

He jerked the book back—too hard.

Her foot slid on the top step.

Her eyes widened.

And then she was falling.

Tumbling down the stairs.

Thud. Crack. Thud. Crack.

The last sound was unmistakable. A wet, splintering *snap*, like firewood breaking under a boot.

Silence.

Matt stood frozen, heart hammering, bile rising in his

throat.

*Oh God.*

The book was already laughing.

*"That's two now, Matt,"* it cooed in his mind. *"Mommy and daughter. Punched the girl who wouldn't spread her legs, cracked Mommy's skull open on her own stairs… Think prison's gonna be fun for you?"*

Matt's hands trembled.

"I guess we'll both be locked up then."

He pushed through the kitchen door, blood smearing the knob, and limped out toward the car.

Toward the box.

Toward the end of this.

# Chapter 21: RUN

1

Ed pulled up to the Callahans' just in time to see Matt's car peel away—fast, tires screeching, a trail of blood smeared from the porch to the end of the driveway.

His heart sank.

He slammed the truck into park, flung open the door, and stepped out, phone already in his hand. His boots squelched against something wet—blood. A lot of it.

He didn't get far before Maya barreled into him from the shadows of the porch, half-blinded by tears. Her white dress was streaked in red—spattered, smeared. Her face was a cracked mask of dried blood and panic.

"Holy shit—Maya?" Ed grabbed her by the arms to steady her. "Are you okay?"

"He has it," she gasped. "Ed—he has *me*—no, *it*. The *book*." Her voice was shaking. Disjointed. "We need to stop him—*now*."

Ed blinked, trying to process her words. His thumb was already hitting 9-1-1.

"I need to call the police—"

"No, *we don't have time!*" she screamed, grabbing his collar, dragging him close. "You don't understand—if he seals it—if he *reads it;* we're all dead."

The dispatcher's voice crackled from his phone speaker.

"Nine-one-one, what's your emergency?"

Ed glanced at the house.

He didn't know what was inside. Not about Miranda at the foot of the basement stairs. Not about Evelyn, barely clinging on.

That's what he'd tell the sheriffs later—when they asked why he hung up. Why he didn't wait. Or why he turned off his phone and threw it into the center console as if it were a cursed thing.

Maya grabbed the keys from his hands and ran toward the truck before he could say a word. He followed as fast as possible.

She drove.

God help them.

2

Matt saw Ed's truck crest the hill—and floored it.

Well, *tried* to. In a Chevy Cruze, flooring it translated to a mild protest and a hopeful whine. Still, to its credit, the tires chirped once, and within seconds he was barreling south at sixty-five, maybe seventy, the speedometer needle twitching like it wasn't used to this kind of exertion.

Why Rome, New York? No damn clue—except it had a UPS store. And Matt had a plan.

Not a good plan. Not even a finished plan. But a plan.

The box sat on the passenger seat, gleaming as if it were proud of itself.

The book lay right next to it. Still loose. Still whispering…laughing and fucking with him when it could. Not inside yet—because Ed had shown up just before Matt could drop the little bastard in.

He needed to pull over, and the sooner the better. Get it in the box. Say the damn prayer. Lock it down. Maybe even mail it to some dead-end P.O. box in Montana— some place Maya would never find it. Just in case. Because something in his gut told him. This wasn't over. Not by a long shot.

He could feel it still—like a tongue pressed against his brain, whispering, mocking.

His thigh screamed with every bump in the road. Blood had seeped through the fresh bandage. If he got pulled over like this—bleeding, wild-eyed, possibly wanted for murder—it was over. He'd be on the news before dinner.

He needed new pants. A fresh shirt. Hell, a whole new identity.

He needed to *think*.

But the book wouldn't let him.

It messed with the radio—flipping stations until it landed, yet again, on that fucking song.

*Love is the sweetest thing…*

The horn beeped. Once. Twice. A long, mournful third.

Matt slammed the steering wheel. "Shut the fuck up!"

The book chuckled, silk-smooth in his head.

*"Just pull over, Matt. Let Maya kill you quick—it'll be kinder than what's waiting in prison. Twenty-five to life, minimum. New York doesn't play around when it comes to corrections."*

The voice purred, as if it *cared.*

Matt gritted his teeth and pressed harder on the gas. "I'll take my chances."

*"You always do... Just remember, when your cellmate lets you choose the nighttime activity—your asshole doesn't have taste buds."* The book broke out in thunderous laughter at that.

Matt winced; at the joke or the pain, he didn't know.

Then he saw it.

A big brown sign on the shoulder, like a gift from the universe:

### *LAKE DELTA STATE PARK — 15 MILES*

A plan clicked into place—not perfect, but something. Campers meant people. People meant unattended coolers, backpacks, maybe even a fresh pair of jeans drying on a line. It was early in the season, sure. His luck would have to do a 180. But the park was open, and better yet, it was *free.*

He could pull in, clean up his leg, find some clothes, and—most importantly—put that damn book where it belonged.

Back in its box.

The thought brought a shaky smile to his face. For the first time in what felt like hours, he saw a path forward—

however muddy and insane.

He eased off the gas, eyes scanning the tree line, looking for signs of the lake.

The book, for once, was silent.

And that, somehow, was worse.

The kind of silence that made your ears itch. Like the air was waiting for something awful.

He shoved the thought aside and pressed the accelerator. The little engine groaned, surged forward. A plan—half-formed and desperate—was taking shape in his mind.

Then, in the mirror, a flicker of green.

A truck. Old. F-150.

It slipped into view like a shadow that had always been there, just waiting for him to look. Too far back to see the driver. Close enough to be intentional.

Matt's hands tightened on the wheel.

*How long has it been that close?*

He didn't know.

But the book did.

And it was smiling.

3

"Jesus *fucking* Christ, Maya, slow down!"

Ed again. Not the first time. More like the tenth.

She wanted to yell back, *I would if I could!*
But her mouth wasn't listening.

Maya wasn't driving.
Maya *B* was.

And Maya B didn't give a shit about speed limits—or Ed's nerves.

The book was screaming now. Not out loud, but inside. Its voice curling in her skull like smoke. Demanding they catch Matt. Demanding she take him down before he reached the box.

Maya could only watch from behind her own eyes, like someone stuck in the back row of a terrible movie she couldn't leave.

It felt like watching the Sox down 3-0 in the ALCS again—the one her dad always talked about. Comeback of the century against the hated Yankees. But this wasn't baseball…and she didn't have a beer.

*God, what I wouldn't give for a beer!*

Weird—the things your brain clings to when you're watching yourself on autopilot, possessed by something that wanted the world to end.

The truck fishtailed, tires screaming on the blacktop, but to Maya's surprise, her imposter kept it steady.

*How the fuck…?*

Somehow, Maya B held the line.

Was it the book? Did it jack her reflexes up to *Fast &*

*Furious* levels? Or were they just riding the ragged edge of disaster and hadn't rolled the dice wrong—*yet?*

Maya wanted to believe it was skill.
But she was from just outside Boston. Yeah, she *knew* how to drive—but in the same way that someone who plays *Call of Duty* "knows" how to be a soldier. They'd seen the guns. Maybe even knew how to aim one.
Didn't mean you dropped them into Kandahar.

Didn't mean *she* belonged in a high-speed chase on backwoods roads with blood in the trunk and a demon in the passenger seat of her brain.

Still, here they were.
Maya clung to every twitch of muscle memory. Every garbage trick from Driver's Ed. Every close call on the 93. Anything that might help the bitch at the wheel keep them alive.

Because if they crashed, Maya was pretty sure she'd feel every goddamn second of it.

No—not *pretty sure.*

She *knew.*

The book would make damn sure they both suffered for letting it down. Probably on a loop. Set to that fucking song.

And for the first time, Maya felt herself rooting— *actually rooting*—for the thing wearing her skin. Cheering on that smug bitch behind her own eyes.

That thought alone was almost worse than the demon.

She just wanted the *Fast & Furious* bullshit to end.

She just wanted to walk again. Like a human being.
Not like a possessed action figure with a front-row seat to her
own damn murder.
Like Mother Nature intended.
*Assuming Mother Nature was still watching.*

4

Ed felt the truck fishtail and instinctively grabbed
what he called the *oh shit* bar—the handle on the passenger
door that helped people climb in or, in this case, survive a
possessed twenty-something behind the wheel.

Each time they started to catch up to Matt, Maya
would either over-correct or slam the brakes too hard,
sending them skidding just enough to lose ground again.

He thought about telling her to slow down—again—
but what was the point? She'd ignore him. Or worse, the
book would chime in and tell him to shut up.

So instead, he just held on tight and prayed the truck
would blow a gasket.
Honestly, at this point, being reduced to a mindless husk
almost sounded like mercy.

Maya glanced over and saw Ed gripping the handle
again. It irritated her.

She wasn't *that* bad behind the wheel. In fact,
considering the situation, she thought she was doing pretty
damn well, thank you very much.

Just as that thought crossed her mind, the tires lost traction.
The truck swerved hard to the left.

She yanked the wheel, over-correcting, and nearly launched them into a ditch.

"Shut up, Ed! I know!" she snapped—*before* he even opened his mouth.

She eased off the gas. Barely.

But the book screamed again.
*Faster. Faster. FASTER!*

And of course it won.

Her foot slammed back down on the pedal.
The speedometer needle climbed past 75. The old truck groaned like a dying animal.
If it could talk, it'd be screaming for mercy.

The temperature gauge was climbing too. Fast.

Maya didn't know much about cars, but she knew one thing: *Red is bad.*
And every needle on the dash was heading straight for it.

---

Then—hope.
Matt's shitty little Chevy flickered into view again. She saw it for just a second, and her chest flared with adrenaline.

Then it vanished around a bend.
And with it, the hope popped like a balloon.

*Gone again.*
*Fuck.*

But then—brake lights.

He pulled in somewhere. A campground—no, a state park. Lake Delta State Park, to be exact.

There was a dented brown metal sign. Faded.
She spotted a bent telephone pole that was still waiting to be repaired. Broken glass still littered the edge of the road, and yes, a few red pieces of what had to be a Tesla.

That's when it hit her.

She looked over at Ed.
His face had gone paper-white, lips pressed tight.
This was it.
Amanda had died here.
Or close enough to stain the air.
Maya thought about reaching for his hand—but didn't.
Some ghosts didn't want witnesses.

Instead, she just turned into the state park. She eased the truck off the main road, tires crunching over gravel, glass, and memory.
She followed Matt. One way or another, this was all going to end here.

---

Maya watched from her cell as it all played out—thankful, at least, that the goddamn Boonville 500 was over.

For now.

Deep somewhere inside, she knew Amanda had died near here.

Not remembered. Not guessed.

*Knew.*

This place—this lake, this patch of rotted earth—felt wrong.
In her chest. Her bones. Whatever was left of her.

Her soul?

She didn't believe in that shit.

…Right?

Fuck it. Maybe she did now.
There were black books that could bend reality and hijack your body—so, sure, screw it. A soul wasn't the weirdest thing anymore.

But whatever it was, she felt *something* here.
Something in the water.
It was wrong.

She didn't know what that meant—only that it *mattered.*
It felt like water was the answer, somehow.
And she hated not knowing the questions.

---

*"Never mind all of that."*
The book's voice buzzed through the loudspeaker in her skull again. Cold. Coiled.

---

"What's wrong?" Maya snapped. Arms crossed.
"Worried I might figure you out?"

*"Figure me out?"* the book purred. Mocking.
*"That's cute. Girl, you can't even figure out your college major. You're gonna crack me?"*

Maya's mouth tightened. She hated how right it was in that moment.

*"And stop fucking with Maya B while you're at it."*
She stepped closer to the imaginary wall, looking up at the speaker, fists clenched.
*"Your little 'driving tips' nearly wrecked her half a dozen times."*

The book's tone shifted. Cooler. Meaner.

*"You're not helpful, Maya. Accept it. You're obsolete. Old firmware. Maya 2.0 doesn't second-guess. She just drives… That's why I like her better."*

A pause.

*"And if you keep making noise, I'll rewrite the code again. This time without you in it."*

No purr now. No teasing.

Just promise.

And for the first time in days, Maya shivered.

Not from cold.

But from the hard realization:

It could—and worst of all, it would.
And she would never even know she was gone.

5

Matt didn't pull into Lake Delta State Park.
He *slammed* the wheel hard right—tires squealing, leaving angry black skid marks across the asphalt as he veered

through the entrance.

They were behind him. He didn't need to check the mirror to know it. He could feel it.

No one at the welcome station. Good… No, *great*— maybe his luck was finally changing.

He blew past it, ignoring the 10 MPH sign like it was a suggestion made by someone who'd never bled out in a Chevy Cruze. The engine whined as he pushed it—30, maybe more—his wheels lifting slightly over the first hill.

Then—parking lots. Trail signs. A fork in the road.

He jerked the wheel again, pulled into the first lot. Killed the engine. The car shuddered to silence.

Matt grabbed the book.

The horn blared.

He jumped—screamed—and dropped the goddamn thing.

"FUCK YOU!" he shouted, not caring if anyone heard.

He reached down—but the moment his fingers touched the book, it went ice cold. Not metaphorically.

*Arctic.*

He looked at his hand—and froze.

Literally.

His fingers stiffened. His joints locked. Skin turned pale, then blue, then— *Crack.*

He watched in horror as his hand shattered, fracturing

at the wrist. Bone. Skin. Tendons. A thousand blood-speckled shards exploded like crystal across the car's floor.

He didn't even have time to scream.

*"Oh nooo,"* the book hissed inside his skull.
*"Matt! How are you going to jerk off now?"*
It cackled—deep, gleeful, wrong.

Pain surged up his arm like fire and frost at once. His vision blurred.

But somewhere in the back of his mind—Matt *knew*.

It wasn't real…couldn't have been real.

None of this was real.

He focused and prayed that he was right. Reached down with his very real, very intact hand—and slammed it into the stab wound on his thigh.

Agony bloomed. Hot and wet.

Reality snapped back like a rubber band.

His hand—still there. Bleeding, but whole.

The book squirmed on the passenger floorboard, pulsing with wrongness. He grabbed it, fingers burning, and slammed it into the box.

The book screamed.

Not in his head.

*Out loud.*

Like a living thing being stuffed back into its cage.

He ignored it.

SLAM.

The lid closed.

Silence.

Blessed, aching silence.

Matt sagged back in the seat, panting. The pain was still there, the bleeding still real, but the voice—the presence—was gone.

For now.

Matt slumped back in the seat, gasping like he'd just outrun death.

The box was shut.

The book was in.

It was over.

Or—it *should've* been.

That's when he noticed.

His eyes drifted to the passenger seat…then the cup holder…then the floorboards.

His stomach dropped.

The lock was gone.

The small brass padlock—the only thing that kept the box sealed, really sealed—was just…*missing*.

He checked again, frantically. Under the seat. In the center console. The glove box.

Nothing.

"No…no no no—"

He looked around the car, wild-eyed, as if it might

magically appear on the dashboard, or dangling from the rearview mirror like a sick joke.

But it wasn't there.

Something must have knocked it loose in all the chaos—the screaming, the blood, and the fucking hallucinations.

Or the book made it disappear.

Matt didn't know much about a lot of things, but he knew *this*:

That box?

Without the lock, it was just wishful thinking.

And until he said the prayer...

Until that lock *clicked* shut?

This nightmare wasn't over.

Not even close, his eyes fluttered and his vision dimmed at the edges. The blood loss was taking its toll. He felt the adrenaline slowly leave his battered body as his eyelids slid shut.

# Chapter 22: LEGACIES

1

**T**rooper Timothy Webb had only been out of the academy a few months, but he was a quick study. Friendly, sharp, clean-cut. Everyone liked him.

It didn't hurt that his great-grandfather had been a local legend—Captain Leon Webb, shot and killed in the line of duty taking down some madman back in the '30s. The story still floated through academy lectures and late-night barroom tales like a ghost.

That name got him the Lee Barracks post—his grandfather's old beat.

But the rest? That was up to him.

And Tim Webb was going to prove he was every bit as good—maybe better.

So when the 9-1-1 hang-up came from Boonville, it pinged his radar. He was already in the area. It wasn't urgent, not yet, but procedure was procedure. They had also dispatched a sheriff's deputy—to knock and talk, standard procedure.

Most of the time, these calls were nothing. A drunk husband. A scared wife. A kid playing with the phone. But it never hurt to have backup on a domestic.

Webb hit the lights, took the curve off Route 26 a

little hot, and reached the property in minutes.

Most people don't realize their phones still ping after a hang-up. These days, the second a call drops, dispatch has a GPS trace within three feet. And if that phone gets turned off right after the call? That's when people pay attention.

Because if it *is* a domestic—and someone hangs up *and* powers off?

That's not an accident. That's a problem.

Tim spotted the deputy as he pulled in. A guy he didn't know—but that didn't matter. They both wore the badge. That was enough.

Together, they approached the Airbnb. An enormous place. Quiet. No movement. No voices.

Tim knocked once, firm.

That's when he noticed it.

Blood.

A smear across the door handle. Faint, but fresh. Still wet.

Something in his chest twisted.

This wasn't a routine knock anymore.

He rested his hand on his sidearm.

The door creaked slightly under his knuckles, as if it were waiting.

Tim looked at the other guy, who nodded and called it in as he opened the door, sliding his service weapon from its holster.

"New York State Troopers!" Tim called, stepping over the threshold. His voice was clear, firm, commanding. "If you're in here, I need you to announce yourself—*now*. Don't make me find you."

He moved slowly and steadily through the entryway, checking corners, eyes sweeping every shadow. Standard procedure. Muscle memory.

The sheriff's deputy peeled off and headed upstairs, clearing room by room. Tim stayed on the main floor. Living room, kitchen, hall—nothing. All quiet. All wrong.

He was just about to lower his weapon when he heard it.

A sound.

Soft. Wet.

A moan—coming from the basement stairs.

His heart sank.

He turned, flashlight in one hand, sidearm in the other, and aimed the beam downward.

At the bottom of the stairs lay an older woman. Twisted. Still. The position of her neck said everything.

He keyed his radio.

"Dispatch, this is Trooper Webb—confirming one DOA at my location. Female. Appears to have fallen down the stairs." He paused, forcing his breath to steady. "Basement access point. I'm making entry to clear."

He moved slowly down the narrow steps, boots sticking slightly where blood had dried. The air was heavy, metallic.

He swept the flashlight across the room.

Basement.

Old boiler. Stone walls. Dirt floor.

And—another body.

A girl this time. Late teens. Maybe early twenties. Curled on the floor, breathing shallow. Head matted with blood.

"Shit," Tim breathed. He moved toward her, checking the space first—corners, behind the furnace. No one else.

"Dispatch, I've got another. Still breathing. Head trauma. Request EMS immediately. The scene is secure."

He knelt beside her, gently trying to rouse her.

Her lips moved. Barely.

"Matt...Matt..."

He leaned closer. "What's your name? Who's Matt? Is he here?"

Nothing. Just that name. Repeatedly. Like a broken prayer.

Tim glanced toward the stairs, relief blooming in his chest as he heard footsteps—backup, finally arriving.

Whoever Matt was, he'd just become the center of this whole goddamn nightmare.

And Webb? He was going to find him.

2

Lenore Morgan sat at her campsite, watching the fire spit sparks into the dark, and silently thanked whatever god was listening that the family reunion was finally winding down.

The Morgans of the Northeast had chosen this shithole of a state park for their grand get-together. In May. She sighed and, not for the first time, wondered if it was time for an Ancestry DNA test—just to be sure.

She hadn't wanted to come.
No, she'd wanted to spend what little summer break she had doing literally anything else. Not stuck in what had to be one of the worst state parks New York had to offer.

The lake was man made, for shit's sake.

She'd planned to hang out with her friends. Maybe, if the stars aligned for once, finally get laid.
Not that you could do that at a family reunion.
Well, you could—but this wasn't *that* kind of state.

She chuckled to herself.
Then her mother's voice barged in.

"You missed the last one, Lily! What if you die? Won't you regret not seeing everyone one last time?"

It echoed in her skull like a curse.

As if she were going to die anytime soon. She was twenty. Invincible. Her twenty-first birthday was around the corner, and she had it all planned—she and the girls, bar-hopping through Burlington like queens.

She ran a brush through her black hair, wincing as it snagged. The fire popped.

From the old, rotting picnic table, her dad's ancient camping radio crackled to life—catching some rogue signal through the trees.

*Love is the sweetest thing...*

Lenore froze.

The melody oozed from the speaker in a soft, tinny hush—too clear for a signal this deep in the woods. Too *perfect.*

A shiver threaded up her spine.

She looked at the radio. It just sat there. Still. Innocent.

Her arms broke out in goosebumps.

"Nope," she muttered, standing. "I'm not sticking around for whatever Stephen King shit this is."

She grabbed her flashlight and turned toward the trail. One last walk before they left this mosquito-infested hellhole.

To say goodbye to the bugs. They'd practically become family.

3

Matt snapped awake.

It felt like he'd been out for days—but his watch said otherwise.

Three minutes. That's all it had been.

Still, enough time for Maya and Ed to catch up.

His head swam. His leg throbbed. And worst of all—
the book.
He could hear it again.

Muffled. Faint. But rising.
Like something waking up in the dark.

He had to finish the prayer. Even without the lock,
maybe it would be enough. Enough to buy a little time.
Enough to *survive*.

He turned off the engine—only now realizing the car
was still idling—grabbed the box from the passenger seat,
and threw the door open.

The moment he stepped out—agony.

His leg seized, the muscle locking around the shard of
metal still buried deep in the bone.

It buckled.

Matt went down—hard.

The box tumbled with him.

He hit the ground, and all he could do was watch as
the box bounced once—twice—and on the third—it cracked
open.

The sound was soft. Almost delicate.

The effect was anything but.

The book's voice exploded in his skull.
A wrecking ball of pressure and static and dark, jagged
laughter.

And just like that, it was awake again.

Matt scrambled.

The song was screaming in his head now, warping into a twisted lullaby.
Visions of Evelyn's rotting corpse flickered behind his eyes—her broken body sprawled in her mother's basement like a marionette dropped mid-dance.

He couldn't see.

The book had blinded him again, dragging him down into its hell.

He clawed at the blacktop, crawling on his belly, sweeping his hands blindly, hoping the box hadn't bounced all the way to Boston.

Somewhere, distant but inside him, he was back in the basement.

Of course.
The book couldn't control him—but it could mess with his mind.
And right now, it was pulling out all the stops.

"This isn't real," Matt muttered, voice shaking as he groped blindly.

The book laughed.

*"As real as it needs to be, Matt. What is reality anyway? Ever been to a psych ward? Go ahead. Ask around. You would be amazed by what people consider 'real' down there."*

A new vision bled in—worse than the last.

Evelyn.

Her skull caved in, her hair matted with blood and bone. She crawled toward him, reaching out with pale, broken fingers.

"Give me a kiss, sweetie," she whispered, lips bloody and trembling.

Matt gagged—but kept crawling. Ignored her. Ignored it.

He swept his arm out again—and then—contact.

The box. Still intact.

"Thank God," he gasped, flipping it open.

Empty.

The book was gone.

*"Oh noooo,"* the voice cooed. *"Where did I go, Matt? Where did I gooooo… Your mind is failing, your arms are flailing…"*

It sang the last part in a tuneless, mocking melody.

Matt's hand clenched into a fist.

"Shut the fuck up," he growled. "When this is over—"

But then—it did.

It stopped.

Because Matt's hand closed around something cold and pulsing.

The book.

Before it could twist reality again—before it could react—he shoved it back into the box and slammed the lid shut.

Muffled silence.

The visions vanished.

The parking lot returned. The trees. The early evening air.

No blood. No corpse.
Just Matt, panting on the asphalt, clutching the box like it might float away.

"Fuck this book…"

4

Maya yanked the wheel, following the not-so-subtle skid marks snaking into the state park—the unmistakable trail of Matt's shitty little car.

The book hissed in her head.
*"Faster."*

She punched the gas.

The old truck groaned in protest, but still managed to hit twenty-five as it barreled up the incline. Her fingers locked on the wheel. The trees blurred by.

Then she hit the first turn.

And everything stopped.

The scream hit her brain like a thunderclap.

The book didn't whisper this time. It shrieked. A sound too big to fit in her head, tearing through her like glass.

Everything went white.

No control. No body. No thought.

Just static. Cold and blinding.

And thank God—for her and for Ed—her foot didn't stay on the gas.

It slipped off the pedal.

The truck coasted forward, slowing, drifting helplessly as the wheel jerked in her slack hands.

It rolled gently into the ditch with a muffled crunch, nose-first.

And stopped.

Still. Silent.

Not like Amanda.

---

Ed woke up first.

His head throbbed like a bad hangover, and it took him a second to realize they weren't moving anymore.

The truck was still. Quiet.

He turned—and saw Maya slumped over against the steering wheel, her hair falling across her face, her breathing shallow but steady.

He reached over and gently shook her shoulder. "Maya?"

Her eyes fluttered open, unfocused at first. Then they locked on his—and he saw it.

Her.

The real Maya.

For the first time since she'd touched that damn book.

"You okay?" he asked, voice rough.

She blinked, then winced. "I think so. My head feels like the day after spring break."

She looked around slowly, taking in the ditch, the quiet, the stalled truck. "Did Matt...?"

Ed shook his head. "Don't know. We lost him."

Maya unbuckled her seatbelt and slid toward him, gravity doing half the work. Ed caught her without thinking—and was startled by how natural it still felt.

She didn't pull away.

He didn't let go right away.

And for one fragile, terrifying second, he let himself wonder—maybe the book hadn't taken everything from them. Maybe something real was still buried under all this madness.

But that thought was for later.

Right now, they had to move.

The truck was stuck—well and truly nose-down in the ditch.

Ed looked at the woods ahead, then back toward the road.

"Come on," he said. "Let's find him."

They climbed out of the ditch, boots slipping slightly on the gravel shoulder as they reached the road.

The sun was almost gone now, sinking low behind the treetops. The air had that dusky hush that came right before nightfall, and a few old streetlights had blinked to life—casting long, pale halos on the road and through the trees.

Everything had that strange, too-quiet glow. Like the world was holding its breath.

Maya stepped closer to Ed, her body tense. Her eyes kept flicking to the trees, like she sensed something he didn't.

It bothered him more than he wanted to admit.

"What is it?" he asked finally.

She shook her head. "I don't know. This place...just feels wrong."

Then, without hesitation, she reached for his hand. He took it.

And then—like lightning—it hit.

A thunderclap that wasn't sound at all, but thought. Screamed into his brain.

The book.

Back. Loud. Unhinged.

*"KILL HIM! KILL HIM! FUCKING KILL MATT!"*

It shrieked in an endless loop, like a siren right behind his eyes.

Ed doubled over, clutching his skull. Beside him, Maya was doing the same—hands pressed tight to her temples, her teeth clenched against the pain.

They moved forward anyway.

Staggering down the road, toward some unseen beacon, the book was broadcasting. Its hate felt like it had mass now. Like gravity.

Ed looked at Maya—and his stomach turned. Her face had changed. Not fully the other Maya yet, but her eyes were darkening. Her jaw set. Her grip on his hand was tight enough to hurt.

The thought crept in, awful and quiet:
*If Matt were standing here right now...*

Ed couldn't finish it.

Didn't have to.

He saw it on Maya's face.

She would kill him. Right now. No hesitation.

He didn't blame her.

And just as they reached the crest of the hill—just as Ed's legs sprinted forward without him—the screaming stopped.

Cut off like a radio.

Ed dropped to his knees, gasping, hands clawed into his scalp.

The silence that followed was almost worse.

Maya sank down beside him, her arms sliding around his shoulders. She held on—tight.

Ed didn't know if she was comforting him or clinging for her own sake.

Didn't matter.

In that moment, the contact was enough.
Warm. Real. Human.
And he needed it more than he wanted to admit.

5

Trooper Webb jotted down a few last notes as the paramedics loaded Evelyn Callahan into the ambulance and closed the doors. She was stable—for now. But with closed head injuries, anything could happen. At least that's what the paramedic told him, and Tim didn't argue. He'd seen too many cases turn in the span of a heartbeat.

He turned back to his notebook as a neighbor gave her statement: she'd seen a car speed off, followed shortly by a truck, both heading south down the road like bats out of hell.

He had a feeling that those were the people he needed to talk to.

Webb called it in—told dispatch he was RTB—and added a note to ping him if anything else came up.

He walked back to his Dodge Charger, tossed his campaign hat into the passenger seat, and slid in behind the wheel.

He'd barely reached for his seatbelt when a new call came through: street racing reported on Route 46, heading toward Rome.

Too close. Too perfect.

Too much to be a coincidence.

And Trooper Tim Webb didn't believe in coincidence. Not tonight.

He keyed his mic.
"This is 13-Webb. I'm already in the area. I'll take a look."

The Charger's engine rumbled to life, and with a flick of the lights, Webb pulled onto the road.

There was a weight in the air now. A charge he couldn't name, but felt in his bones.

With a resolve that another Webb might've recognized, he headed south—down the same stretch of asphalt that had once taken his grandfather to an early grave.

# Chapter 23: THE TURTLE'S BACK

1

Matt lay on his back, panting, arms wrapped tight around the box like it might try to escape. He could still hear it—muffled, furious, snarling inside his head—but he figured that was just proximity. The thing hated being close to him now. Hated being trapped.

Once he finished the prayer—maybe even found a new lock—this would be over. At least for him.

Maybe for Maya too.

He sat up slowly. His head spun; his stomach rolled. The blood loss was catching up. But youth had its advantages—you could ignore things like trauma and internal bleeding for a while. At least, that was the hope.

He set the box down gently, making damn sure it stayed closed. Then, he pushed himself to his feet.

The world tilted. Vision swam. But he stayed upright.

He bent, picked up the box again, and started limping toward the trail.

Once on the trail, Matt limped forward, scanning for signs of a campsite—somewhere people had been recently. Maybe they'd left something behind. A cooler. A pack. Clothes.

Then he saw it: a flickering fire off in the distance.

And music.

That goddamn song.

"Fine," he muttered. "That's the one."

He picked up his pace, stumbling toward the glow.

*"That's right, Matt,"* the book cooed in his head. *"I'm sure they've got a nice little brass lock just for me."*

"Do you ever shut the fuck up?" Matt snapped out loud—then winced. He didn't need to speak. Thinking worked just fine.

The blood loss was getting to him. He could feel it in his limbs. In his thoughts. Like static on a dying radio.

*"What's the matter, Matt?"* the book purred. *"Feeling light-headed? Maybe take a little nap. Bleed out. Do the world a favor."*

*No, I'm good, thanks.* This time, he thought the words.

He stepped onto the campsite. It was quiet, empty. The radio sat on a warped picnic table, its dial glowing faintly as *"Love Is the Sweetest Thing"* drifted from the speakers like a curse.

Matt seriously considered smashing it.

Instead, he just sat down heavily on the bench and set the box next to him.

He glanced around—no people. No first-aid kit. No brass lock.

Just the fire. The woods. The damn song.

For a second, the idea came: throw it in the flames.

"Do it," the book whispered, its voice thick with

amusement. "Set me to burn and watch what happens next."

"Yeah," Matt muttered. "Then you burn the only thing that keeps you somewhat quiet. No, thank you."

The fire crackled. The radio crooned. Matt looked down at the box, heart pounding.

First aid could wait.

It was time to say the prayer.

Time to put the book to sleep.

2

Ed glanced at Maya as they moved closer to where Matt must be—and with each step, he saw it happening again. Her shoulders squared. Her expression tightened. The warmth drained from her eyes, replaced by something colder, harder. Not quite her.

That decided it.

Maya couldn't get any closer to the book. Not while it was still in the box.

"Hey," Ed said gently. "Let's head back to the truck. My phone's still in the glove compartment."

Maya looked at him, and for a heartbeat, he saw two people behind her eyes. The look she gave him was half relief, half frustration. A silent war.

"What if we lose him?" she asked, taking a step toward the lot where Matt's car was parked crooked and empty.

"He's not going anywhere. The car's still here. Come on—I need my phone, Maya."

He reached for her hand.

To his surprise, she took it.

Let him pull her back down the hill, away from the book's signal, back toward the old green truck still stuck in the ditch. With every step, she seemed to soften. The hard lines of her face eased. Her eyes lost that flicker of unnatural sharpness.

"How's your head?" he asked after a stretch of silence.

Maya didn't answer at first.

Then: "My head's fine, Ed. Probably the same as yours. Every time we get close to that goddamn book…"

She trailed off.

But she didn't have to finish.

He knew.

They couldn't help Matt. Not directly. Not like this. If they got too close, there was a real chance they'd hurt him instead. Fight for the book. Rescue it.

*Serve it.*

Ed sighed as they reached the truck. The thing was listing slightly, tires sunk deep in mud.

He climbed in and reached across the seat. The glove compartment creaked open, and he pulled out his phone.

He turned it on, already bracing for what he'd have to do next.

3

Trooper Timothy Webb's radio chirped as he cruised down Route 46. The update was short, but it made his fingers tighten on the wheel.

The phone that made the 9-1-1 call? It just turned back on.
Current location: Lake Delta State Park.

Well, wasn't that convenient?

He was already heading that way thanks to the street-racing tip. But now? Now it felt like something more.

The pieces were lining up too neatly. The hang-up. The phone power-off. The sudden silence. And now this.

That old EMT saying floated through his head: *When you hear hoofbeats, think horses, not zebras.*

It applied just as well to police work.

Coincidences were rare. Connections weren't.

He pressed the accelerator and flipped on the lights. The Charger surged forward as red and blue flashed off the trees.

Keying his mic, he called it in. Calm and clipped.

"Dispatch, this is Webb. I'm en route to Lake Delta State Park. The suspect's phone from earlier pinged active in that location. Requesting backup—any available units."

His eyes narrowed on the road ahead.

Whatever this was—it wasn't just a domestic call anymore—attempted murder maybe, but not a simple domestic.

---

Meanwhile, just south of Lake Delta State Park, Officer Richard McConoughey sat in his Rome Police Department Tahoe—a bulky SUV that smelled like stale coffee, fur, and fast food. In the back, his K-9 partner, Jeter, panted happily, tail thumping against the crate bars.

Everyone on the force agreed Jeter was a hell of a dog—smart, fast, loyal.

And, if they were honest, probably smarter than old Dick.

But Officer McConoughey tried hard. For a small-city cop, he did okay. He'd just finished his second lunch and handed Jeter a plain donut—no glaze, department policy—when the backup request came across the police band.

Webb. State Trooper. Sounded urgent.

Richard sighed.

Jeter wagged.

"10-4, en route to Delta State Park," McConoughey said into his radio. "ETA five mikes."

He tossed the rest of the donut out the window and pulled out of the Dunkin' on Black River Boulevard—forgetting, in his haste, to hit the lights. He cut across traffic and nearly sideswiped a Honda Civic. Laid on the horn as if it were *their* fault.

Then he remembered. Hit the lights. Flipped on the

siren.

Dispatch crackled in his ear. "Unit 21, cancel lights and siren. You'll alert suspects."

"Roger that," he mumbled, reaching to silence the wailing speaker—*after* it had already echoed across two blocks.

He figured the trooper would have it all under control before he even got there anyway. He straightened out the Tahoe and got the beast moving toward the lake—a stretch he hated this time of year. The black flies were everywhere, Central New York's unofficial state bird as far as Richard was concerned.

Cars moved over as he surged past, red-and-blues flashing. In no time, the big SUV was pushing fifty and climbing. The first stoplight came and went in a blur—he blew through it without even a tap on the brakes. Horns blared. Tires squealed.

Cost of doing business, Richard figured.

He flew past the school zone—thankfully empty this time of day—and soon the city gave way to the edge of town. Houses thinned out, yards turned to trees, and the four-lane boulevard narrowed to a two-lane ribbon of pavement winding through the suburbs.

He eased off the gas. A little.

Jeter barked once from the back.

"Yeah, yeah," Richard muttered. "I know. Sixty's pushing it."

4

Maya B sat in the glass prison that bitch Maya had made for her, watching with seething contempt as she walked toward the truck *holding Ed's hand*—like she had any right to him.
Jealousy flared in her chest like a match to dry leaves.

"Just wait," she spat, pacing. "The book will get out. And when it does…"

She didn't finish the sentence. She didn't need to.

The loudspeaker above—now redesigned into the shape of a middle finger—crackled, then came to life. No static. Just Maya's voice, clear and calm.

"If wishing made it true, sweetie," the voice said. "And if that happens…I'm sure we'll fight again. Let the better bitch win."

Maya B snarled and kicked the wall. "Let me out of here!"

"No. And stop kicking the wall—it's pointless. Trust me," Maya's voice replied with just enough pity to infuriate her. "You're lucky I don't know how to *get rid* of you, or you'd already be gone."
A pause.
"You've done enough damage."

"What damage?" Maya B fired back, arms flailing. "Getting you a *real* man for once? One that won't cheat on you or use you?"
She kicked the wall again, harder.
"Tell me, Maya, what damage did I actually do—*beyond*

screwing up your walking wallet with a car Matt was too dumb to dodge?"

Silence.
The speaker didn't respond this time.

Maya B scowled, stomped back to the bed, and threw herself onto it in one long, dramatic motion. Arms crossed. Eyes burning.

Let the better bitch win.
She intended to.

---

Maya listened to Maya B pout in the back of her mind and wondered briefly if this is what Maya B had to deal with every time *she* pouted.
The thought made her laugh—then she quickly decided she didn't give a single shit about Maya B's comfort. Let her stew.

She turned her attention to Ed, who was scrolling on his phone like they weren't in the middle of a supernatural hellscape.

"Ed, I don't think now's the best time to check your email," she said, dry as dust.

He didn't answer.

That meant it was probably important. Or at least not worth interrupting. So she left him to it and wandered off a few steps toward the edge of the trees, where the lake glimmered through the branches like a secret.

She'd parked the truck—well, "crashed" might be more accurate—just up the road. From here, she could just see the water.

It was pretty; she supposed. In its own dull, man-made way.

But it still felt wrong.

The air was heavier here. Thicker. Like it didn't want her there. Like it was holding its breath.

And whatever it was holding back...
She had the sick feeling they were about to meet it.

Then Maya saw them.

Red and blue lights slashed through the trees as a black-and-white Chevy Tahoe screamed up the road and slammed on the brakes at the park entrance below the hill. Gravel and rubber exploded in every direction.

She heard a dog barking—loud, frenzied.

Right behind it, a blue-and-gold Dodge Charger pulled in. That one came in smooth, controlled, almost surgical.

The Tahoe, not so much.

It roared up the hill toward them like a freight train, then screeched to a stop in front of the truck. The driver's door flew open, and a slightly overweight officer stumbled out—struggling with his seatbelt, still half-strapped in.

Maya couldn't help herself.

She chuckled.

Which, of course, only pissed him off more.

"GET ON THE FUCKING GROUND!" he bellowed, face flushed beet-red—part exertion, part embarrassment. The K-9 in the back lost its mind, barking furiously.

Still grinning, Maya raised her hands and dropped to the grass, arms out to the side, palms open. She wasn't about to argue with a cop and a German shepherd in full freakout mode.

Then it hit her.

*They'd been to the house.*

She watched the other cop—tall, sharp, calm in that ex-military way—quietly cuff Ed and guide him into the back of his patrol car. No shouting. No drama. Just practiced movements and calm authority.

Meanwhile, *her* cop was still screaming like she'd just assassinated the mayor and he'd cracked the case wide open.

She lay in the grass, stunned, not sure what the hell was happening.

Then she saw it.

The calm cop—the tall one—walked over, placed a hand on the red-faced officer's shoulder, and leaned in. Just a few words. Maya couldn't hear them, but whatever he said, it worked.

Just like that, the fury drained out of the guy. His entire posture sagged.

He holstered his gun.

Walked back to the Tahoe.

And let the dog out.

To Maya's surprise, the calm cop—the tall one— reached down and helped her to her feet.

"I'm Trooper Timothy Webb," he said, voice steady and measured. "Your friend's in custody for now until we get some answers. Mind telling me why he called 9-1-1, hung up, and then turned off his phone?"

"I… We needed to…" Maya started, but the words stuck in her throat.

Webb held up a hand. "Let's start with this—do you need medical attention?"

Maya blinked. Her face hurt. Her head throbbed. Her stomach was doing flips. And Matt… She couldn't help him like this. Standing out here, trying to explain the unexplainable—it would only get worse.

So yeah, she needed something. Probably more than she wanted to admit.

She nodded.

Webb gave a soft sigh, then keyed his radio. "Dispatch, send EMS to my location. I've got one MVA, requesting medical."

He guided her gently to the bumper of his cruiser. Let her sit. Gave her space.

Then: "Did that gentleman hit you?"

Maya's eyes snapped up. "No! God, no—it wasn't him."

Then Maya froze.

She'd heard the words *as* she said them—*It wasn't him.*

Not "I hit my head in the crash."
Not "No one hit me."

It just *wasn't him.*

And she knew exactly what the next question would be—before he even asked it.

"So then…who hit you?" Trooper Webb said quietly. "And what happened in that house?"

Maya looked at him, really looked at him—and felt the floor of her world shift again. She could lie. Protect Matt. Pretend it was all a misunderstanding.

But Matt was up there somewhere, bleeding out with a piece of metal still jammed into his leg. Half-crazy from blood loss. Probably hearing that goddamn song.

He was screwed no matter what.
Book or no book.
And the truth?

Yeah. The truth was…
Matt *did* hit her.

Maybe it was Maya B he hit. Maybe it wasn't really *her.* But that was splitting hairs—and there was no box on the police report for *"possessed by an ancient evil."*

She couldn't tell Trooper Webb that it was okay, that Matt had punched her *because* she was possessed.

And anyway—the bruise didn't care about nuance. Neither did the blood on her dress. And sure as hell, neither would Trooper Webb.

She sighed and took a deep breath.

5

Matt sat at the table and pulled out his phone.
He opened the notepad app and found the file—the prayer
he'd transcribed from some corner of the internet. He *hoped* it
would work.
Because, honestly?
It was all guesswork at this point.

He glanced at the box. Made the sign of the cross.

*"Is that supposed to scare me, Matt?"*
The book hissed in his head.

"I don't care if it does or doesn't," Matt muttered,
scrolling.

*"Before you begin, just remember—the last person who tried
this didn't fare so well."*

It laughed. Low. Hateful.

Matt ignored it. Stood. His leg flared with pain and he
nearly stumbled, catching himself on the table.

Then, he began.

"Behold, I have given you dominion—over serpents,
over scorpions, over the might of the enemy.
No harm shall touch you while this seal holds."

The book screamed in his skull. His leg locked—
muscle cramping hard.

"Fear not, for I am with you."

*"Shut your fucking mouth, Matt! Or you'll regret this day!"*
The voice cracked. Thinner now. Less sure.

"Be not broken, for I am your God. I will give you strength. I will stand beside you. I will raise you with My right hand, righteous and unyielding."

Matt's voice steadied—louder now. Stronger.

"Burn the idols of the false. Touch not their silver. Desire not their gold. For these things are foul in the eyes of the Most High."

"For we war not with flesh and blood — but with dominions and dark rulers... with unseen thrones and ancient powers... with spirits of wickedness in the heights beyond the veil."

"By these words, let this box be sealed. Let no hand open it that walks in shadow. Let no voice call forth what lies within."

"So it is spoken. So it is bound. By flame. By truth. By the hand of the Most High."

By the end, he was screaming. His whole body shook. Then—he collapsed.

Blood ran from his leg again.
His head spun.
But he wasn't done.

Not yet.

The box was closed.

Now, it needed to be buried.

Standing once more, he picked up the box.

And for the first time, it felt like just a box.

Not a voice.

Not a weight in his mind.
Just…a thing.

His thing.
His choice.

He took a breath—shaky, but his. Then he limped back toward the hiking trail, searching for a place—quiet, hidden—where he could finally bury this cursed thing.

# Chapter 24: LILIES AND DOGS

1

Evening had fallen over the state park as Lenore Morgan made her way back toward the campsite. She figured her family had returned by now from whatever "super exciting" thing they'd gone to do in Rome.

Something about a fort.

Yawn.

She'd seen everything this park had to offer—trees and boredom—and was ready to fake a migraine if anyone suggested a campfire singalong.

That's when she saw him.

Up ahead.

A guy was walking the path alone.

She slowed.

Something about the way he moved—staggering, stiff, like each step cost him—put her on edge.

He was carrying a box.

That was creepy enough.

Who just…walks around a park carrying a box?

Immediately her brain supplied answers she hadn't asked for.

A box full of human teeth.

Or eyeballs.

Or...fingers in formaldehyde.

Lily grimaced.

Her imagination had always been overactive—she'd been the kid riding her bike up and down Main Street pretending she was a superhero, defending New Hampshire from evil.

But she wasn't a superhero.

And that guy up ahead?

He looked dangerous.

She slipped off the trail, ducking low into the underbrush, heart picking up speed.

Just in case.

Then he passed by, and she saw it.

His leg—bleeding.

Badly.

A dark smear soaked through the torn fabric of his jeans, and he was mumbling to himself, low and fast, like he was arguing with someone who wasn't there.

Lenore froze. Her first instinct was to bolt—run back to the campsite, grab her phone — only then did she realize she didn't have it.

Of course.

But then...something stopped her.

Not fear. Not curiosity.

Something else.

A whisper just beneath her thoughts—like a voice she couldn't quite hear, but couldn't ignore either.

*Follow.*

She didn't know why.
Couldn't explain it.

But against every shred of better judgment she had left, Lenore crept through the trees, trailing just off the path. Quiet. Hidden.

Following the bleeding man and the box he carried.

2

Jeter was a good boy.

That's what they told him, and so he believed it— kept his nose low to the ground, sniffing with purpose, waiting for the command.

He already had the scent. Human blood.

He'd picked it up the moment they pulled in, but his human had been busy yelling, so Jeter waited. And sniffed. And waited some more.

It wasn't a bad life. Donuts, belly rubs, the occasional chance to tackle someone—that part was always fun.

So when his human finally gave the order— "Track!"—Jeter didn't hesitate.

He knew exactly where to start: the parking lot at the top of the hill.

He bounded forward, tail high, nose twitching. His human would catch up. Eventually.

He always did.

They always got the guy in the end.

"Woof."

That should be enough to let them know he meant business.

Jeter circled the car, nose to the ground, tail flicking with purpose. He found it—blood. Faint but fresh. Just enough.

He looked back. His human was finally cresting the hill, panting, red-faced, slow.

Another firm, "Woof." Just in case.

Then he took off down the campers' path, ears forward, eyes sharp, nose leading the way.

Because he was a good boy.
And good boys get their man.

3

Matt hobbled along the trail, searching for a place— any place—to bury the cursed box and end this nightmare.

Well, most of it. He knew better.

Down the path, consequences waited. No prayer would bury those. Evelyn. Her mother. Maybe even Maya— he'd be blamed for all of it.

But at least the book would be done.

He stepped off the trail, breathing hard, unaware that

he had a witness.

And farther back—padding through the dusk—came a keen-nosed German shepherd and the far less eager cop trying to keep up.

He scanned the woods until he spotted a patch of earth that looked soft enough to dig—maybe, just maybe, he could make a dent in it with his bare hands.

Dragging himself over, he knelt—his wounded leg spasming in protest—and dropped the box beside him. The ground was damp beneath a blanket of decaying leaves, pliant in a way that gave him hope.

With shaking fingers, he swept the debris aside, exposing dark soil beneath. Then he began to claw.

Fistfuls of earth came up slowly, painfully, his fingernails tearing into the dirt, pulling it back one clump at a time.

The box sat nearby, silently waiting.

That's when he heard it.
A bark—loud, sharp, and unmistakably serious. The kind of bark that only came from a big dog trained not to play games.

Matt froze.
His heart thundered against his ribs, pumping the last dregs of blood through a body already running on fumes. His brain dumped another shot of adrenaline into his system, and he started digging faster—frenzied, desperate.

He didn't notice when the first fingernail tore free. Or the second. Just felt the sting, the warm blood slicking the dirt.

Then his fingers struck something solid. A rock.

He gritted his teeth, felt around it with ruined hands, trying to find the edge. Somewhere in the back of his mind, he thought: *I must look insane.* But there was no time for sanity now.

He worked around the rock—slow at first, then faster—until it finally came loose. He tossed it over his shoulder into the trees.

It nearly hit a girl.

She ducked back, heart pounding—but Matt never even saw her. He was very close. Too goddamn close.

"There," he whispered. Or maybe shouted. He wasn't sure.

He grabbed the box, slick with his own blood, and lowered it into the shallow grave he'd torn into the earth. His fingers smeared crimson across the wood as he pressed it into place.

Then — A low growl.

Matt froze.

It was right behind him.

Matt could feel the dog's breath on his neck.
Hot. Steady. Close.
He didn't dare move.

He stared down at the blood-slicked box in the hole, its dark wood smudged with red. It looked back at him like an eye—mocking, grinning. Inside, he could *feel* the book laughing at him.

*So close.* And this goddamn dog was going to ruin it all.

"Don't move a muscle, son."
A voice behind him. Firm. Male. Cop.

"Listen… I just need to—"

"You need to shut the fuck up and do *exactly* what I say," the officer snapped. "Or my dog is gonna take a chunk outta your ass. Jeter, to me."

The dog pulled away—Matt heard claws on leaves— and he dared a motion, just reaching to push dirt onto the box —

"*What the fuck did I just say?*" the cop barked, and Matt froze as he heard the unmistakable click of a sidearm being drawn.
"Do it again, and I'll order this dog to hold you. Now stand up. Slow. Hands where I can see them. Walk back toward my voice."

Matt glanced at the box one last time—just a thin layer of dirt now. He prayed it was enough.
*Please let it be enough.*

He stood. The world tilted. Darkness rushed in from the edges of his vision, but he stayed upright.

One step. Another. Backward. Onto the trail.

Then, hands grabbed his wrists, rough and fast. Cold metal snapped tight.

He didn't fight.
Didn't speak.
The cop—who Matt would later learn was significantly dumber than his dog—marched him down the path without a

second glance toward the cursed patch of earth he'd bled over.

And behind them, in the woods, the box lay half-buried.
But not forgotten.


4


Lily watched wide-eyed as the entire scene played out. The cop, the dog, and, hell, the entire arrest that followed. It felt like something out of a movie—one of those streaming originals where everything looks normal until suddenly it's not.

She was amazed that the dog hadn't come after her. It *had* looked her way once, sharp ears twitching—but the cop was too focused on his shiny new arrest to care about anything else.
He called the dog, and it followed, obedient and eager.

She didn't move.
Not for a long time.
The woods pressed in around her like a held breath.

But eventually, curiosity won.

*Don't,* a voice inside her whispered. *Just go back to camp. Go to sleep. Leave in the morning like you planned. Let this be someone else's story.*

She ignored it.

Creeping forward through the brush, she retraced the man's path until she reached the spot—the hollow, ragged hole clawed into the earth.

She knelt beside it.

The forest was silent. The air felt heavier here.

Something had happened. Something big.

She slowly reached into the hole and brushed away the remaining dirt, her fingers trembling. The soil was damp and clung to her skin like something alive.

Her hand touched something smooth. Wood. Cold.

She gripped it, pulled, and the box came free.

For a moment, she just stared at it—sitting there in her lap as if it had been waiting for her.

The sun had slipped below the horizon, and the woods were pitch-black now. Still, she could swear she saw a faint shimmer ripple across the surface of the box. Like heat off pavement. Like breath on glass.

She swallowed.

Every instinct told her to drop it. To run.

Instead, she stood.

She didn't open it. Not here. Not yet.

She tucked the box against her chest and turned back toward the trail, heading for the campsite. The wind picked up behind her, rustling the leaves like a whisper.

She didn't look back.

Instead, she dug into her jacket pocket, pulled out the small flashlight, and flicked it on. It sputtered once…twice…then held steady. Good enough.

She followed the trail back toward the campsite, the familiar voices of her family drifting through the trees. The fire was still going, crackling and warm. Her aunts and cousins laughed over something, someone popped open a can of soda, and everything looked painfully normal.

"Hey, Lily," her mother called. "What have you got there?"

"Just a box," Lily said, holding it up. "I'm gonna turn it into a jewelry thing."

It was a lie. She didn't know why she had lied.

"I think I'm gonna call it an early night. Want to head back to Vermont first thing tomorrow. It was great seeing everyone."

That was another lie. But at least she knew why she had told that one.

"Okay, sweetie. Love you," her father said quickly, cutting off her mother before she could protest.

Ever the peacekeeper.

Lily smiled and nodded. "Love you too. Goodnight."

She turned and ducked into her tent, the box clutched tightly in her hands.

5

Ed and Maya watched as the police brought Matt down in handcuffs. He was limping. Pale. Eyes locked on the ground like he couldn't bear to meet theirs.

Maya felt the instinct to run to him—but the moment passed
before she could act.
An officer guided him into the back of an ambulance, and
just like that, he was gone.

She didn't know what she'd hoped to do—say
goodbye? Say nothing? Ask why he never told the truth?

Now she had her own paramedic to deal with—and
Ed, hovering close like he could will her bruises away.

"Are you sure that's all you remember, ma'am?"
Trooper Webb asked for the third time.

"Yes." Maya sighed. "I told you—we came here to
buy rare books. I spent too much money. Matt got upset. I
went to try to sell the books back to Ed, and that's how we all
ended up together—ow!"

She winced as the paramedic started an IV. The
needle burned.

"Anyway… That hurt," she muttered, then went on.
"Matt got upset. We had a fight. You can ask around
Boonville—people at the bar saw it. Then Ms. Rodrick—rest
her soul—found out I was going to try to get my money back
and, well…she wasn't thrilled."

She stared down the road where the ambulance had
vanished. A long silence stretched.

"It all boiled over at the Airbnb. After Matt's card got
declined, Evelyn's mom threatened him. I guess that just…set
him off. I've never seen him like that before."

Her voice thinned out at the end. Saying it out loud
didn't make it real—it just made it worse.
She felt grimy.

Not because she was lying. But because, somehow it still felt like the truth.

What else could she say? That a book told Evelyn to stab Matt, so he hit Maya in the face? That she had another version of herself living in her head and—most days—she wasn't the one driving?
No.
Then they'd all end up in the same padded room.

So she told the story again, hoping Trooper Webb would buy it and just let her and Ed go to the hospital. Her face hurt. Her migraine was building. And the adrenaline had long worn off.

Webb nodded and closed his notepad. He handed each of them a card.

"If either of you remembers anything else, give me a call. I'm sure the DA will be in touch."

He turned without another word and walked back to his cruiser.

# Chapter 25: NIGHTMARES AND DREAMSCAPES

1

Maya tossed and turned in the bed.

It wasn't a bad bed—Ed kept his guest room clean and comfortable—but she couldn't settle. Truth be told, she'd thought about asking if he'd mind some company. Just someone to share the quiet with.

But she shoved the thought away almost as quickly as it came.

It wasn't the time to shack up with a widower whose wife's body was barely cold. The police still looked at her sideways whenever her name came up in the case files—even if Matt wasn't saying much to them, which she didn't understand.

He owed her that, didn't he?

She rolled onto her side and stared out the window, replaying everything that had happened over the past few days. A talking book. A possession. A passenger in her head that wouldn't leave.

Maya B.

Still there. Still whispering. Still reminding her how great Ed was, as if Maya needed reminding.

He'd been incredible—even at the hospital, where he waited through the endless forms and made sure the bill was in his name. He didn't have to do that.

She wasn't used to men treating her like...anything more than a good time.

Matt had—once. And she'd taken advantage of it. The guilt rose cold in her chest, washing her hollow.

She was still pissed he hit her.

Her nose wasn't perfect anymore. Ed swore it looked fine, said it gave her "character," but she could see it in the mirror—just slightly off now, tilted left.

It shouldn't matter. But it did.

She closed her eyes and tried—really tried—to sleep, hoping the pain meds they'd given her for her face would kick in soon.

Eventually, they did.

Warmth settled over her. Her limbs grew heavy. The world folded inward, soft and dark. For the first time since Boston, she felt...safe.

Until the black veil closed in completely.

She was sitting in class again, typing code into her laptop while her professor droned at the front of the room. Everything felt normal. Familiar.

Then she looked down at her screen.

The project file: *The Black Book.*

Her breath caught. She looked up—and the classroom was empty.

On the whiteboard, a message scrawled in blood-red text.

Latin. She knew the words.

She stood quickly, her chair scraping the floor. Her laptop fell and bounced off the tile with a hollow clatter.

"Hello?" she called, voice small in the vast silence.

No answer.

She knelt to gather her things, though she didn't know why. She wanted to run, but her body moved on autopilot, stuffing her belongings into her bag.

Then she saw it.

Beneath her bag, pulsing faintly like a heartbeat—*the book.*

Her hand reached for it, even as her mind screamed to stop. *No. Not again. Not after everything. I was free.*

Her fingers touched the cover.

Electricity ripped through her.

She shot upright in bed, gasping.

Sunlight poured through the window. Her sheets were damp with sweat. Her heart thudded against her ribs.

She looked around, disoriented but slowly grounding herself in the safety of Ed's guest room.

"Fucking nightmare," she muttered.

Maya slowly got out of bed, her hair stuck to her

sweat-slicked brow. Her legs ached as if she'd run a marathon, and her face throbbed as if she'd gone three rounds in a UFC cage.

She didn't want to look in the mirror.

But she needed to.

She shuffled down the hall to the second bathroom, each step heavy and uneven. At the sink, she hesitated, then forced herself to look.

The face staring back barely looked like her.

Both eyes were bruised, swollen and discolored. Her nose was slightly off-center, the swelling hiding the full extent of the damage. Her lips were cracked. A faint trail of dried blood still clung to the corner of her mouth.

She blinked.

Her reflection didn't.

For a fleeting moment, too quick to be certain, she believed she saw Maya B staring back.

She gripped the edge of the sink until her knuckles turned white.

"Still me," she whispered. "Still here."

But the mirror didn't answer.

2

Ed sat alone in the living room, a beer in his hand, six empty cans lined up like tombstones on the coffee table in front of him.

He stared up at the ceiling, wondering if Maya had fallen asleep yet. Wondering if he should check on her.

In the end, he just took another long drink.

He didn't replay the last week—no, that would've been too easy. He rewound further. Years back. Because that fucking book hadn't just ruined a few days.

It had been there his whole life. Pressing down. Shaping things. Breaking things.

His family.
His future.

And now… what? It was gone?

That was the problem. It didn't *feel* gone.

Ed had grown up around that book—read it, feared it, hated it. Played with it when he was too young to know better. Let it mold him. And he knew, with a certainty he couldn't explain, that it wasn't finished.

Matt might've weakened it. Maybe even put it to sleep for a while.

But it was still here. Somewhere.

Ed could feel it. Like the pressure drop before a storm.

He got up, wandered into the kitchen, and grabbed another beer. His hand paused when he saw the bottle of Jack Daniel's on the counter.

He stared at it for a second, then shrugged. Grabbed that too.

Back in the living room, he sank into his chair, cracked the beer, and took a long, healthy swig.

"Fucking book," he muttered to no one.

Then he uncapped the Jack and brought the bottle to his lips.

The amber burn slid down his throat—warm and familiar. Too familiar. It brought comfort, and that comfort was starting to worry him. But that was a problem for tomorrow.

Tonight was about forgetting.

And Jack was damn good at helping you forget.

He took another pull, coughed a little, and chased it with a swig of beer. His head began to hum, as if a nest of bees had settled behind his eyes.

Just the way he liked it.

Ed leaned back in the chair, set the whiskey bottle on the floor, and kept the beer in hand.

He closed his eyes, trying to think of Amanda.

But it didn't take long before Maya took her place.

---

Ed didn't *drift* off to sleep—any drunk will tell you there's no drifting. You're just awake one second, dreaming the next.

Tonight was no exception.

Jack didn't help him forget. In fact, it seemed to do the opposite.

He walked along a familiar trail in the state park…only it wasn't the park anymore. The lake was gone, replaced by a slow-moving river. The path curved beside it, quiet and shadowed.

Then he saw it—a hole.

He knew what it was, or what it had to be.

He knelt beside it, expecting to see the box.

But instead, inside the hole…was a portal to a face.

A girl's face. Pale. Motionless. Staring up at him from a steel morgue table.

A voice—cold, distant, almost clinical—whispered from the darkness:

"Lenore Morgan, 21, female. Cause of death unknown. Pronounced by Dr. Wade Johnson at 14:23, April 24th, 2024. No signs of trauma to the head, neck, arms, or hands."

The head's eyes opened.

Ed screamed.

And woke up.

Beer spilled down his shirt and onto the floor. His heart pounded, his mouth was dry. The first rays of sunlight filtered through the window.

The hangover had already begun.

And the nightmare was already fading.

3

Matt lay in a bed at Rome Memorial Hospital, his leg bandaged, his wrist cuffed to the bedrail.
He had a private room—one of the perks of being in the headlines; he guessed. At least for now.

Dressed in a stiff hospital gown, he stared at the ceiling and tried not to think. But that was impossible.

His public defender had told him not to talk to anyone. So he didn't. Not even to him.
Except to say one thing: he was guilty.

Guilty of hurting Evelyn. Guilty of hitting Maya.
He'd take whatever punishment the DA handed down. No sense crying about it.

He'd punched Maya. He'd pushed Evelyn.
No jury in the world would believe they'd attacked him first.
And no one—*no one*—would believe the part about a demonic book.

But he wouldn't take the fall for Evelyn's mother.
That had been an accident.
That much he'd made clear.

His lawyer argued they should fight. Said the stab wound counted for something. Maybe it did.
But Matt was tired.
Tired of fighting.
Tired of explaining.
And honestly, if getting stabbed was the worst of it…maybe he got off easy.

The thing that still messed with him?

The nurses.
How they looked at him.

Like he was a thing. A monster.
Every time they came in—checking vitals, changing
bandages—it was the same. Cold eyes. Barely masked disgust.

He didn't blame them. But it still hurt.

He'd always been the good guy. The helper. The one
girls came to for advice, not to be afraid of.
Now he was just a creep who hit women.
He knew prison would be worse. Guys who hurt women
didn't get much sympathy behind bars.
That thought made his blood run cold.

A nurse came in—one he hadn't seen before—and
silently pushed something into his IV. She checked his
bandages, nodded, and left without a word.

The drugs hit quick.
His eyes grew heavy. The edges of the world blurred.

He was sinking.

Deeper.

Into nothing.

---

Matt woke on a beach at sunset. Evelyn sat beside
him, humming that same tune—the one that used to drive
him crazy.
Now he was just glad to see her.

"Eve?"

She smiled. "Pretty out here, huh?"

He blinked. "Are you...okay?"

"Why wouldn't I be?" she asked, still humming. "It's not like you bashed my skull in."

"I... It was an accident."

"What was?" She turned toward him, confused. Part of her skull was caved in. Blood matted her hair. One pupil was blown, black and wide. She kept smiling.

Matt reached for her. But suddenly she was farther away. Then farther still.

"I'm sorry."

"For what? Just a little bump on the head. The book said I'd be fine... as long as you didn't hurt the book."

Evelyn's tone darkened. Blood dripped down her face.

"You didn't hurt the book... did you?"

"Eve, I... Maya needed—"

A crack of thunder split the sky.

"MAYA!" she screamed. "It's always Maya with you!"

She stood, fists clenched, looming over him.

"You killed me for her. Crushed my skull for her. Murdered me. For her."

Matt scrambled backward. "I—"

"TAKE A HARD LOOK, MATT."

She lunged, grabbed him, shaking him violently—he woke up screaming.

A team of nurses and doctors swarmed the room.
Lights flashed. Alarms beeped.
Matt gasped, his vision swimming.

The nurse who'd "treated" him earlier?

Not a nurse.

The medication?

No painkillers.

They said it was meant to kill him. That she almost succeeded.

But the nightmare?

That part worked exactly as intended.

4

Lily lay curled in her sleeping bag, the box tucked close beside her.
She didn't know why exactly—only that she *wanted* it near.
*Needed* it near.

She'd cleaned off the mud. And what looked like blood.
But her brain refused to do the math. It wasn't blood.
Couldn't be.
Just…darker mud. That's all.

It was clean now. Tucked safely under her pillow.
She'd thought about opening it, but something had stopped her. Not fear, exactly.
Something softer. A sense of timing.

Like waiting for the right moment.

Maybe she'd open it when she got back to Vermont, back in her apartment with her two roommates buzzing around and the comfort of normal life pressing back in.
But for now…
It was enough just to have it close.

It felt warm under her pillow. Like a hot water bottle.
Or a sleeping pet.
Familiar. Comforting.

Sleep, which usually came hard, came easily that night.
She lay in the soft dark, staring up at the nylon tent roof, listening to the hum of insects outside.
Her eyelids grew heavy.
Heavier.
Heavier still.

---

Lily dreamed she was eight again, riding her bike down Main Street.
She'd just gotten braces—still sore, still shiny—and to cheer her up, her mom had let her ride her bike like a big kid, up and down the sidewalk as fast as she wanted.

Her black hair streamed behind her, her bike her spaceship to adventure.
She didn't see the chunk missing from the concrete.
Misjudged. Over-corrected.
Went down hard.

Blood. Tears. The works.
She was sure she'd be in trouble—until a man in scrubs rushed out of the new clinic on the corner.

Doctor Timothy Clarke knelt beside her, calm and smiling.

"You'll survive," he said, inspecting her knee.

He cleaned the scrape, dabbed on Neosporin, and pressed a Spider-Man Band-Aid over it. Then he handed her a cherry-red lollipop.

Lily accepted it carefully.

He was a doctor.

And doctors were safe.

"No scars?" she asked, blinking up at him with teary eyes.

"No scars," he promised, helping her to her feet and steadying her bike.

She sniffled. Nodded fiercely.

And rode off—hair flying behind her like a banner of defiance.

---

But the street didn't end.

She kept riding.

She got older.

Her legs got too long for the bike. She was too big.

She was no longer eight years old—she had grown up.

So she stepped off the bike, letting it vanish behind her.

She was standing in the middle of the road.

And there it was.

The box.

Sitting there. Waiting.

A note lay on top:

*Open me.*

Lily looked around.
Doctor Clarke's office door creaked open slowly.

She carried the box through the doorway and into the quiet reception area.
It was empty.
But she could feel it now—a faint hum, vibrating through her fingertips.

She set the box on the desk.

"Hello?" she called. "Doctor Clarke? It's Lily Morgan… Lenore… You know my mom, I think…"

No answer.

Just the hum.

She reached for the lid—slowly.
She lifted the lid — music blasted

Her phone alarm.
6:00 a.m.

Lily blinked, heart racing, the dream fading like mist.
She reached under her pillow.
The box was still there.

And it was still warm.

She packed quietly before anyone else was awake.
By the time the first birds were stirring, she was already on the road—the box buckled into the passenger seat like it might start picking the road tunes.

Lily tried not to think about it.

She turned onto Route 46 heading north and checked

the GPS.

Three hours and fifty minutes.

If she were lucky.

And today?

She was feeling lucky.

She turned the radio on and pressed the accelerator.

It was right around Gifford Hill Road that the song came on — "Love Is the Sweetest Thing."

It played once.

She frowned, shrugged it off.

But it wouldn't be the last time she heard it.

# AUTHOR'S NOTE

This story blends historical fact with fiction. While some events—particularly the 1933 New York State Milk Strike—are rooted in genuine history, many elements are purely imagined. I encourage you to explore that moment in time; it's a fascinating and often overlooked piece of American labor history.

The town of Boonville, NY, and the surrounding areas are also real—and are amazing places. I've visited many times and hope you get the chance to as well. Just be wary of any black books you might stumble upon.

While the story may not always paint the area of Boonville or its people in the most flattering light, please know that's a creative choice, not a reflection of reality. The people of that region are kind, generous, and deeply welcoming.

This novel also takes place on lands traditionally belonging to the Oneida Nation. A version of their Creation Story appears on these pages, shared with deep respect and the intent to honor the cultural heritage of the Haudenosaunee people. I do not claim ownership of this sacred narrative, which belongs to the Oneida people and their oral tradition. I encourage readers to seek out authentic retellings and support Indigenous storytellers and historians.

So, if you ever find yourself in Upstate New York and in the mood for a burger or a beer, stop by one of the area's many local spots. You'll be glad you did.